THE PRICE OF DECEIT

A John Deacon Action Adventure

Mike Boshier

Author's Other Books

High Seas Hijack - Short Story

The Jaws of Revenge

Terror of the Innocent

Crossing a Line

Acknowledgements

I would like to thank Sandra van Eekeren for her assistance and support in completing this book.

Eternal thanks to my wife and daughters who support me in my dreams.

If you liked reading this book, please leave feedback on whatever system you purchased this from.

Check out the rear pages of this book for details of other releases, information and free stuff.

1

It was very quiet as Deacon slipped out of one entrance door and made his way to the next. Some of the wounded were crying, and he could hear a male shouting at the hostages to keep quiet. Careful to ensure his footwear didn't squeak on the shiny marble floor, he edged along the glass-fronted window.

The day had started normally. He'd been minding his own business walking through the shopping mall when the explosion occurred near the main entrance. The shopping mall itself, St Jude's, was fairly old. Built in the '80s, it was more bricks and mortar than today's all glass and steel structures. Built with a long paved pedestrian approach from the nearest road, the outer doors were individual 'push' doors with the glass supported on metal frames and the inner doors were electric sliding types. The mall was also quite small with only thirty or so outlets, which is nothing compared to today's massive complexes. Apart from fire exits, the only way in or out was through the main entrance and along the concourse.

Seconds after the explosive blast, five men wearing face masks and heavy jackets had pulled automatic weapons and grabbed a number of customers as hostages, dragging them further into the mall and hitting the fire alarm to evacuate the remaining shoppers with a few bursts of automatic fire at the ceilings to speed them on. They had also called the local TV station and made their demands.

They'd stated there were five of them, armed with handguns and semi-automatic rifles and also claiming to have explosives. They were holding over a dozen hostages in an electronics shop within the mall, and their demands were simple. The release, live on national television, of four specific prisoners being held in Guantanamo Bay. The U.S. Government had one hour to agree and release them, or the terrorists would start executing one hostage every five minutes. They claimed to have supporters watching the area and any effort by the police or other groups to storm the mall would be met with resistance and the immediate executions of the hostages. Their message was clear. If power was cut to the mall or if anyone approached the building, executions would commence immediately.

To make matters worse, deliveries to the mall usually took place out-of-hours as vehicles needed to approach the rear via a service road adjoining the main entrance. Supporters of the terrorists, in contact with them by phone and radio, would see any approach by the authorities and again, executions would commence immediately. The fire exits also led to the same service road easily monitored by their supporters.

All vehicles outside had to be cleared away, and only television trucks would be allowed to park on the road outside. No one was to approach or walk on the pedestrian walkway or, no surprise; executions would commence immediately.

Their final demand was the live broadcast of their streaming video from within the mall. To prove they were serious they had filmed the execution of one female hostage, and the upload had instantly gone viral.

Immediately after Deacon had seen the men drag the hostages inside he had darted into the nearest shop and waited. Some of the ceilings had collapsed, and there was twisted metal and glass everywhere. Some of the people injured or killed in the initial blast were lying on the floor near the entrance, while some of the less injured were trying to help them move away.

All Deacon had was his Sig-Sauer handgun hidden in his belt. He was wearing casual clothes of jeans and a shirt, with a lightweight jacket over, and trainers on his feet.

It was the trainers causing him issues now. The rubber soles tended to squeak on the polished floor, but he couldn't slip them off because of the amount of glass from the broken windows strewn about. Hidden in a clothing outlet, he'd watched the terrorists bundle their hostages towards the electronics shop. Counting, he quickly identified the five wearing masks and the thirteen hostages. From where he was hiding the hostage group seemed to consist of five males and four females. The males were all teenagers while the females looked to be slightly older and he guessed them to be young mothers with their offspring, along with four children aged under ten.

The mall itself was quiet now. The alarms had been silenced, and all remaining shoppers and staff had run and evacuated immediately after the bomb blast. Deacon had used the eight minutes since the explosion to observe the terrorists next move. It was all too easy to rush in and get himself and the remaining hostages killed.

The electronics shop entrance was over one-hundred feet away from Deacon and had been carefully selected. Its position gave a clear view from its doorway down the length of the concourse and out past the main center doors. It also provided a clear onward view across the paved walkway out to the road making any movement or planned assault by the security services easy to see. From Deacon's position further along the concourse he could hear, but not see, the leader shouting his demands to the police by phone. The glow of the television screens showing the live newsfeed from outside flickered and danced off the broken glass, and he quietly approached.

Deacon knew he was at a significant disadvantage. From his position, he couldn't see all of the hostages nor how many were guarding them and exactly where they were located. However, he could see the feet of a young woman assumed to be the first hostage they'd murdered. She was face down, and blood was still pooling around her body.

Generally in a situation like this, he would have been happy to leave everything to the police and hostage negotiation people, but the moment one of the hostages had been murdered it had all changed. He'd heard the shot and the terrified screams of those remaining and knew he had to act and act fast. One against five wasn't good odds and, although armed, he wasn't wearing any type of protective vest although he suspected the terrorists were.

The terrorists would be expecting the police and authorities to comply and release the prisoners from Guantanamo or for them to try and talk them into submission, possibly by tiring them out over a day or two before maybe storming the mall later. However, it would take the police some time to get organized and what they wouldn't be expecting so soon after the site had been seized, was any type of assault this early in the game, and certainly not after a hostage had been killed with it being shown live on social media.

This was in Deacon's favor and helped balance the odds a little.

Moving sideways and forward slowly from the doorway where he was concealed, he edged closer before sliding down low behind a large decorative pot plant with the stalk and large leaves obscuring any view of him. The two terrorists standing guard just inside the shop doorway were looking towards the main entrance and away from him, not expecting anyone to approach from that direction. They were both wearing long jackets and were carrying AR-15 semi-automatic rifles.

There was a risk any shot from Deacon through the toughened glass door could be deflected and miss. What he needed was less distance between the glass and the targets, so grabbing a coin from his pocket he tossed it underarm to bounce and clatter further along the atrium.

The sudden noise made one of the guards lean forward to look, and as he moved closer to the glass, Deacon shot him in the head. As the terrorist fell back and the shattered glass of the shop door landed on him, the second terrorist swung around and loosed off a series of wild shots in Deacon's direction. Amidst a mass of falling green foliage and the heavy thumping of rounds hitting the other side of the pot plant, Deacon dived left and fired twice through the empty doorway. His first shot missed, but the next caught the second terrorist high in the shoulder exploding the bone and muscle, forcing him to fall back and his rifle slide away. Rushing towards the doorway while trying not to lose his footing on the glass strewn about, he quickly finished off the wounded terrorist with a headshot before leaping over the fallen bodies and clearing the doorway.

Two down, three to go.

Diving to the side, he crept along one of the aisles until he could peer through the small gaps between various boxes stacked on the shelves. Careful not to make a noise, he could see a group of people sitting on the floor with their hands on their heads. Moving slightly for a better view he could see they were huddled in a corner with two terrorists guarding them, rifles aimed and arguing. Lying at their feet was the body of a woman with blood and grey matter leaking from a massive head wound.

The guards had heard a shot from near their two accomplices by the door, followed by a brief burst from an AR-15, followed by more single shots and then silence. Calling out to them and receiving no answer they shouted at their other colleague to go and check.

Not sure where the third terrorist was, Deacon silently laid down on the floor, weapon drawn. The terrorist was creeping along the aisle two over from Deacon, towards the doorway, calling out his colleague's names when Deacon fired once through the gap at floor level, shattering his left ankle.

With a scream, he fell and as the remainder of his body bounced on the showroom floor, Deacon fired two more quick shots under the shelving into his chest.

Three down.

Scrambling to his feet, Deacon rushed back along the aisle just as the fourth terrorist let loose a complete magazine where he'd been hiding. Any noise Deacon made was drowned out by the repetitive bursts of firing coupled with the screams of the hostages.

Leaping across the end of one aisle to the next, he could see the fourth terrorist side-on. A quick shot to the TV screen to the right and the falling glass made the gunman swing around, exposing his front.

Deacon fired once, quickly, hitting the gunman in the chest, but the gunman merely staggered back, Deacon's round lodged firmly in his protective vest. However, it allowed Deacon to sight again and his second 9 mm round hit the gunman dead center in the forehead, exploding a pink mist out towards the wall.

Four down, one to go.

The last gunman, slightly younger than his colleagues, grabbed the nearest female hostage, pulled her to her feet and jammed his rifle up under her jaw. A small boy, maybe her son, aged around seven clutching a Barney Dinosaur stuffed toy scrambled up next to her.

"It's over," Deacon called, "you're the only one left. Put the gun down and surrender. It's over."

"I'll kill her. Back off. I'll kill her."

"Look, pal; there's more police coming. You can't get away. There's no need to die needlessly. Surrender now. There's no way out."

"I'll kill her. Come another step closer and I'll kill her."

"Live or die, pal, it's your choice. Surrender and you live. Hurt her and you die. Your choice."

"I'll kill her. I'll kill them all."

"No one else needs to get hur--"

As the gunman's gun began to waver Deacon's round entered his face just below his nostrils through his septum, through his upper jaw and straight through his medulla oblongata exploding his brainstem out through the back of his head. All bodily functions ceased immediately with no chance of a trigger pull. As the gunman's body collapsed and the woman began to scream, Deacon rushed forward to rescue the hostages when the young boy smiled as he raised and pointed the stuffed toy towards him.

Before Deacon could fully comprehend, the boy fired at him twice from point-blank range. Both rounds slammed into Deacon's chest, and he was hurled violently backward from the force of the shots. As his body bounced off the shelving, the last thing he felt was an immense pain as he saw bits of stuffing and purple fabric filling the air, and he wished he'd worn a protective vest as everything went black.

2

Surmi Reef, South China Sea

For as long as they could all remember, life on the small island had been harsh but simple. The three families living there lived happily in harmony with each other. One of the couples had two teenage sons while the second was older and past child-rearing age, their daughters already sold off into marriages to men across the seas. The last couple's son had left and married but had come back with his new bride over a year before. Eager to carry on the family's fishing tradition, they now had a six-month-old daughter. The males scratched a living as fishermen with the shallow seas around the island supplying a myriad of fish in abundance, while the women worked just as hard keeping house. The island wasn't large being just a little over six hectares, but it contained a multitude of plants and palm trees supplying ample provisions and shelter. The inhabitants had learned long ago how to utilize everything nature provided, passing the information down through the generations.

Just about everything the island produced could be used. The coconut palm trees were the main providers. The coconuts themselves provided ample food and drink. Coconut water is high in nutrients, and the milk could be turned into cream for cooking. The meat, or flesh, is pure protein and if crushed, produces a smooth oil for food. The husks were used for fiber matting and brushes, with longer strands being woven into ropes and fishing nets. The trunk, fronds, and leaves could be used to build simple homes and furniture with smaller offcuts making utensils. Coconut sap could even be boiled to make a fermented wine. With the abundance of fish, birds, and turtles, and a number of small fresh-water sources, the fishermen and their families had a simple, meager life.

The older couple had a small skiff type boat with an ancient outboard engine. What remained of the paint was faded and worn, but the old engine still ran almost as sweetly as when it had been made. Sure, it took a few extra pulls on the cord to fire it into life, but when it ran, its rhythm was regular and strong.

When the gods saw fit to provide a bigger catch, the two boys would salt the excess fish, load them into homemade baskets and launch the boat before venturing the two-hour journey to the neighboring island where the fish would be sold or swapped for flour, rice, fuel for the outboard, or whatever else was needed.

With a number of eligible young girls on the other islands, their parents knew the day would come sometime soon for their sons to choose not to return and life would become harder for those remaining, but hopefully, at least one of the sons would bring a bride back and continue in the tradition.

In the spring of 1945 American Forces had landed on the island and departed again soon after but not before drilling a deep-sunk well providing access to fresh water from large underground pools. As often during the war, when the Americans left they discarded unwanted pieces of equipment - a generator here, an outboard motor there, tins of food ... .

When the fighting finally ended, and peace prevailed, the fishermen returned. The older couple were direct descendants of those that returned. Any booty found had been lavishly used and the generator had run for years providing power for lighting before a lack of servicing and fresh oil had caused it finally to seize solid. However, the abandoned outboard had received better maintenance. Life had quickly returned to normal, and the few islanders went back to using coconut oil to cook with, and light lamps and their existence had again become meager but satisfactory.

Twice in living memory, the island had almost been swept clean by typhoons. Because the highest part of the land was only nine meters above normal sea level, any storm brought waves and winds that cleared anything in its path. It was only from the skills learned over the years to read the sky and foresee the coming storms that they had been able to secure as much as they could, but both times their simple homes had been wrecked and possessions lost.

However, the island people were nothing if not resilient. They foraged, rebuilt and started again. Each time stronger than the last. Their lives would never be great, but simple lives suit some, and food, water and shelter were all they needed.

That had changed finally in 1991 when military forces had landed and requisitioned the island. It was reported the inhabitants were relocated away and a small garrison of soldiers were stationed there. In 2009 scientists and engineers arrived and new plans were drawn up. Twenty dredging ships came in 2011, and within eighteen months the island had more than tripled in size and work began on building an infrastructure. The military island now included docking facilities for small to medium-sized ships as well as a 2,000-meter long runway. Various buildings were erected, and currently, over 150 troops were permanently stationed on the island operating the radar systems as well as overseeing the current building expansion work.

3

North-east region of Nigeria

Colonel Kolade Ganda stormed into the room, slammed the door and started shouting. Self-proclaimed, he'd never received formal officer training, merely rising through the ranks by natural progression and the violent murder of fellow colleagues. In a region where violence was a major part of its history, he'd been born to a mother who had died when he was three-years-old. He, like many others, had only existed by the kindness handed down by villagers.

He never knew his father. In fact, his mother had only met him once. The day he and another thirty or so fanatical jihadist soldiers had stormed the village killing and looting. At the time she'd felt herself lucky. The village elders had been mercilessly executed, many of the male villagers also. Any teenager males had been given a simple choice, either pick up arms and join the army or receive a bullet in the head. The women were given no choices. Older ones were ignored. Younger ones still of childbearing age were raped. Girls over ten were taken and sold into slavery. Kolade's mother had been repeatedly raped and her eleven-year-old daughter taken. They never saw each other again. Shamed by her pregnancy from rape, his mother had tried many times to end her life or cause a miscarriage, but nine months after that fateful event, Kolade had been born. Shunned and ignored by many in the village, his mother had struggled with her emotions to raise him. Suffering from malaria, she'd finally succumbed to peace in her sleep, leaving

Kolade to be raised by others. With no-one to love or guide him, he'd quickly learned the only things worth having were those he stole and as he grew he listened to the stories. Stories that made the sound of life with the jihadists exciting.

Joining them when he was seven he spent his formative years learning how to fight and take what he wanted, how a knife or gun could be used to threaten those weaker. He'd beaten and stabbed many people by the time he was ten, but his first killing wasn't until he began to grow pubic hair. They'd raided a village, and an old man was wearing a silver neck chain. Kolade wanted it. When the elder wouldn't hand it over, Kolade had tried to snatch it. His outstretched arm had been swiped aside, and an open palm had landed on his cheek as the old man swore at him. With anger in his veins and with his cheek still stinging he could hear the laughter from his colleagues.

Kolade had been stopped by an old man!

Kolade had been slapped!

An old man had said 'No' to Kolade!

With tears of embarrassment beginning to seep into his eyes he pulled the 12-inch blade from its leather sheath hanging around his neck and, with a flick of his wrist, the razor-sharp point traced a fine red line across the old man's stomach.

The old man looked down as, with a low bubbling sound, his greyish purple intestines spilled down over his legs to land on the dirty floor.

With a cry, the old man fell to his knees as he tried to scoop his innards back inside. Yanking the old guy's head forcibly back, and with a cry of rage, Kolade jammed the blade of his knife so hard up into the bottom of the old man's chin, up through his tongue, the roof of his mouth, and up into the central parts of his brain, that the tip came to rest protruding a half-inch through the top of the old man's skull.

Since then, killing had come easy to him. He'd taken the silver chain and the old man's AK-47 as a prize. Old and weathered, the wooden stock had lost its varnish, but the weapon still worked well. Cleaned and oiled the mechanism racked back-and-forth as it ejected its 7.62 mm rounds with ease and Kolade had kept it as his favored stolen weapon.

His anger and violence had grown with the years and he even surprised his fellow fighters with his methods of killing. A particularly cruel act was to mutilate those he left alive by chopping their arms off at the elbows. Totally dependent on others to help even the most basic of tasks, victims would often suffer a painful and slow death from infection or starvation. Others he would kill either quickly by beheading or slowly by slicing open their stomachs. It could take as long as twenty minutes for someone to die that way, writhing on the ground with their intestines trailing behind while Kolade looked on, laughing.

"You, you, you two, you and you," he said, pointing around the room at various girls.

Four armed guards grabbed the upper arms and shoulders of the girls and dragged them, screaming and crying, out through the door. As they were marched outside, they could see the browns and greens of camouflage across the truck's tailgate. Pushed, kicked and punched, they were loaded on board before two of the guards climbed in beside them and the tailboard was raised.

Threatened with a beating or even death if they made a noise, the girls were sitting huddled together quietly sobbing on the truck floor as their journey started deep into the forest along dirt tracks barely wide enough to take a vehicle. For the first hour, the track was exactly that

- a rough-hewn track better suited to hoofed or four-legged animals before eventually, it joined up with a loose tarmac road. Two hours later the road slowly improved and the truck sped up a little.

Basic food consisting of stale bread and some semi-rotten fruit, along with refilled bottles of water had been stored on board, and the truck stopped four times for toilet breaks. The truck would slow and turn off the road and head over bumpy ground before finally stopping. The driver and guard up front would come and lower the tailgate and the other two guards would climb down. After checking the area was secure and setting a guarded perimeter, the girls were allowed to climb down and perform their toilet breaks and stretch their legs. Five minutes later, they'd be forced back on board and the journey would continue.

Six times during the journey the girls' hopes were raised as the truck approached Army-patrolled roadblocks. Each time the guards in the rear would raise their weapons towards the girls, making it clear any noise would generate painful or fateful consequences. Each time the girls felt their hopes dashed as they could hear the driver pass over paperwork, a discussion then took place between the driver and the checkpoint soldiers, before they heard the rustle of paper being passed back and the noise of the engine being put in gear then the truck accelerating away.

With everyone tired and exhausted after twenty-two hours since the journey began, the truck turned sharply in through a gated wall, bumped over some rough ground and finally stopped.

The sobbing girls were ushered down. They could see the gates were already closed, and in the loom of lights from windows, they saw they were in a large courtyard. The sky had an orange glow, so they knew they were close to a bigger town or city, but the wall that surrounded the courtyard was at least eight feet high.

Ushered through a side door and down a dark flight of steps to a basement, the girls ended up together in the underground cellar of a large house. An old woman holding a bamboo cane was waiting for them and introduced herself as Ezinne, meaning 'Good Mother'. Looking around, the girls could see the large room had six simple bunk beds, each containing a filthy mattress with a threadbare grey blanket and an even filthier pillow. The room had no windows, being below ground level, and just two bare bulb ceiling lights casting a dim shadow around the room. At the far end a doorway led to a toilet and shower room, and even in the gloom, they could see the cockroaches scurrying across the floor.

With a faint swish followed by a louder 'crack', Ezinne flicked the bamboo cane across the legs of the nearest girl. Pointing at an old table with a large dish of rice with some meat sticking out of it, some bread equally as stale as they'd had on their journey, a metal pitcher full of water and metal cups alongside, she told them to eat, sleep and wash themselves in the morning. There would be a guard outside the door at all hours so anyone making trouble, shouting, or disobeying orders would be severely punished.

Leaving the girls crying, Ezinne then walked to the exit, closed and locked the door behind her and left them to their fate.

Realizing they had little choice, the girls eventually started to eat some of the food before choosing a bed each and settling down for the night.

4

The White House, Washington

Thomas Wexford had woken early this morning. Usually waking at six a.m., today he was already dressed and showered and moving towards his study by the time the clock hands moved into line. He'd always been rich. His family had enjoyed the trappings of wealth his father, a self-made real-estate multi-millionaire, had earned. By the time the young President-to-be was ready to launch his own career in real estate, he had grown accustomed to everything unlimited money could buy. Including people.

His family had always employed servants, so the young man destined to become the most powerful leader in the world was used to having everything done for him, but even he was surprised by the service offered to the person that held the title of President of the United States. Normal people may make their own breakfast and brew their own coffee - they might lay out their own clothes or perhaps open their own doors, but there is nothing normal about his role. As he reached the door from his bedroom, it opened. Walking through without breaking stride he turned sharply left and continued down the corridor, the words 'Good Morning, Mr. President' already fading in his ears.

As he reached the door from the corridor, it again opened automatically, the Navy steward having already been alerted to the President's movements. Greeting the steward with a nod of his head, POTUS moved to the table where his breakfast of fresh orange juice, oats, fruit and toast was waiting. Sometimes he preferred eggs and maybe even steak or bacon, but his wife, the First Lady, kept a close eye on his diet and few Navy stewards would choose to openly defy her instructions.

Not a career politician, he reveled in the glamour and prestige the role of President afforded him. Most people admitted he was a good businessman. He used some of his parents' money to build, then lose, then build again his personal fortune, now rumored to be in the region of several billion dollars. Always craving attention he'd never been one to keep quiet about his accomplishments. He'd regularly been on the front pages of Newsweek, Forbes, and other magazines, as well as hosting a television show.

Good at business where you make the decisions and can hire 'yes' men to support you and fire those that don't, the limitations of public service had come as quite a shock. When elected, Wexford knew he still had a lot to learn about the workings of Washington and the government at large, but he chose to run roughshod over the normal practices of statesmanship and foreign affairs. He didn't care whom he upset, and he didn't care who knew it. Used to fawning admiration he found it hard to accept criticism and the intensive scrutiny of the press, preferring instead to use social media.

He also made a concerted effort to rid the White House of those who disagreed with him, preferring the sycophantic nods and smiles of those matching his views.

A creature of habit, he always liked to scan *The Washington Post* and *The New York Times* briefly while eating breakfast to get a feel of where the day may be heading. He would usually have *Fox News* playing in the background to understand what was being reported about him by his favorite news station. Thirty minutes later, after finishing his second cup of coffee, he moved to a more comfortable chair and picked up the President's Daily Brief or PDB.

The PDB is generated in the early hours of each morning and comes from the Office of the Director of National Intelligence. It is their job to sift and sort the masses of data available from the various intelligence agencies and put it into a sensible summary for the President. Some of the data is hard facts; some are only strong rumors. Many of the rumors may be false but contain enough substance to cause unrest in regions of the world where Americans might be placed in harm's way.

Reading through this morning's PDB, he was thankful that little had appeared to have changed overnight. Israel was still deploying their military to the Gaza border and some skirmishes had broken out; the ongoing conflicts in Syria, Iraq and Afghanistan were continuing, but nothing major had occurred; and the other conflicts, skirmishes and world's problems were much as they had been when he went to bed just over six hours ago. In particular, the Middle East Gulf region was as static as it had been for many weeks.

One item did draw his attention, however, and he made a mental note to raise it.

Walking into the Oval Office at seven-fifty, he sat at his desk and quickly scanned his daily calendar located immediately in front of him. Pressing the intercom button, he said, "G'Morning Angela. Are they here yet?"

"Good morning, Mr. President," his secretary answered. She'd been at her desk for over 30-minutes and already has his day organized. "Generals' Dreiberg, Tarrant and Mansfield are already here, sir."

"Send them in and have Alex and Bill Casler join us."

Seconds later, the door opened and Lt. General Warwick Dreiberg - Director of National Intelligence, General Melvin Tarrant - Secretary of Defense, and

General Ulysses Mansfield - Chairman of the Joint Chiefs of Staff entered, shook hands with the President and took their seats on the sofas.

By the time the steward had served coffee, the President's chief of staff, Alex Simpson, had arrived. Simpson was the only member of the White House permitted to enter the Oval Office unannounced, usually from his own office adjoining it.

"Gentlemen," the President began, "I've asked for Bill to join us, but until he arrives let's get on with the briefing."

For the next fifteen minutes or so, they jointly discussed the contents of the PDB and debated any potential options. They had just finished talking about Russia's ongoing military build-up and what it could mean for the immediate future when the intercom buzzed.

"Mr. President. Secretary Casler is here," and moments later Bill Casler - the newly appointed Secretary of State after his predecessor had disagreed with the President - walked into the Oval Office.

"Mr. President, sorry to have missed the beginning of the meeting."

"No worries, Bill. I wanted you here about Nigeria. This latest report about Boko Haram moving six girls - tell me more."

"Mr. President. We believe facets of Boko Haram are planning to raise additional funds by selling off some of the girls they've taken either as brides, into prostitution or as slaves. This group is headed by Colonel Kolade Ganda who is one of their divisional leaders based in north-east Kano. The NSA intercepted radio traffic confirming the movement of the girls and of a bidding session planned for two days' time."

"Can't their army rescue these girls, Bill?"

"The Nigerian army is rife with BH supporters. Any time any mission is planned Boko get wind of it, and usually, they've moved on by the time the army gets there. Or they reinforce their position so well the army takes masses of casualties. It causes embarrassment to their government. I've even spoken to Nigeria's foreign minister and offered our assistance, but he and his president are concerned that any outside interference by the U.S. would make their army look even worse. Having to rely on outside help for what is seen as an internal problem."

Raising a hand to make it obvious to all those in attendance to remain quiet, POTUS sat in silence for almost a minute. Finally, looking up, he said, "What if we could help without being seen to help?"

5

FBI Headquarters, Quantico

Standing in the shower with the hot water cascading down over his head and shoulders, Deacon gingerly rubbed the two pairs of red burn marks on his chest. The center of the marks was blackened where the skin had burnt away, while the angry tissue surrounding it faded from bright red in color close to the middle, back to dark yellow and blue four inches or so away as the bruising gradually came out. The muscles surrounding the entire area were still swollen and sore, and he couldn't help wincing as he raised his arms up to shoulder height to wash his hair.

Rinsing off the remaining suds he opened the cubicle and grabbed a towel. Standing by his locker waiting for him was Troy Kemple, the lead weapons instructor at FBI Quantico.

"Sore?"

"Sure is!"

"Gone are the days we used life-size cardboard images of gangsters or mothers with babies. IVRS training really puts you out there."

"Eyevers?"

"Yeah, IVRS - Immersive Virtual Reality Simulation. As close to real life as we can currently make it. Problem with the old system was if you screwed up we just reset the test and you started again. Now you screw up and you suffer. Like in real life."

"Where did the idea come from?" Deacon asked.

"Pilots have been using this sort of gear for years. Used for training and for re-certification it's obviously far cheaper than actual flying. What they've reported on the newer systems that have excellent graphics and full-motion movement is they forget they are in a simulator. Looking out through the windshield, the images are so real and life-like. Even the vibrations and movements of a flying plane are produced so accurately that the pilots become fully immersed. You see pilots come out of stress testing shaking and covered in sweat. When the doors of the simulator shut it's so realistic it's as if they're really there. Well, we've just taken that idea, along with input from video game manufacturers, to make a fully interactive immersive simulation. It uses some of the very latest technology. S'no good having you sitting on a comfy chair shooting at bad guys. You need to be in the thick of it. The sight, sound, smells . . . and movement. You need to be fully immersed. The walls, doorways and furniture or shelves ... everything is totally movable. Your VR headset and earpieces project the images and sounds we want you to see and hear. We even spray relevant smells. In minutes, your brain becomes totally fooled. You become completely engaged, and you forget it's just a simulation as you move through the building. We can even control the temperature and include rain. The images are all computer generated but they are so good you can't distinguish from reality."

"My chest hurting isn't simulation. It really is hurting," Deacon said, gently massaging his chest.

"The technology leap that made the pilots training so real was the motion feedback. That, along with sight and sound is what fools the brain. That's what pilots reported back, that once that had been included, the perception of reality changed. No point having you go through all this if you don't get the full feedback. So we provide you with the same. The nylon bodysuit you wore under your clothes was connected wirelessly to the same computer system. Electrodes were touching multiple parts of your body. As long as you didn't get shot there'd be no problem. As soon as you were hit, the computer generated the relevant amount of impact pain to the same area of your body where you were hit. You received Taser equivalent blasts to your chest where the rounds would have penetrated. Pretty real life, huh?"

"Two hours ago and still damn sore."

"Well, it was only simulation. In reality, two chest shots without a vest on and you'd be dead. What would you prefer? Tickled with a feather?" Kemble said with a smile.

"Nah, I'm good. So why use the kid?"

"So far, however good our trainees are, everyone forgets to check the kid. They all assume, like you did, that he was one of the hostages. Everyone assumes only the adults are the bad guys. In Afghanistan and also Syria we're getting reports of more and more kids being used as jihadists. Sometimes alongside adults, sometimes on their own. A favorite trick is having a child wandering along a deserted road. Soldiers stop to check everything OK and the kid's handler watching from a distance triggers the vest remotely. So in this test, there were six terrorists, not five. Even if you had guessed, I was in the control room and would have gotten you with a seventh hidden behind an air vent. Don't worry, you did better than everyone else who's used this system so far. It's only been operational just over a week."

Grabbing his clothes, Deacon quickly dressed while continuing on the conversation. "I'm very impressed. You're right about them using kids, but it's awkward to accept an innocent looking kid could have evil intent. This is just the sort of training we need in the SEALs."

23

"Yeah, not just you guys. We're hoping on replicating this in various locations around the country. We've had a lot of interest from SWAT and hostage teams, as well as various special forces. Even some standard Police Forces. However, you're a civilian - usually this department is only available to government agencies. You must have some high-level connections?" Kemble added, raising an eyebrow.

"The company I represent offers security and close personal protection to visiting businessmen, film and music stars, and to diplomats preferring U.S. security over their own," Deacon said, "but you're right, connections help."

Before finishing the sentence, Deacon's mobile phone rang. Excusing himself and having seen the number dialed from, he answered.

"John. Just got a call from Mitch. Admiral Carter wants you at the Pentagon a-sap."

Thanking the caller before hanging up, Deacon finished dressing before shaking hands with Troy and heading out to his truck for the fifty-minute journey along I-95.

Climbing into his dark blue F-150 crew cab, Deacon settled back, turned the radio down and headed for Washington. His life had changed drastically in the past eight months. For his last mission while still a full SEAL member he'd had to go underground and join the very people he was tasked with fighting. But, as always with all of his missions, he'd had to improvise. His success, he believed, came from a mixture of planning, skill, improvising, bravado, timing and good old-fashioned luck.

His last two major missions had come to the direct notice of the previous President and the then President-Elect. Eight months ago he'd accepted the offer to work directly for the new President via Admiral Carter, and he hadn't looked back since. Jointly he and the Admiral had decided on the best set-up and cover story. Shortly after, he'd resigned from the U.S. Navy. Now holding the rank of 'Honorary Lieutenant Commander', Deacon set up a company called Phylax, offering close personal protection and bodyguarding.

Phylax being ancient Greek meaning guardian or sentinel, and with an office located in Dupont Circle, close to the major embassies, business began to roll in. Funds to set up the company came in the form of a low-interest loan through an offshore bank in the Cayman Islands, funded by a shell company in the Bahamas with many layers of isolation between it and the U.S. Government. Phylax was registered as a fully legitimate company offering close protection services to visiting elite business people and diplomats. Private endorsements by the President guaranteed success and Phylax had already expanded to provide long-term in-country protection with customers based in the Middle East. Deacon's role within Phylax was CEO with most of his time spent either in the office or traveling marketing his company's services. Using only staff personally vetted by him, Phylax offered the highest quality of personal service. Staff included Gina Panaterri - an ex-Secret Service agent who ran the office in his absence and had just made the call to him, and Sean Martock - ex-Navy SEAL, as well as twenty-five other employees registered on their books, all being ex-Army, Special Forces, or similar. Some had even signed up from foreign agencies such as the British SAS, the German GSG 9, and the French DGSE.

With a blue-chip client list growing rapidly and excellent references from satisfied customers, Phylax was on target to become a major success.

Only Gina Panaterri and Sean Martock knew that although Phylax was a legitimate company, it was also a front for services directly to the President, via Admiral Carter - Chief of Naval Operations at the Pentagon. As and when the President deemed necessary, Phylax and its employees would be available for specific government-designated 'black-level' work. However, in this role, Phylax would be considered a private company and not able to call on the normal protection of the U.S. Government. If injured or captured, individuals would be held accountable to the laws and legal sentences of that country. In practice, the U.S. Government would totally disown them.

Only the President and a very few in his inner circle were aware of Phylax and its capabilities.

6

Hong Kong

Junior Grade Lieutenant Zhang Su Ming arrived fifteen minutes early for work, as she did most days. Working on various projects and based at the People's Liberation Army Navy (PLAN) Hong Kong Garrison, the twenty-eight-year-old was enjoying life to the full. The vibrant, exciting city of Hong Kong had everything a young woman could possibly want. Within yards of her apartment, there were numerous bars and restaurants to call on. The city also enjoys an exciting nightlife, mainly from its time as a western-influenced British Dependent Territory. With a large collection of both male and female friends, she didn't believe life could get much better.

Her department was in charge of provisions delivery and ships resources allocated to Surmi Reef. Her specific role was in ensuring adequate food, mechanical spares and fuel were always available. Currently, four large floating dredgers were working around-the-clock dredging sand, shale and coral to continue building up the island base. However, round-the-clock working meant routine maintenance was being overlooked, and machinery was beginning to wear out and break down. Today's task was in sourcing replacement digger jaws and teeth from the manufacturing company based in Tianjin, near Beijing. The coral and shale would quickly blunt the digger teeth and, once blunted, the teeth themselves would easily break. Missing maintenance schedules merely exasperated the problem, but the senior officers in charge just kept pushing for more and more work, and so the problems escalated. With schedules to keep and broken equipment slowing them down, additional crews had been drafted in to run the bulldozers and compactors to flatten the newly reclaimed land.

Su Ming had been at her desk for almost two hours when her phone rang. She'd already been onto the digger manufacturer, receiving their promises and guarantees that replacement teeth would be available and could be shipped directly to Hong Kong, but she knew from experience that it was a lie. Had she been a man then promises would likely have been kept, but as a mere woman, even a Lieutenant in the PLAN, arguing with a senior manager of production was a waste of time, and she'd need to follow up daily with stronger and stronger threats.

Grabbing the ringing phone, she lifted it to her ear, but before she could state her name or title, the guttural voice of the Captain in charge of the overall department blurted out demanding she come to his desk.

Captain Gao's small office was only thirty feet or so away but she felt all eyes on her as she answered his summons. He rarely called people in, and when he did, it was usually for a severe reprimand. He lecherously watched her walk the last ten feet until she stood in front of his desk and saluted. He was a small man with poor skin and bad teeth. He had bad BO and suffered from extreme halitosis which anyone stood close enough to him would happily corroborate. But he fancied himself and would letch and flirt with all the young women working for him, Su Ming in particular.

"Yes Captain," Su Ming said.

Looking her up and down in a provocatively sexual way, his eyes finally fastened on her breasts. She was slim with normal womanly dimensions and wearing a nonflattering uniform, but still his eyes bored into her, and she felt the revulsion in the pit of her stomach.

"Captain, you wanted to see me?" she tried again, his eyes never moving from their focus.

Finally, after what seemed an age to her, he managed to peel his eyes away and glance at her face as he blurted out, "Lieutenant, your grandfather is very ill. I've been ordered to allow you to go to him. You may leave. Dismissed."

Trying not to show tears partly of relief but also of sadness about the news, Su Ming saluted, spun around and walked quickly back towards her desk. She knew from experience he would be watching her backside as she walked, his lips slightly parted with just the tip of his tongue caressing and wetting them.

Changing her screen to a search engine, she found the booking number for Air China, picked up her phone and dialed it. Two hours later, she was walking along the air-bridge boarding her 12:35 flight from Chek Lap Kok Airport to the public and military combined airport at Quanzhou Jinjiang. Her grandfather had lived his entire life in the hills above Quanzhou. In days long past, the family he had raised had lived in a small building, almost a shack by today's standards, but some wealth had slowly come to the family and he and his wife, Su Ming's grandmother, had moved into their current home almost twenty years before. High in the hills facing east, the home was wooden built in traditional style, and Su Ming had fond memories of enjoyable summers spent being spoiled by her grandparents.

Hailing a taxicab at Jinjiang airport, she shivered slightly. The air temperature was made cooler here by a sea breeze, and she knew it would drop even more so as they climbed into the hills. The driver made good time, and they arrived at the family house in less than an hour. Paying him, she stepped out directly into the arms of the tear-streaked face of her grandmother. It had been over six months since Su Ming had last visited and she felt the guilt weigh heavily on her shoulders now.

After a few minutes talking and hugging, her grandmother took her hand and walked her slowly through the home to the bedroom she had shared for so many years with her loving husband. Her grandfather was very weak. He could still talk, albeit with difficulty, but the end of his life was very near. He'd insisted, though, that he had something vital to tell Su Ming, hence his dying request to see her again. Trying to hold back the tears, Su Ming took the hand of the old man she loved so much. His eyes flickered open and searched the room. Coming to rest on Su Ming's face, his old leathery face cracked into a faint smile and a tear of joy squeezed out of the corner of an eye.

Instructing the nurses and his wife to leave them, he beckoned Su Ming closer. With her sitting on his bed he motioned with a wrinkled old finger for her to lay next to him. With her head so close to his, he didn't need to strain so much to talk, and the two of them stayed undisturbed.

Three hours later, sitting with her grandmother both of them in tears, and holding the cooling hand of her dead grandfather, she still couldn't believe what he'd told her.

7

The Pentagon, Washington

Parking in one of the allocated visitors' spaces, Deacon walked towards the main entrance to the outer security station and showed his pass. Cleared, he walked through to the second desk where the receptionist picked up the phone, dialed a number, and within a few moments, a female petty officer came and collected him. Walking along the corridors and up the ramps, Deacon made idle chat with his hostess while looking around. Although he'd visited many times, he still couldn't help but marvel at the structure of the world-famous building.

Rumored to be one of the most secure buildings in the USA, the structure is shaped like a pentagon. With 17.5 miles of corridors and a floor space of over 6.6 million square feet, housing over 23,000 workers each day, it's one of the largest offices in the world. With five floors above ground and two floors below, it's made up of five concentric rings labeled A through E from inside to out. Built during WWII when steel was in short supply and needed for ships and weaponry, there are no elevators in the building, only ramps, stairs and escalators.

Arriving at Admiral Carter's office, the petty officer knocked once before opening the door and waving Deacon to enter. Lieutenant Mitchel Stringer (Mitch to his friends) put the phone down, walked around the desk and clasped his friend's hand warmly.

"Good to see you again, John. Sorry I couldn't come down - tied up on the phone."

"Excuses ... excuses. No worry pal. I've already got your number, but you're not my type. Now I have Sandra Teasman's as well," Deacon said, smiling and pocketing the card she'd given him, as he watched the pretty petty officer walk away.

Punching Deacon lightly on the shoulder, Mitch turned and opened the door into Admiral Carter's inner sanctum. Completely different from any other Pentagon office Deacon had ever seen, this was a room with a long window and a view outside looking across the Pentagon Lagoon Yacht Basin to the Potomac River beyond. The walls were painted in the standard pale color, but the Admiral had clearly made the room his own. The expected photographs of the Admiral shaking hands with the various Presidents he'd served under adorned the wall behind his desk. Along the adjacent wall were photos of various naval aircraft in flight and of ships he'd served on. Directly opposite the Admiral's desk was a large painting of the Admiral's last sea command and the United States' first nuclear-powered aircraft carrier, the USS Enterprise.

Rising to his feet from behind his large wooden desk, rumored to have been hand-built for the Admiral with reclaimed wood from the USS Maine — the U.S. battleship sunk in mysterious circumstances in Havana harbor on February 15th, 1898 — the Admiral stood as Deacon saluted and returned the salute, before taking Deacon's hand and shaking it warmly.

"Deacon, my pleasure. How did it go at Quantico?"

"Very well, sir. Learned lots, which was the intention. Got caught by their new IVRS but passed everything," he said, gently rubbing the two sore patches under his shirt.

"Yeah, I heard," the Admiral said. "Kemble emailed me your report. Passed everything with flying colors and Troy admitted he deliberately put the kid with the gun in the sim. Said he couldn't let you pass everything with 100 percent as you might get big-headed," he laughed.

"I'll remember that," Deacon said, smiling as the Admiral guided them over towards a small coffee table in the corner grouped alongside four comfy chairs.

Petty Officer Teasman re-entered the office again carrying a tray loaded with coffee and cups, set it down on the table, looked and smiled at Deacon before exiting again.

"So why am I here, Admiral?" he asked.

"Before we go into that, what do you know about Boko Haram?" the Admiral asked.

"Uhh, never needed to fight them directly. Formed in 2002, I think. Called something else originally before they became Boko or BH as they're now known. Followers of al-Qaeda under Osama bin-Laden and likewise of ISIS, they're heavy in northern Nigeria."

"Hmmm, not bad. Mitch. Fill in the details please," the Admiral said.

Picking up a folder Mitch began to read out loud, "The group commonly known as Boko Haram started life in 2002 as 'Jamā'at Ahl as-Sunnah lid-Da'wah wa'l-Jihād' or 'Group of the people of Sunnah for Preaching and Jihad'. They became known as Boko Haram, and that has stuck ever since. The original leader, Mohammed Yusuf, was captured by Nigerian Forces and executed in 2009. A new leader, Abubakar Shekau, took control. A follower and supporter of Osama bin Laden, he became more violent and sadistic. Boko Haram has killed tens of thousands of civilians and displaced almost 2.5 million. The entire north-eastern region of Nigeria, including parts of the adjoining countries of Niger, Chad and Cameroon are totally controlled by Boko Haram. In 2015 they were ranked as the world's deadliest terror group, overtaken in 2016 and '17 by ISIS.

"In 2015, Abubakar Shekau pledged full allegiance to ISIS (Islamic State of Iraq and the Levant) and became known as the Islamic State in West Africa. However, they are still known by everyone as Boko Haram.

"With over half of the northern region of Nigeria already operating under Sharia law, the areas covered by Boko Haram are the most extreme. In April 2014, they obtained international fame for the kidnapping of 276 schoolgirls from the town of Chibok, in eastern Nigeria. The plan was to sell them into slavery, but over 50 managed to escape, leaving a total of 219 in captivity. Since then over 100 have been freed in exchange for Boko Haram militants, but over 100 are still missing. Most by now, we believe, will have been sold into marriage or slavery. There have been countless attempts to find the girls or obtain information about where they are being held, but the locals are terrified of violent reprisals, and the Nigerian Army and police forces have been heavily infiltrated. Also, offers of help from the U.S. Government along with the British SAS have been rejected for political reasons. With the amount of spending by the Nigerian Government on their military and police, the public is outraged when their own soldiers are stood down in favor of us or the Brits."

Putting down his coffee cup Deacon said, "Ok, that's their history. So what's happened?"

Mitch pulled out a couple of sheets of paper and passed them over, saying, "Intelligence has uncovered a plot to sell six girls to rich Arabs for slavery and 'personal use'. The local BH area commander, Kolade Ganda, a particularly vicious bastard, had them moved yesterday to a secure house on the outskirts of Kano. Rich middle-eastern businessmen are flying in the day after tomorrow. The Nigerian leader, President Buhari, has been on the phone to 'State and he wants the U.S. to help, but can't be seen to be asking. Likewise, U.S. Forces can't be seen to be involved without the permission of Buhari."

Admiral Carter took over the conversation, saying, "John, this is where Phylax comes in. We need you to lead a small team in and rescue the girls. Your men need to believe this is being funded by a rich Nigerian businessman whose daughter is one of the kidnapped. As before, you and your men will be on your own. If you are captured, the President needs to be able to deny all knowledge to save embarrassment to himself and Buhari. You need to fly tonight. The NSA has identified where the girls are being temporarily held in Kano and our best intelligence shows between twelve and fourteen guards. Once rescued, you need to get the girls to the Sheraton Abuja hotel where TV and news people will be waiting. Abuja is over 400km from Kano by road, about four hours at top speed, or a forty-five-minute flight. I'll leave it to you to sort out the logistics. It goes without saying that you and your people must remain anonymous. Mitch has all the information we currently have and will be your point of contact, as normal. The CIA has in-country assets, and they'll meet you at Kano airport with weapons and gear."

With copies of the intelligence reports, a data file and photograph of his CIA contact, as well as aerial photos of the girls' suspected location, Deacon headed back out to his truck.

Sitting in the cab with the engine running he called Gina Panaterri instructing her to call Roberts, Canetti, Martock, Stockwell and Maričić to the office with full travel gear for 16:00 hours today. Finishing that call, he immediately dialed the number for Hank Pechnik, one of the best Navy pilots he'd ever come across and one of his earliest recruits to Phylax.

"Hank, charter a private executive jet flying from Washington to Kano, Nigeria, tonight. Preferably a Gulfstream 550 or similar. Returning within 36 hours. We need it fueled, and flight-plans booked ready to leave at 19:00. OK?"

As he put the phone down, he knew Hank would already be making the necessary calls.

8

High over the North Atlantic

Stretching out his six-foot-two-inch frame as he reclined the leather seat down, Deacon smiled as he listened to the chatter of his five colleagues. Hank had done a good job in chartering the aircraft at such short notice. He'd managed to acquire the Gulfstream 650 model, a faster, slightly larger and more comfortable version of the extremely popular 550 executive jet. Usually, the jet would come with its own crew of pilot, co-pilot and stewardess, but they'd rented it bare. Deacon was relying on Hank's ability not to need a co-pilot, and he knew his people would fetch their own food and drinks.

As always, the flight to a mission would be alcohol dry, but he'd made sure there would be plenty of beer for the return journey. Hank reported over the intercom system that they were now at 48,000 feet but fighting a strong headwind so the 5,500-mile journey over the inky black and cold North Atlantic would take just over ten hours. Their cruising height was well above the normal commercial airliner flight corridors, so he was expecting a quiet and uneventful flight.

Deacon would give them an hour to enjoy a meal before calling them to order and running through the plan one last time. They'd already covered it twice in detail in the secure inner conference room in Dupont Circle, but he always believed in as much preparation as possible. However, from many years of experience, he also firmly believed in Helmuth von Moltke's, a 19th-century head of the Prussian army, famous observation that 'No battle plan ever survives first contact with the enemy'.

The 'official' story that Deacon, Martock and Gina had put forward to the other members of the team was one of the many girls kidnapped was the daughter of a rich Nigerian businessman. He had received a ransom demand from Boko Haram saying his daughter, along with another five, were being moved to Kano to be sold as sex slaves. He could pay a ransom for his daughter's release, but not for the other five. He'd decided to approach Deacon and Phylax and was willing to pay them to try and rescue all six girls. Deacon had accepted and was bringing a team of people with him to assist.

Having gone through the plan a third and final time, and after carefully examining all available aerial photographs and mugshots of known senior BH terrorists, the discussion moved onto weapons. They all knew BH wasn't going to give up their hostages easily and without a fight but they couldn't take their weaponry with them. Deacon knew they'd have to clear Nigerian customs and he had no license to carry weapons into Nigeria. Although many of the police and customs officials were badly corrupt, they couldn't take any chances. Also, a team of military-age male Americans carrying weapons entering the country into the middle of Boko Haram territory would quickly get back to the terrorists. Therefore, Deacon had made other arrangements.

The only problem was, he didn't know what quality of weapons they'd be getting.

Ten and a half hours after lifting clear of the runway in Washington the thump of the landing gear being lowered brought a faint cheer from those on board. After a near-perfect landing, Hank taxied the Gulfstream to International Arrivals at Mallam Aminu Kano

International Airport. As the dying whine of the engines spooled down, Martock pressed a button, and the access door opened, and the steps unfolded themselves down to the tarmac.

The local time was 13:37 and the first thing that hit them was a sudden gust of extremely hot, humid air. Dust clouds circled around a military-style jeep fast approaching. It screeched to a stop near the steps and two soldiers carrying automatic weapons leaped from the back of the vehicle taking up positions on either side of the stairway. Seconds later, a rear door of the jeep opened, and a short, dark-skinned man wearing full military uniform stepped out. After carefully adjusting his cap, he approached.

Climbing the stairs, he was followed by the two guards. Stepping into the cabin, he said abruptly, "I am Captain Kemi Fashola. Papers!"

Deacon stepped forward, smiled and passed over the required paperwork. After carefully looking through and checking each person's passport, he tossed them on to a nearby table.

"What are you doing here in Nigeria?"

Offering his hand that was ignored, Deacon said, "Captain, my men and I are lead engineers for an American peanut growing company exploring the possibility of intensive farming in the northern Nigerian countryside. We are here to scope out favorable locations."

"Do you have weapons with you?"

"No Captain, only scientific instruments and cameras."

"Show me!"

Leading the way, Deacon headed down the steps and moved to the rear of the airplane to the cargo hatch.

Opening it, he was pushed brusquely aside by the two armed guards who climbed inside.

"Please be careful." Deacon shouted, "Those are delicate," as the guards started pulling boxes and Pelicases about.

Taking them carefully, Deacon laid them down on the tarmac and opened them. From one he took a laser theodolite, and from the other, he took two laptop computers and a GPS unit.

"Captain, these are used to measure and map exactly where we are."

Captain Fashola looked on, not sure of how to proceed. Undoubtedly, Nigeria was always looking for more foreign investment, and peanut growing and production was being seen as a savior for the Nigerian farming industry. He knew if he failed to allow them to proceed he could be in trouble with his superiors but as with most corrupt officials, he wanted something for his trouble.

The guards reported there was no contraband in any of the carryalls, so he motioned for Deacon to head back into the cabin.

Knowing the power the Captain possessed to delay or obstruct them, Deacon moved to one of the galley lockers and pulled out a bottle of Johnnie Walker Black Label whiskey that was quietly handed over to Fashola along with an envelope containing one hundred US dollars, and three cartons of Marlboro Light cigarettes.

Finally, the table was repeatedly thumped as the passports received their required stamps and the aircraft paperwork was signed and authorized, before a smiling Captain stomped back down the aircraft steps, climbed back into his jeep and shouted at his guards to follow.

Exhaling a sigh of relief, Deacon waited until the jeep had headed away before making a quick phone call.

Minutes later two taxis approached, stopped alongside and a thin, gaunt-looking man stepped out of the lead car.

"John Deacon? Bob Bowker."

"Bob, have you been briefed?" Deacon said, stepping off the aircraft steps and extending a hand. He'd already checked the image in the CIA photograph against the person.

"Everything's arranged. I work for Charles Ingram's department. If you're ready, we need to head off."

Deacon confirmed for Hank to get the aircraft refueled and then stay and sleep on board to guarantee no one interfered with it, while the others grabbed their bags and climbed into the waiting taxis. The plan was for them to be back by early morning.

Climbing into the lead taxi, Bowker ordered them to head out. They drove through the airport gates before passing through a small industrial area. Finally, after a number of twists and turns, they ended up at the rear of a dilapidated badly weathered dirty building behind large, closed doors.

With no weapons, they all felt uneasy. Was it a trap? Climbing out of the taxis and grabbing their bags, the taxis quickly drove away leaving just the six of them and Bowker. Smiling, he led them towards one of the large doors which, surprisingly, slid open easily on well-oiled rollers.

Inside were two beat-up, rusted, Toyota Hiace minibusses. Walking over towards them the team could see both had cracked windshields and one had a wiper blade missing. They were both badly dented and had ripped seats.

"Do they even run?" Deacon said, raising an eyebrow.

"Hey, don't judge by looks. They're both good runners. They're reliable. They just look like crap, but they blend in well over here. They are also one of the most common vehicles in this country. Anything clean and modern stands out. The windows are darkened but just look dirty. Each seat back and headrest, as well as the side panels and front and rear doors, are reinforced with 2 inches of African Blackwood - one of the hardest woods you can get. Poor man's armor plating, but almost as good as steel. It'll stop an AK-47 round at three yards. Heavy, so it will slow you down a little, but worth it. The weapons you requested are at the farm. Climb in; we need to go," he said.

Both vehicles started on the first turn of the ignition and with Bob Bowker at the controls of one bus Sean Martock followed driving the other. The rest of them slouched down low in their seats, almost completely hidden from any prying eyes, as Bowker led them through the streets out of the city to the north-east.

"What do you think?"

"I was expecting it to be raining?" Deacon said towards Bowker.

"Yeah, the rainy season's just about finished. A bit early this year. A fortnight back a lot of this was flooded, but now it's just turning back into its normal dust bowl, but I meant about the vehicles?"

"They don't seem to have any power. But I guess they'll have to do," Deacon said.

"They were all I could muster at short notice, but you're right - all that extra weight of the wood has crippled them."

Almost an hour later, they turned off a small road onto a dusty dirt track that led finally to an isolated farm. Driving behind the main building, Bowker headed into an old barn, before stopping the bus and climbing out.

"CIA safe house. It's isolated enough you won't be seen here," he said.

Walking over to the other side of the barn, he pulled open a trapdoor and started down the wooden steps.

"This is a sound-proof range. You can test your weapons here," he continued.

Between them, the team pulled all the weapons out of a wooden crate and laid them on a bench. In total, there were six handguns with suppressors, mostly Colts; four shotguns, and six Heckler & Koch assault rifles with suppressors and night scopes. Also included were flash-bang and tear-gas grenades, as well as four night-vision headsets, plus small low-power radios, earpieces and throat mics. There were also boxes of ammunition, spare magazines, numerous bottles of water, high-energy food bars, six large blankets and a first-aid bag.

"This should be enough to start WW3," Martock said, checking over one of the H&K's.

"Guys, you know the drill. Grab a weapon, strip it down, clean it, oil it, test it. Make sure you're happy with it. Your life may depend on it later today."

After spending two hours cleaning, checking and firing the weapons, Deacon wanted to go through the plan once more this time with the latest satellite info provided from Bowker. With the middle-eastern buyers expected to arrive before 09:00 the following morning, the rescue would have to occur this coming evening, which left little time for any changes.

With the aerial photographs projected up onto the wall, Bowker ran through what he knew.

"The girls are being held in this building here," he said indicating the center building of three in a walled compound. "This area is a village. Quiet and away from the main road. This whole north-eastern region is pro BH. Gunfire noise will travel, and locals will likely be up against you within minutes. We believe the girls are still located in the basement, but at least they are all together.

Six were counted arriving, and they've not left yet. The auction tomorrow is planned to take place at the compound. Four guards arrived with them and are still there. The local Boko leader, Colonel Kolade Ganda, is staying in one of the buildings - we believe it to be this one," he said pointing to a smaller adjoining room.

"There are four additional guards plus two women - a cook and an old woman called Ezinne who looks after the girls. There's an older guy who looks after the building, more like a gardener come handyman. We don't think he's armed. All the other males will be. Bear in mind, these are all murderers and terrorists and Kolade Ganda is a particularly vicious bastard."

Bowker passed around other photos of the buildings and grounds and also additional aerial views while explaining, "Upstairs is the guards' living quarters. This one is the main dining room for them and the kitchen. This is a toilet and shower block at the rear. This first building is for visitors, and that's where Ganda will be holding the auction. The guard routine normally is two on, two off, on four-hour watches, but now three guards are patrolling and at least one more is on duty inside while the others are sleeping or off duty. The rest is up to you. I can't be involved. The weapons are all unmarked and the vehicles are clean," he finished.

Deacon and his men spent a few more minutes looking, but nothing major had changed from what they had expected.

He stood and recited the plan one final time. Deacon and Martock would be the drivers. Pointing to the map, he confirmed, "We head along Kano Gumel Rd, and head to here. We leave both vehicles. Andy and Goran stay with them. We head one mile across country to here," he said pointing to an enlarged image, "and hit the target. When called, they bring both vehicles to here," he said, pointing, "then Goran drives straight to the airport with the girls with Jose and Bill. Andy, Sean and I will follow and run any interference. Clear?" With no negative response, he continued.

"Now for the attack on the compound . . ."

Finally, Bowker turned to Deacon and said, "How do you plan to get the girls to Abuja?"

"Hank will be refueled and waiting. As soon as we're clear, we'll head straight back to the airport for a quick flight down. Then drop them off and we head home."

"Good - I've arranged a bus to pick them up and transport them to the Sheraton for a press conference. That's obviously top secret for now - only the Police Commissioner has the details. The only other police you can trust are those under direct orders in Abuja and within the federal capital territory. All the others between Abuja and here are suspect. Some are good, but many have been bribed either just as informants or to look away at the right time. Some are even soldiers of BH. Trust no one.

"If you get into trouble before you get to Abuja, you're on your own. You'll be seen as armed foreign mercenary insurgents and treated accordingly. The U.S. Government will not come to your aid," Bowker said, "but you've got my cell number if you need to contact me," he added, before shaking each of them by the hand and wishing them good luck.

After a final check and the need to have a one-pass reconnoiter of the area in daylight, they packed up ready to leave. At this time of the year and this latitude twilight came early, so after stowing what they needed and grabbing some energy bars, they piled into the minibusses, started the engines and headed out.

9

Northeast region of Nigeria
As the minute hand on Deacon's watch swept up to 03:00, their attack began. The drive-by earlier had proven fruitful as they'd seen the condition of the local roads, being mainly dirt tracks full of potholes and ruts. It would make any fast getaway impossible because they had to cover the first two miles until they got back onto the main Kano Gumel Rd, the nearest suitable road with blacktop.

The two minibusses had been left parked in the shade of a large tree almost a mile from the walled compound with Andy Stockwell and Goran Maričić standing guard. The locals lived in either cinder block or tin shack houses but the nearest was over 400 yards away and none had lights showing. The area seemed alive with wild dogs mostly all barking and howling at once, but the advantage was the locals had become immune to their noises and any faint disturbance from Deacon and his men was lost in the background.

As they headed toward the target a large alpha dog leading his pack approached, teeth bared and snarling. Not willing to take any chances, Bill Roberts dispatched him with a suppressed round from his rifle, the animal dropping in its tracks with the remainder of the pack turning, sniffing the air and running away. The soft phut of the weapon was not heard more than a few feet away. The dry, dusty earth gave the advantage of deadening any sound produced by their feet as they carefully edged closer while the mainly overcast sky sat solemnly overhead and hid them from view.

The pale green glow from their night vision goggles clearly illuminated the paths and tracks, and although they checked carefully for any tripwires or early warning sensors, they found none. As they approached the compound wall, all except Martock and Roberts stayed low in the scrub bushes. After a final sight check in either direction, the two of them moved forward until they were crouching down next to it. The wall itself was fairly thick and rough textured. At ten feet, it was too high to easily scale, and they'd chosen not to use any form of grappling hook due to the sound it might make. Bending slightly, Martock joined his hands together and Roberts slipped his right foot onto them. Careful not to make a noise, he lifted Roberts until his outstretched hands just cleared the wall. Pulling himself up a little, Roberts could see broken glass cemented along the crown of the wall. He could also see a pair of guards casually walking towards his position, maybe twenty seconds away. Dropping back down he quietly spoke into the radio mouthpiece, at the same time unfastening his backpack and pulling out two thick grey heavy blankets.

Forty seconds later, he was back up level with the wall and could see the guards further along their route. Laying the two blankets double thickness across the glass gave enough protection and he quietly slipped over, dropping down the other side into the compound before taking position behind a nearby bush.

After checking the guards were still patrolling, Roberts gave the 'all clear' signal and moments later Deacon's head appeared at the wall top before Canetti joined him there. Leaning down they gripped Martock's outstretched hands and with one swift pull all three of them were sitting straddling the blankets, before they also slipped quietly down. Splitting into two teams, they moved towards the far corners of the compound grounds. In the inky darkness the red glow of the guard's cigarette would have shown anyway, however, through their NVG's it was as bright as a flashlight. The green image showed a guard sloppily dressed, smoking, and leaning casually against the wall. His weapon, what looked to be an AK-47, was propped up behind him. There was a sweet smell of marijuana in the air as the other two guards carried on their patrol, weapons slung loosely over their shoulders and speaking in low tones.

Martock and Canetti crept up towards the patrolling guards while Roberts waited. As the smoker drew deeply and the cigarette end glowed brighter, Roberts shot him a single tap in the forehead with his suppressed rifle. The rumpled noise of the body collapsing muffled the soft plop from Roberts' rifle and less than three seconds later Martock and Canetti also dispatched both patrolling guards with headshots.

Not bothering to move the bodies as the plan was for a rapid in and out, Deacon headed towards the end dwelling just as the skies cleared overhead allowing the stars to shine through.

Colonel Kolade Ganda had been sleeping but he'd had a restless night. A number of times he'd risen, grabbed a drink, or a cigarette and waited for tiredness to overcome him. Now, sitting up in bed smoking but with the lights out, he again felt restless. Maybe it was intuition or maybe it was whatever instinct had kept him alive all these years that was keeping him awake now, but sitting there he suddenly saw the outline shadow of Deacon pass along the outside of his window. Grabbing his weapon, he leaped off the bed and started shouting.

Alerted by the Colonel's shouting, another guard came running out of the main building straight into two rounds from Martock into his chest. Martock, Canetti and Roberts raced towards the guards' building, kicked open the door and rushed upstairs. The off-duty guards were still coming awake and scrabbling for their weapons as the door was kicked open and two flash-bang grenades were thrown in. Completely disoriented by the sudden violent blast and brightness, they were no match for the pinpoint accuracy of Roberts and Martock's aimed rounds. One guard, quicker off the mark than his colleagues, opened fire with his AK-47 before a well-placed double-tap from Martock exploded his forehead. Canetti ran on, chasing the one last guard who'd managed to escape into the adjoining room. As Canetti leaped in through the doorway, the frame disintegrated under multiple AK-47 hits, two of them snicking at his clothes as he dove to the floor. As the guard lowered his rifle barrel towards Canetti, Martock followed up with one in the guard's chest followed by a second in the head.

Deacon shouted at Roberts and Canetti to track down Colonel Ganda as he pressed the radio transmit button calling for Stockwell and Maričić to get there as quickly as possible. With the element of surprise now gone and lights and lamps coming on in houses nearby, the worry was they could get bogged down in a firefight. With a sudden roar of an engine starting, a dark Mercedes crashed through the door of a lean-to shack and out towards the main gate. Deacon laid down fire and peppered the trunk with the rear window exploding into fragments, but it wasn't enough and the Mercedes hardly faltered before crashing through the main wooden gate, slewed to the left and sped away.

In a rush now before any reinforcements or the police would arrive, Deacon and Martock shot the locks off a door leading down to the basement. The wide-eyed stares of six terrified girls huddled in a corner stared back at them. With English being the most common language spoken in Nigeria, Deacon only had to shout twice before the shock left them and they began to respond. Ushering them upstairs he told them they were being rescued and they must exit the building, just as Goran Maričić pulled up in the lead vehicle outside. As Martock ushered the girls into the lead minibus and they climbed in, Deacon could see Canetti tying the hands of the old gardener behind his back and making him sit. Quickly grabbing any paperwork he could find, plus a laptop belonging to Colonel Ganda, Deacon ran towards the second vehicle just as the old lady guard, Ezinne, came out holding an AK-47. Slapping his hand on the side of the first vehicle, he told Maričić to get to the aircraft just as Canetti and Roberts climbed on board, and with it, the bus left with a wheel spin churning up dust and dirt.

"Boss, look out!" Stockwell shouted as Deacon turned. Seeing Ezinne raising her weapon Deacon didn't hesitate and shot her in the chest. Jumping back in the driver's seat, Stockwell revved the engine as Martock and Deacon climbed on board, Deacon mumbling, "Shit, just like the boy."

Headlights glowing, and churning up clouds of dust to mask their escape, they were just a few hundred yards behind the lead vehicle as they hit the blacktop and swung right back towards Kano and the airport.

With smiles all around, Deacon called Hank from his cell phone.

"Hank, all complete. Get her warmed up for immediate departure."

"Boss, I can't. I've been trying to reach you. The airport has closed the main runway for routine inspection and all flights in or out are barred until 05:30 -- that's sunrise and just over two hours away."

Cursing, and realizing they couldn't wait that long since the alarm was raised, or would be shortly, Deacon realized it was now down to plan B. He ordered Hank to fly down to Abuja as soon as he could get clearance, disconnected the call and pressed his radio transmit button. Radioing the others on a group call he explained what had happened and confirmed the only option was to head to Abuja by road. They were deep inside Boko Haram lines in a heavy Muslim controlled area. Locals couldn't be relied on to assist as most were terrified of reprisals. Even the local police and army had likely been infiltrated hence the need to get the girls to Abuja where international news media were waiting. With no other option, he instructed both drivers to slow down so as not to arouse suspicion and to head southwest towards the A2 highway and Abuja.

Although classified as a highway, roads in Nigeria are slightly less well formed than in western countries. This road was mainly two-lane and contained a number of potholes. It was already fairly busy with trucks and Maričić could only maintain a speed of just over 35 mph, well below the local speed limit of 50.

The girls had been frightened at first, crying or just keeping quiet, but then began shouting and cheering as they realized they were being freed. Canetti and Roberts passed them water and some chocolate and energy bars that had been left on board and had to keep urging them to sit quietly so as not to draw attention to themselves. The entire north-eastern region of Nigeria is under heavy Boko Haram rule who impose strict sharia law and the kidnappings were currently featuring in the news. The sight of six Nigerian girls laughing and shouting in a minibus driven by white men would surely raise an alarm.

Stockwell had finally managed to overtake a group of trucks weaving to miss the potholes and had finally caught up with the lead vehicle and he was now just a hundred yards or so behind it. The risk of pursuit was high but more so in the first hour, and he kept one eye on the rearview mirror as they made their escape.

Twice he thought he could make out shapes of motorbikes.

"Boss, I think we've got bikes tailing us."

Martock was in the rear and was peering through the dirty window. The glow of trucks headlights made it impossible to see clearly, but he also thought he could see at least one darkened motorbike show up as a silhouette as it weaved in front of the trucks.

"Andy's right, boss. At least one tango on a bike, maybe more."

Realizing there was little they could do to evade pursuit, Deacon instructed them just to carry on while he kept a lookout for the police or Boko Haram roadblocks.

Logically, what they were doing in heading by road to Abuja was insane. It was almost 280 miles and would take at least five hours, maybe more. The A2 primary road was better beyond Kano but still only average compared to roads in the West and there was a high chance they would be stopped at one of the BH checkpoints. Deacon knew logically they should have taken the girls to the central police station in Kano and released them there. However, his instructions were to get them to Abuja as the intelligence suggested the local police were corrupt, and that was what he intended to do.

He was counting on the escaped Colonel Ganda assuming the rescue had been actioned by Nigerian military forces. Deacon was hoping by the time Ganda realized, through his contacts, that he'd been duped and the rescue had been carried out by bought-in western forces and not the Nigerian military, they'd be too far away to catch.

The first problem occurred as they were passing the township of Zaria two hours later. They needed to stop as Stockwell's vehicle was overheating. The water temperature gauge was hard over into the red, the minibus having been driven hard. Two of the girls were desperate for a bathroom break, and all six were complaining of hunger. Pulling in to a Total gas station just as daylight was breaking, Stockwell drove around the rear, while Maričić parked his vehicle at the side of the building.

Moments later, two motorcycles pulled to the other side of the dusty road, and one of the riders pulled out a cell phone and made a call.

Jose Canetti escorted the girls to the toilet, telling them yet again to keep quiet as they still had a long way to go, but they were excited and started gabbling away in their local dialect of Hausa. Canetti shushed them and they quietened down, but not before one of the staff had overheard them. In the meantime, Maričić and Stockwell had topped up both radiators with water and Deacon had purchased dried packet foods of chips and cookies, and more water before distributing them amongst everyone.

As they pulled away back onto the A2 south five minutes later, Deacon thought he saw the sales employee using the phone just as the motorcycles took up position a few hundred yards behind them again.

Thirty minutes later Martock alerted Deacon they were being followed. Two Toyota Land Cruisers full of bodies were keeping pace with them two hundred yards back.

They were still over thirty minutes away from Kaduna and almost three hours from Abuja.

10

With the better quality road and now two-lanes in both directions, their speed had finally increased. Maričić and Stockwell had slowly accelerated until both vehicles were doing almost 60 mph, but their pursuers were also keeping pace. On an open road the Land Cruisers could easily have overhauled them, but now the amount of traffic was actually helping them. Everyone was weaving in and out and it was almost impossible to go any faster than they already were.

"Where did these bastards come from?" Stockwell asked, almost to himself.

"Those bikes were tailing us. We're on the main road. It's pretty obvious where we heading. We're lucky it's taken them this long to catch up," Deacon replied. "They might be local BH, but my bet is they're from Kano and Ganda's on board."

Racing past the small township of Jaji, Deacon grabbed the large scale map and spent a few moments looking.

Turning to Stockwell, he said, "If I were the local BH warlord or Ganda himself, I'd arrange a roadblock and force us to stop. Now he's close behind he can box us in. This road joins another major one a few miles on by a town called Katabu. He'll get reinforcements there and block the road."

Stockwell glanced at him, his eyes still mainly on the road and watching the traffic, "So what are we gonna do, boss?"

"Now we go off-road," Deacon said with a grin.

Thumbing the radio transmit button, he said, "Goran, keep your foot down. There's a dirt track on the right in about a mile. Don't indicate - just go for it. Over the railway track then sharp left - keep going. Don't stop for anything - even police. Shoot any civilians who try to stop you but not police or army.

A minute later approaching the dirt track, Maričić jammed the brakes on and slewed onto the track. Brown red dust kicked up everywhere making it awkward as Stockwell followed suit. Being the lead vehicle, Maričić could see as he accelerated away but Stockwell couldn't and began to slow.

"No, don't slow. Close up," Deacon shouted.

As his minibus gained speed again, Deacon looked out the rear window and all he could see was a mass cloud of red-brown dust. They closed on the lead minibus until only a couple of feet behind and at that distance the dust from Maričić wasn't so bad, but the combined vehicles churned up major dirt storm.

Still making almost 40 mph, they kept this up for almost two minutes before the track raised above the level of the surrounding fields and the dust began to thin. Suddenly the rear window of Deacon's minibus exploded and the rhythmic chatter of AK-47's could be heard. One side window also exploded and two rounds hit the front windshield causing it to crack. Climbing over the seats to the rear, Deacon joined Martock and together they kicked out the remaining glass in the rear door before opening fire through the thinning dust cloud. As the vehicles twisted and turned to follow the track, they got glimpses of the Land Cruisers chasing them and Martock managed to sight on the lead one and give it one long burst, emptying his magazine.

At this distance Martock couldn't miss and he smiled as both front tires exploded. The Land Cruiser hood was peppered with bullet holes and the blood-spattered windshield shattered and collapsed into the cabin. The severely injured driver lost control and the Land Cruiser careered off the dirt track into a cornfield before finally stopping. With a loud whumf fire enveloped the engine compartment and the remaining gunmen could be seen trying to get out.

The second cruiser that had dropped back when Martock and Deacon had started firing now accelerated again with a gunman at each window firing at the minibus. More rounds started to strike exploding the remaining side windows and peppering the rear door with loud thuds.

"I hope Bowker was right about that African Blackwood," Martock said raising his weapon and firing again, just before cursing as a bullet passed through his exposed jacket sleeve grazing his arm. It didn't draw blood but the heat from the round burned and blistered his skin.

"Shit, that was fuckin' close," he said.

Radioing Maričić to keep going and stay off the main road until after Katabu, then just drive all the way to Abuja, Deacon shouted at Stockwell to slow.

"You fucking mad?"

"Keep your head down and just drive, but slow down."

As the Land Cruiser approached through the now thinning dirt cloud, with rounds hitting the rear door of the minibus, Martock and Deacon crouched down low on the floor in front of the rear seats for added protection. Deacon suddenly shouted, "Now!" and as Stockwell stamped his foot on the accelerator and the Hiace leaped forward, he and Martock both tossed grenades out the rear window before rising up and opening fire. After each discharged almost a full magazine at their pursuer, the return fire slackened as two of the gunmen were hit, and the grenades exploded. The driver had seen the grenades being thrown and stomped on the brakes before swerving to the left, so their explosions only caused minimal damage to his vehicle, but their intense fire had taken effect.

As Stockwell slewed around another corner, they all looked back and could see their second pursuer stopped with smoke coming up from the hood and angry looking men kicking at it. At least three bodies were visible lying in the dirt and one of those still standing was using either a cell phone or a hand-held radio.

Accelerating hard, within minutes Stockwell had caught up with the lead minibus and together they slowed to a safer speed.

Six minutes later, with all the windows of Deacon's vehicle bullet-crazed, or missing, the radio crackled to life and Maričić's voice came on saying, "The engine's overheating and faltering. We're going to have to stop before it seizes entirely."

11

Eight hundred yards further on Maričić finally stopped his minibus. The girls had been screaming and crying at the sounds of the gunfire, especially when rounds had been hitting their bus, but they'd quietened down as it had moved out of range. The minibus stopping suddenly raised their fears again and Canetti and Roberts had to physically stop them from panicking and trying to get out and run.

As Deacon and his men arrived, they could already see Maričić opening the minibus's engine compartment to let the steam escape.

The last two hundred yards in their vehicle had been particularly bumpy, and after Maričić inspected the rest of the vehicle, it was obvious why. The rear tire on the passenger side was shredded. It had been hit by one of the pursuer's rounds and deflated. Driving with it flat on the steel rim had caused it to shred completely and there was hardly any rubber remaining.

With both minibusses temporarily at least out of order, Deacon reassessed the situation.

"We've over 140 miles to go. We're in the middle of nowhere and we're being pursued. Bill, Jose - head back 500 yards to provide rear cover - they might be chasing on foot. Sean - you go forward 500 and keep an eye out. Andy - you and I'll change the wheel and Goran, get that engine cooled and some fucking water into that radiator."

Turning to the six girls huddled in the lead bus, he continued, "Girls, keep quiet, all of you. Listen. If you make a run for it they'll catch you and kill you. Get down on the seats and stay quiet. We'll be moving again in five and you'll be safe."

As his men split up and moved away, Stockwell was already ripping up the rear floor cover to get to the spare tire.

"Fuck it, it's flat," he cursed, looking at the bullet-ridden rubber.

The spare wheel on the lead minibus wasn't much better. The rim was rusty and the tire itself was almost bald of tread, but at least it was still inflated. It took them less than five minutes to have their bus jacked up, the wheel removed and replaced and the jack removed.

Stockwell was just tightening the wheel nuts for the final time when Maričić called that the pressure had reduced and at last he could undo the radiator cap. Using all the remaining water from the drink bottles, he refilled it and estimated it was almost seven-eighths full, so he tried re-starting the engine. It turned over but refused to start, before eventually catching and misfiring. Maričić guessed it was only firing on three of the four cylinders but pumped the accelerator hoping it would improve.

Deacon told Maričić and Stockwell to drive on slowly with the girls and pick up Martock while he waited for Roberts and Canetti to join up with him, having already radioed them. A few minutes later Canetti eased into the driver's seat as Deacon and Bill Roberts took defensive positions in the rear and they hurried to catch up with the lead minibus. Keeping the speed down to around 20 mph over the rough dirt tracks as fast as could safely drive, worried that another puncture would be disastrous, but as they drove away the dirt cloud they raised behind them could be seen from many miles away.

With the track still raised higher than the surrounding fields it was impossible to mask the direction they were taking. However, navigating by map and GPS Deacon managed to follow a winding path well away from the main expressway but in roughly the right direction.

They had to slow when passing through the many small villages that littered the track, partly because chickens and livestock roamed freely but also because bare-footed children would run alongside the buses shouting and clapping, while women sat at cooking pots, merely observing. Older village men, most of them smoking pungent-smelling cigarettes would look on without comment at the battle-scarred second vehicle, dented and battered, minus most of its glass and with multiple bullet holes in the rear. However, the villagers seemed more surprised to have visitors passing through their village than worrying about the condition of their transport.

Eventually, after almost an hour wasted at slow speed, the two minibusses finally bounced back onto the expressway blacktop and their journey on to Kaduna and Abuja continued.

Slowly increasing speed while watching the water-temperature indicator climb, Maričić estimated 40 mph was about the fastest he could go without the engine overheating again. Canetti, driving behind him, reported the oil pressure lamp on his engine kept flickering.

Deciding it was better to continue without stopping and also knowing the local police couldn't be trusted, they made slow but safe progress towards Abuja, with Deacon and Roberts keeping watch at the rear.

Guessing Ganda and his followers would keep trying, Deacon grabbed a satellite phone from his bag and dialed an international number. He spoke for over five minutes and repeatedly examined his map. Finally putting the phone down he, at last, had a smile on his face.

Knowing their rescue of the girls had been detected, he tuned the bus radio to check on traffic.

Ninety minutes later he realized he'd guessed correctly. He knew Boko Haram wouldn't give up the prize of the girls that easily but they needed somewhere they could effectively block and guard the road. The radio announcer was talking of a vehicle fire at Jere Junction and of all traffic being halted. Six miles before that location, just as they passed over the River Gurara, Deacon radioed and instructed both vehicles to turn off left onto yet another mud-covered dirt track.

A few hundred yards further on they approached the railway and turned south parallel to it. What was a rough track became worse, full of ruts, stones and potholes. Reducing speed to 10 mph, it took almost eight painful minutes before they approached a cattle bridge over the railway. Driving across it they came to a wider rough track. Following its twists and turns they finally joined the Tasha-Bwari road, which was two-laned, semi-blacktopped, and virtually empty of traffic, where they could increase their speed back up as fast as possible.

However, their trip along the dirt tracks had been spotted. Two more Toyotas had been in pursuit, each filled with four gunmen, but keeping their distance. Neither Deacon or Roberts had identified them amongst the throng of other traffic. Their orders from Colonel Ganda had been to stop the girls at all costs and their plan was to trap and box in the rescuers at the Jere Junction. Twenty BH soldiers had already blocked the road and set fire to a number of old tires. The south-bound road was closed entirely and the guards were making their way back through the building traffic queue. If Deacon and his team of rescuers had been caught in the jam, they would have had no way to escape.

Soon after the two minibusses had turned off the main road, the rising dust from the track had given their new direction away. Knowing how vicious Ganda could be, no

62

one wanted to be the person telling him they'd escaped, so, with tires screaming they gave chase. Less than four miles separated them as they sped, bouncing and shaking on the rough track, after the escaping vehicles and they quickly began to gain ground.

As the Toyota's exited onto the Tasha-Bwari road and accelerated hard, they could see their prey far in the distance, now just over two miles away. As they gained ground, the gunmen leaned out of their windows and started firing as soon as they thought they were in range.

Radioing through, Deacon urged Maričić to go as fast as he could while he and Roberts would run interference and try and keep the pursuers at bay.

As bullets began to chew into the rear door and roof of the minibus, Canetti slewed it left and right to try to offer protection to the girls' bus in front, but rounds still got past. Their rear window shattered and the screams of the girls' could be clearly heard. Martock's voice could be made out shouting at the girls to keep their heads down, as he and Stockwell took positions at either rear side window and began firing past Deacon's bus, but it was clear they couldn't last long.

As they rounded the next corner, Maričić saw a barrier with police in the distance blocking the road and thought it was all over. Radioing Deacon for instructions, he was surprised to hear Deacon's voice calmly come back through his earpiece telling him they were friendlies and they would let them through.

A sudden burst of heavier fire exploded the dashboard of Deacon's bus and continued through into the engine compartment, wounding Canetti with flying shattered plastic, but miraculously no rounds struck him. As the engine sputtered and faltered and their speed dropped away, Deacon smiled as he saw the barrier being moved for the girls' minibus to pass.

Shouting at Canetti to slew left and roll the bus to block the road, Deacon and Roberts quickly jumped out the side door and took defensive positions on the ground at the front and rear of the overturned minibus as it finally ended its journey for the last time. Canetti kicked out the shattered windshield and climbed out to join them, three against eight. With only half-empty magazines between them, they knew they couldn't hold the pursuers off for long.

After the rush of the pursuit, the silence seemed deafening, broken only by the wheezing and creaking of their minibus as its engine finally succumbed to over-revving, bullet holes and lack of oil. The adversaries, one chasing, the other being chased, stood weapons aimed a mere fifty yards apart.

Finally, after a three-minute stand-off that seemed far longer, the leader of the pursuers shouted a command and his men returned to their vehicles, started the engines, reverse turned and drove away.

Walking the last few hundred feet to the police barrier, Deacon relaxed when he saw Robert Bowker smiling.

Extending a handshake, Bowker began, "You are now in Federal Capital Territory. The Chief of Police is happy to take the girls to the Sheraton where he will attend a press conference extolling the virtues of his department, and the brave actions of his fellow officers in the rescue and release of six hostages about to be sold into prostitution and slavery. Unfortunately, a number of the kidnappers were killed in the rescue, but all the hostages and police officers were unharmed."

The girls were all being consoled and had blankets wrapped around themselves. They each had a bottle of water and were gabbling away in a local dialect Deacon didn't recognize.

Knowing they were now all safe, he said, "Yeah, that's exactly how it went down."

Leaving all the weapons behind in the safekeeping of Bowker, Deacon and his men took the remaining minibus and drove it slowly towards the airport, flanked by two police motorcycle outriders.

An official in uniform was waiting at the airfield security gate, stamped their exit visas in their passports, expressed his hope that their visit had been prosperous, and bade them 'Bon Voyage'. As they walked towards the waiting Gulfstream and climbed the steps into the cabin, Hank had already laid out sandwiches and beer.

Finally sitting down and relaxing with a cold one in his hand, Deacon smiled to himself at another job well done as the engine noise increased, the brakes were released, and the Gulfstream starting racing down the runway.

12

Dubai

The China Eastern Airlines Airbus A330 landed at Dubai International Airport slightly ahead of schedule. Junior-Grade Lieutenant Zhang Su Ming was amongst the twenty-strong Chinese delegation attending the 5-day biennial Dubai Airshow. China's government employees are allowed to travel business class when traveling on official business, so they received a personal escort down the long concourse and escalators to the immigration desks.

Although not directly involved, the rank of her father in the PLAN almost guaranteed her involvement in anything she found interesting. She had received much of her education abroad in both Europe and California and she still hankered after more travel. Although her role involved naval projects, she had a personal interest in aircraft and a deeper interest in the vast array of fashion shops on offer in Dubai.

It was expected some of the latest US and European fighters would be on show and demonstrated here. In particular, Raytheon was demonstrating their advanced quantum radar allegedly capable of detecting fully stealth-enabled aircraft.

China and the United Arab Emirates have deep commercial ties, China being the largest trading partner with Dubai since 2014; and the second-largest trading partner of the whole UAE since 2011.

With such close and friendly relations, the clearing of customs and immigration became a mere formality, under the personal supervision of Crown Prince Hamid bin Mohammed al Makani. After clearing customs, the delegation made their way to the executive exit where a fleet of luxury limousines was waiting to take them to the Radisson Hotel, one of a number of major hotels in Dubai owned by the Chinese company HNA Group.

After checking in and with time to shower and freshen up, the group met and headed to the restaurant for a light lunch. With a security officer in tow, Su Ming declined the planned afternoon and evening's entertainment at the Motiongate Theme Park, preferring to explore the city's shopping malls. Hong Kong shopping was fine, as was Shanghai's, with all major western stores available, but the sheer size and opulence of Dubai always impressed her.

Today she would visit the Mall of the Emirates. One of her favorite pastimes in Dubai was to sit drinking coffee in the massive shopping mall while watching people wearing thick clothes playing in an indoor ski run. It still amazed her having falling snow indoors with temperatures sometimes of over 50 degrees centigrade outside. Luckily, at this time of the year, although considerably warmer than Hong Kong, the weather was more comfortable than during the major heat of July and August.

Walking around the mall, her bodyguard walked closely to her side and slightly behind. Many of her colleagues could wander freely, but her father always insisted she be accompanied on foreign trips. Whether this was because she was his daughter and he was just being protective as many fathers would be, or because of his rank and title, she never knew. However, there was as much political wrangling, one-upmanship and backstabbing in the Politburo of the Communist Party of China as in any American television series, and there was always a risk, albeit a small one, she could be used as a pawn against her father.

However, Su Ming's social standing and rank allowed her to ignore her guard and he, in turn, would never speak to her without authorization, merely keeping in close proximity. However, in the event of any form of danger he had the authority to take command. She also knew that he would report back to his superiors and her father about her movements and any contact she might have with westerners.

Knowing it would annoy him, but he would be unable to say anything, she chose deliberately to slowly linger and window-shop as much as she could. Finally, she stopped at a Starbucks and ordered a latte while watching the skiing through the windows of Ski Dubai at the world's third largest indoor ski slope, the smile of pleasure evident on her face for anyone to see.

After taking twice as long as necessary to drink her coffee, Su Ming stood, stretched her five-foot-three-inch frame, picked up her purse and headed back out to continue shopping, deliberately walking into ladies fashion shops, knowing her guard would be embarrassed and uncomfortable. The only good thing about having him follow her, she thought, was in making him carry her growing number of shopping bags. Although he still remained vigilant, she could tell he was becoming bored. When she walked into Victoria's Secret she smiled to herself as she saw the red of embarrassment flush his neck and face as he followed her inside and saw the posters on the walls showing scantily dressed women, before being rapidly and forcibly half-carried back outside.

The windows had been covered completely to meet with Sharia Law and he'd just followed her in, forgetting the stricter rules of the Middle East. He'd hardly stepped in through the doorway and through the thick black curtain before a large, muscular Arabic woman grabbed him by the scruff of his neck, spun him around and moments later he found himself back outside under a hail of loud, abusive Arabic. He was trained as a bodyguard and fully conversant with all manner of self-defense, but even he was stunned at the speed and agility of this massive woman in lifting him and depositing him back outside to wait.

Moving to the changing rooms, Su Ming found a young Indian shop assistant and briefly explained she was married, and her husband ensured she was guarded at all times. She even pointed to the fracas that had occurred by the entrance doors to emphasize her point. Begging to use the assistant's cell phone to send a short text, she passed over a fifty Dirham note in thanks. She quickly typed '14:38 Sunday. Stand B17' and sent it to a number she'd memorized days previously, before deleting that message from the phone's memory and passing it back to the shop assistant. Opening the rear door, she scanned the passageway.

As with most shopping centers, the rear passageway was just used for deliveries and for the removal of waste. The general public never saw the less-decorated areas of the mall. This one was no different from thousands of others, just containing empty cardboard boxes waiting to be collected and removed.

Briefly scanning both ways, she could see there were no visible security cameras actually within the passageway; most likely the security would merely consist of the access doors being locked.

Heading back into the shop and pulling the door closed behind her, she spent a few minutes choosing new underwear before paying for it and striding out. Tossing yet another bag at her guard, she turned and walked fast-paced to the limousine drop-off and pick-up point, ignoring the angry looks from him as he almost double stepped in trying to keep up.

13

Washington

In the week since Deacon and his men had landed back at Washington Executive Airport, or Hyde Field, as it's known locally, life had returned to normal. The wound Jose Canetti had suffered from flying plastic had needed a few stitches but was healing well.

Deacon had gone straight to the Pentagon after landing to give a complete debrief to the Admiral. Sitting in one of the Admiral's comfy chairs, enjoying a coffee, he said to the Admiral and Mitch, "Everything was going well until the airport maintenance people decided to close the runway for safety light checks. I planned to head straight back there with the girls and fly down to Abuja – less than an hours' flight. Unfortunately, with the runway closed, we couldn't afford to sit and wait once the alarm had been raised. Hank filed a 'priority flight clearance request' for access as soon as the runway opened, but even that was ignored until other airlines had cleared. Our only choice was down the main roads heavy with BH supporters. The call had gone out, and I was surprised how quickly they picked up our trail, but with only one main road, all they had to do was place observers at different points. After fighting them off the first time I guessed they'd try again and the next location offering the best hijack point was Jere Junction. That's where I would have done it so it seemed the best choice. Luckily, Mitch answered my call and we set up with the Abuja police to meet on the back road on the Federal Capital Territory border. We knew BH wouldn't pursue across that, but it was just a case of getting there in one piece."

With his fingers steepled together, the Admiral smiled before saying, "You and your men did well. The President is very pleased. He received a call of thanks from the Nigerian President whose popularity has increased and with no embarrassment of the mighty US of A having been involved. Send your expenses through to Mitch, as usual, and I'll get them reimbursed."

Deacon knew his people would be happy. Everyone involved in the mission would be receiving a $5,000 bonus as well as normal pay, although only Martock knew it wasn't coming from the alleged Nigerian businessman. The deal Deacon had originally agreed to in leaving the Navy and setting up the company was if any of his team was killed on legitimate Phylax work, Phylax would cover life insurance; but if anyone died on private 'government' work, a government slush fund of $2,000,000 per employee was available for payout to relatives or dependents. Deacon had taken on Sean Martock as his first recruit - a close friend he trusted with his life, and also Gina Panaterri - an ex-Secret Service agent who'd been injured in the line of duty and was no longer fully 100% fit. Gina had been injured while guarding the previous President on a visit to Afghanistan when an IED had exploded and damaged the vehicle she was traveling in. Deacon and some of his team had also been in the convoy and Deacon had helped carry Gina from the wrecked Humvee. She still had minute pieces of shrapnel in her back, close to her spine, meaning she could no longer meet the comprehensive fitness regime all Secret Service agents were required to pass. However, she had excellent managerial and office skills, kept Phylax running smoothly, and could still outshoot both Deacon and Martock with a handgun - something she reveled in and proving regularly. Both Martock and Gina were fully aware of the 'black' relationship Phylax had with the government.

With a gentle pop, Mitch eased the cork from the second bottle of a particularly enjoyable Pinot Noir Deacon had brought with him. Scooping up the last of the thick mushroom sauce with the remnants of a large slice of toasted ciabatta, Deacon gave Helen a massive smile. He and Mitch had known each other for years, and when Mitch had met Helen at a sailing club drinks party and immediately fallen in love with her, he couldn't have been happier. She was a very attractive petite brunette with a lovely smile and personality. The two of them made a perfect pair. After two years, Mitch had finally popped the question and eighteen months later, they'd been married. They now lived in the up-market and trendy Adams Morgan area of Washington. She was quite career-minded and had recently been promoted to a high-level position in a prestigious Washington law firm.

Previously, while stationed in Coronado, Deacon had only managed to see them occasionally. Now, also living in DC, they met regularly and tonight was one of those dates.

Helen had cooked prawns for starters, followed by creamy mushrooms with bacon - one of his favorite meals. He usually tried to do the washing up after, but Helen or Mitch would always shoo him away, so he resorted to bringing the wine and peace reigned all around.

The following morning Deacon arrived in the office for a few days of catching up with paperwork and emails. Gina was excellent in reducing his workload and dealing with the day-to-day stuff, but all major decisions were his and his alone. Unfortunately, this morning Deacon was feeling just a little thick-headed. After the second bottle of wine the previous night, Mitch had brought out the Bourbon. They'd only planned one drink each, but then CNN had run a news item showing the Nigerian President bestowing his gratitude to the Nigerian Police and Army for the release of the six girls. That had caused a slightly merry Mitch to pour another glass, followed by a third.

Now after drinking two full glasses of water and swallowing a pair of headache tablets, Deacon shook his head to try and finally clear it. Two Japanese executives were arriving in Washington the following day and wanted 24-hour armed security. Deacon knew from experience Japanese executives often liked to party well into the early hours, so he'd need three eight-hour shifts of two guys per shift to cover them properly. The executives would then fly to New York for two more days of meetings before heading home to Japan. Deacon decided the numbers needed in both Washington and New York and then passed it to Gina to liaise with the individuals and organize transportations etc. He knew that with Gina's experience and enthusiasm he could leave more and more of the day-to-day running and organizing in her capable hands.

Gina also opened all the mail except anything marked 'private' or 'personal'. One of the many opened letters on his desk had come from the office of the Ministry of the Interior of the United Arab Emirates. Phylax had been requested to quote for a three-year long-term contract offering diplomatic security and close personal protection in the Gulf State of Ras al-Khaimah for a number of senior royalty. Although he could respond by letter, Deacon knew the best way to try and secure the contract would be to visit the UAE in the coming days to meet with the royals and fully discuss their needs. A contract such as this was good long-term revenue for his company and he knew a number of his employees would be eager for these roles.

In practice, close protection bodyguards would get to eat and live almost as well as those they were protecting, living in palaces and traveling in royal private jets, so he knew it wouldn't be a hard sell to whoever he chose for these roles. It was also useful to have these close ties as often other individual work would be requested from diplomats and royalty eager to avoid accountability. Deacon was also aware of the high regard the entire area of Jordan, Saudi, Kuwait, Bahrain, Qatar and the UAE has for both American and British servicemen, with Oman particularly favoring the British SAS.

Calling Gina into his office, he sat and discussed with her the format and contents of their bid, as well as asking her to book his flights to Dubai for a three-day trip to Ras al-Khaimah - a day each end for traveling and a day for high-level meetings and discussions.

14

Dubai

Shane Walker was having a good day. He'd caught the Emirate's flight from Baghdad two days previously to enjoy the freedom of Dubai. He'd been stationed in Dubai for four years carrying the rank of Captain and the role of Military Attaché - standard cover as CIA agents don't hold military rank. However, when he'd moved to Baghdad he'd been promoted to Station Chief, and his duties had expanded, but the freedom he enjoyed in Iraq was far less than here. The US Embassy in Baghdad was one of the largest overseas US embassies, but it was mostly self-contained for security purposes. Many of his fellow Americans never left the security of the walled and heavily guarded compound, preferring safety over freedom. But he was lucky since his role needed him to travel around Baghdad and also further afield into other Iraqi cities, but it obviously came with added risk, although since ISIS had finally been chased out of Iraq, security had improved. Fluent in Arabic, all Middle Eastern cities were comfortable to him, with some far more so than others.

However, Dubai was his favorite, and he was happy to be back.

He'd spent the morning at his old offices in the Consulate General of the United States, near Dubai Creek, and had stopped for coffee in nearby Deira to enjoy the warm afternoon sunshine when his phone chimed. Reading the message perplexed him as he didn't recognize the number it had come from. Finishing the thick, strong black liquid in a single gulp before chasing it down with a small glass of water, within moments he was heading back to the Consulate General offices.

Clearing security, he headed into the center of the building and the secure communications department. He walked over to the supervisor and said, "Andy, I've just received a text from what looks to be a local UAE mobile number. Can you do a reverse trace and tell me the owner?"

Less than a minute later, and after some deft keyboard work, the supervisor, Andy, looked up and said, "It's an Etisalat number, pay-as-you-go, registered to Mahindra Gupta. According to immigration, Miss Gupta is a nineteen-year-old Indian citizen, daughter to an Indian couple working at HSBC bank in Sharjah. They have a younger daughter, Akshaya, who attends school, and they have been here for almost twelve years. Do you want their address?"

Thanking him for the quick search, Shane declined any more information and walked away deep in thought. It could be an accidental text sent to a wrong number or it could be something more . . .

The following day was the opening of the biennial Dubai Airshow and the reason for Shane's journey to Dubai. The five-day event is always busy with up to 80,000 attendees. It's not open to the general public, only to those business professionals within the industry. It was always good to act like a supplier and wander around the stands listening to what he could learn. International buyers from around the world attended and he was always amazed at what tidbits of information he often overheard while standing in queues or sitting in restaurants. His cover was as a salesman for a small petroleum supplier of aviation fuel looking to expand into foreign markets. This gave him enough cover to ask relevant questions. Sometimes groups of people would forget where they were and be quite open in their discussions. He also found listening to conversations between buyers and salespeople on the military stands could benefit him a ream of otherwise confidential information about forthcoming expansion plans or future purchase requirements. Although military dictators wouldn't journey themselves, they often sent emissaries, and although most high-level discussions would be held in private, the old adage of 'loose lips sinks ships' so effectively used in WWII still held true, and he always came away with snippets of useful data.

He also enjoyed watching the aircraft perform their dangerous flypasts and various intricate maneuvers as, like most men, he still had that little bit of young boy in him.

The morning kept him busy touring some of the many hundreds of exhibition stands and he kept his phone on silent, occasionally pretending to talk on a call whilst snapping pictures of many of the visitors. He'd already had Washington hack into the air show registration database, but as he'd learned previously, quite a few people used false identities when attending a show such as this.

Sitting eating a sandwich in one of the many breakout areas, the directional microphone of his modified cell phone picked up and recorded various quiet or whispered conversations within the general hubbub of the place.

At two p.m., the flypasts started and many of the attendees moved outside. Checking his watch in the slightly emptier arena, the hands showed 14:37 and he casually walked along the aisle between stands. B17 was on the left next to yet another catering outlet offering food and drinks, with B18 opposite. He planned to walk past, then double back and sit and have coffee to see if anyone turned up, but as he passed the end of the catering stand a young Chinese woman abruptly stood up and bumped into him.

She immediately apologized and looked both embarrassed and flustered. A tall, thin man sitting at a different table quickly stood as if to say something but the woman had already begun to move away. The thin man followed her and said something to her, but she just waved him off. Shane walked on as if nothing untoward had happened, alarmed at first in case it was an attack. Many agents had been killed over the years by seemingly innocent brush pasts, sometimes jabbed with needles or even sprayed with a fast-acting chemical, but realizing all she had pushed at him under his jacket was a small slip of paper, he was careful not let it fall.

So as not to arouse any suspicion, he wandered around for another fifteen minutes before eventually heading towards a bathroom. Unfolding the paper, he read, 'MotE, rear Vic Sec. 19:00'.

Leaving the air show a few minutes later, he caught a taxi back to the Consulate General offices.

Sitting at an empty terminal, he logged on and was soon connected to the ultra-secure systems in Langley, Virginia.

15

Su Ming stayed at the air show until closing time at 18:00, socializing with other members of the Chinese delegation. Heading out to their waiting limousines, she told them she had more shopping to complete and headed over to the taxi rank. Her reluctant guard followed and flagged down a taxi before instructing the driver to take them to the Mall of the Emirates.

The forty-minute journey was completed in silence, Su Ming in the rear, with the guard sitting up front next to the driver. On arrival, she strode off, leaving her guard to pay. Su Ming walked to the nearest woman's clothing outlet taking her time to look through the items on offer before finally paying and emerging almost ten minutes later. Thrusting the bag towards the guard, she said, "You carry!" leaving no opportunity for him to refuse. After visiting another clothing shop, she headed back towards Victoria's Secret. Having learned his lesson the previous day her guard stopped outside leaning his back against the opaque glass, and waited.

After spending less than a minute rummaging through some underwear on display, Su Ming grabbed two brassieres and headed to the rear changing rooms. Waving her finger to call the same young Indian sales assistant over, Su Ming thrust her handbag into the girl's hands and instructed her to wait there and to let her in when she knocked. She then opened the doors to the rear passageway before stepping outside.

There was rubbish on the floor and empty boxes stacked up ready for collection. She was quite alone. Glancing at her watch, she saw the minute hand click over to 19:01 and was just about to turn and knock on the door when a movement from behind one of the taller boxes further along the passageway made her jump.

A tall sandy-haired man stepped out from behind the boxes smiling as he slowly approached her.

"I think we should introduce ourselves," he said. "I'm Gerald Wagner. And you are . . .?"

"You are Captain Shane Walker of the CIA. You are stationed at the US Embassy in Baghdad."

With his skin prickling, he was immediately on heightened alert. Was this a hit? His cover was obviously blown, what was next? Was she planning to assassinate him? Eyes glancing left and right, he murmured, "Hold," into the throat mic as he stepped back half-a-step, muscles tensed ready to react.

"I am alone, Captain Shane Walker, and I mean you no harm. If you were indeed Gerald Wagner we would not be having this conversation now. I am Junior Lieutenant Zhang Su Ming of the People's Liberation Army Navy, and I want to defect to the United States. Will you help me?"

"Miss, you have mistaken me for someone else. My name is Gerald Wagner, and I'm a salesman for a petroleum company in the US. I'm just here on business and taking a short-cut through this alley," Shane said as he slowly moved away, keeping an alert eye open for any door suddenly opening.

As he moved away out of arms reach, he relaxed slightly. He carried a Sig-Sauer tucked into a hidden shoulder holster which he could draw in less than half-a-second. He was also pretty damn good in unarmed combat. For added support, there were four US marines, dressed in civilian clothes, all carrying hidden sidearms, stationed two at each end of the passageway, ready to intervene if needed.

Over the years, dozens or even hundreds of agents had been compromised to foreign powers. Some were assassinated while others were captured for the intelligence information they held. Earlier in the day Shane had identified Su Ming from her name badge and read her file held at Langley. He knew she was the daughter of Admiral Zhang, therefore receiving far more privileges than her colleagues. She had attended school in both London and Switzerland and university at Stanford. She was fluent in English and had been promoted quicker than expected within the PLAN. Whether this was entirely due to personal achievement or because of her family name was unclear. Why she had deliberately passed him the message was unknown, but her position suggested either some type of private liaison and a honey trap or an attack or kidnapping attempt on him, although why any such attempt would be made in the relatively safe location of Dubai versus the lawless back streets of Baghdad eluded him. If she knew who he was, and she obviously did, then there were far easier places to attack or harm him. Also, nothing in her record suggested any form of spy school or clandestine training.

As he said into his throat mic, "It's a bust, I'm coming ou––," he heard her voice call quietly as she turned and knocked on the outside of the shop door, "I have information. Check it out then wait for my call. There is a Jin-class submarine, the *Xiangliu*, monitoring your Norfolk base."

As he swung around, he saw her step back into the rear of the shop and the door slam shut behind her.

It was 19:04.

Slipping the Indian assistant another fifty Dirham note, she grabbed her handbag and quickly walked out of the store. Her guard still waiting outside was caught unawares by her sudden exit and had to move quickly to keep up.

Arriving back at her hotel she found some of her delegation still eating in the restaurant with the others drinking in the bar. She smiled as she walked in and joined them for the remainder of the evening, ordering a Tsingtao, preferring a simple beer over their favored drinks of Chivas Regal and Green Tea, or the Chinese Vodka equivalent, called Baijiu.

16

Washington

A shocked Shane was back in the US Consulate General offices within fifteen minutes and on a secure line to Langley less than a minute later. He also typed a brief report, marked it 'RED - Flash' and emailed it off to Lieutenant Mitch Stringer at the Pentagon and to Charles Ingram - Director of the CIA at Langley.

It was 19:30 local, 10:30 EST.

<><><>

The morning weather was fine in Washington. Mitch and Helen had risen early for their morning jog and when they'd arrived back at their townhouse, Mitch had prepared breakfast while Helen showered. After finishing their omelets, Mitch had jumped in the shower while Helen tidied up before they both headed off to work. Helen liked to start early so she could leave the office before the late afternoon rush. Just a normal day in the Stringer household.

Mitch was carrying a mug of coffee to his desk when he heard the ping of a new email. He'd been in the office since 07:00 and had just taken a coffee and biscuits into the inner sanctum of Admiral Douglas Carter, Chief of Naval Operations, reporting directly to the President.

Sitting down he opened the new email, briefly smiling when he realized it was from Shane. His smile faded when he saw the RED-Flash classification and his blood felt as if it had frozen as he read the text. Hitting the 'Print' key, he murmured, "Oh fuck," as he grabbed the paper off the printer and knocked before entering the Admiral's office.

"What's up, Mitch?"

"Uhh, sir, you'd better read this. It's RED-Flash from Shane who's currently at the Dubai air show," he said as he passed the paper over.

Ten seconds of silence followed as the Admiral read the email before he crashed his hand down on the desk shouting, "Those slant-eyed motherfuckers better not be. Devious little bastards. Shaking hands with the President one day, butt-fucking him the next. Get me Dick Warrington at Norfolk on the line followed by General Tarrant."

Carter sat there fuming until Mitch signaled he had Captain Richard Warrington, Norfolk Naval Base Commander on the line.

"Dick, just been informed by a reliable source we got goddam Chicoms at the door. Scramble a couple of P-8's and Orion's, will ya? If he's in international waters, scare the fucker off. If he's in ours, sink him," he said before slamming the phone down, yelling, "Where's General Tarrant?"

Two minutes later the phone chimed and Mitch called, "Admiral, General Tarrant on line 2."

Pressing the button, the Admiral began, "General, we may have a problem . . ."

Heading out of the office a few minutes later, he said to Mitch, "Lieutenant, I'm off to Tarrant's office. Get my driver to meet me downstairs and call me if you get any more news," before slamming the door behind him.

Breathing out a sigh of relief, Mitch thought, 'There goes the day'.

<><><>

Just over thirty minutes later, General Tarrant contacted Chief of Staff Alex Simpson to request an urgent meeting with the President, along with General Mansfield, Lt. General Dreiberg, and Secretary of State, Bill Casler.

17

Chinese Submarine, *Xiangliu*

Captain Yin Weimin, commander of the *Xiangliu,* was standing in the control room. The *Xiangliu* was one of the newest and latest Chinese-built SSBN's. The 'SS' stood for 'ship submersible', the 'B' for 'ballistic', and the 'N' for 'nuclear, making it a nuclear-powered submarine capable of carrying ballistic missiles. The *Xiangliu* was currently only carrying torpedoes as she was completing her sea trials, but her nuclear power plant meant she could circumnavigate the world without stopping to refuel. In fact, she could travel continuously for over ten years, the only limiting factor being the humans on board and their need for food. She even produced all her own water needs from a built-in desalination plant.

The name, *Xiangliu,* meant nine-headed dragon and she was living up to her name. When fully equipped she would be armed to the teeth with the very latest weaponry and defenses and would be an extremely formidable foe.

She was also quiet. Very quiet. Earlier submarines had suffered from producing various noises from pumps and machinery which could be monitored and heard underwater, allowing relatively easy detection and tracking. In particular, the large bronze propellers were often slightly unbalanced and the blade tips would produce cavitation. This cavitation, or bubbles, would then pop and the noises easily detected often many miles away. The Americans had joked the early Russian-built submarines were as quiet as a freight train, often sounding like a badly-tuned motorbike. That had all changed with the Russian Kilo class.

These were the first Russian submarines to be designed and produced using the latest computer technology stolen from the West. The computer-controlled milling machines produced components far more accurately than had been possible previously. These latest diesel-electric boats were limited by their need to surface to run their diesels to recharge their batteries, but, when submerged and running under electric power, they were extremely quiet. They were actually quieter than the background noise of the sea. So quiet that most US sonar operators could only find them by listening to the lack of noise they produced - they actually produced a 'dead' spot.

With the decline of the Soviet Union back in the late eighties and early nineties, the Soviet leaders were desperate for money to pay the workers, so they sold working Kilos. Sixteen in total were sold; ten to India, three to Iran, two to China and one to Poland. Although they can travel almost 7,500 miles without refueling, their ability to remain submerged is limited, and the US and the UK manage to track them daily by checking for satellite images of them surfacing to recharge their batteries.

As China often does, it took the two Kilos, operated them, and then listed what they would like to improve. They completely stripped one down to fully understand exactly how it had been made, before building a number of identical models.

They then took the design and augmented it, and, coupled with secret designs of the latest submarines stolen from the British and Americans, simply built their own.

The one drawback with nuclear-powered submarines was some were quite noisy. The pumps needed to pressurize the water and pump the steam around the turbines to make electricity were sometimes so noisy it made detection quite easy. However, the Americans managed to solve that problem in their *Los-Angeles* class nuclear boats and their newer *Virginia* class boats.

The latest Chinese boats, their Jin-class, are the result of many years' work and of many years' spying and stealing secrets. The *Xiangliu* was the very latest model crammed full of the latest technologies. Launched just over six months' previously, she'd completed basic sea-trials and was now undergoing extensive testing.

Fitted with the very latest sonar and underwater listening capabilities, Captain Weimin had exited the secret naval base at Hainan Island, headed south-east and steered his craft across the Pacific, stopping offshore at both Hawaii and San Diego Naval Stations and floated there recording as much underwater sound data of US warships as possible.

Currently located in the Norfolk Canyon, approximately sixty-five miles off the Norfolk coast of the Eastern Seaboard, the *Xiangliu* transited slowly back and forth over a twenty-mile stretch at a depth of just under 300 feet.

The seabed off the Norfolk coast, called Albemarie Shelf Valley, is fairly shallow with an average depth of only 300 feet, before shelving deeply at approximately sixty miles offshore to over 6,000 feet - ideal hiding ground for submarines. Further out, it deepens again to well over 12,000 feet and remains that way for most of the North Atlantic.

The Norfolk Canyon is a deeply jagged spur of over 1,000-foot depth stretching in through the shallows towards shore that extends the ideal operating ground for the *Xiangliu* almost twelve miles further towards land, making the recording of underwater shipping sounds from Norfolk Naval Base easier.

Finally, to make detection even harder, the sea consists of thermal layers - layers of differing temperatures. Sonar and sounds bounce along these layers but rarely penetrate through them. There was a perfect thermal layer at 293 feet, and Captain Weimin kept the *Xiangliu* floating just below this layer, whilst her sonar microphones called hydrophones floated along behind her just above this layer. By keeping the *Xiangliu's* speed to five knots, she was as silent as the grave as she traversed back and forth, recording the signature of every US Naval craft entering or leaving Norfolk Naval Base.

"Captain, sonar. We have sonobuoys being deployed. Very faint, about fifty miles away."

"Sonar, how many?"

"Over a dozen, Captain. But heading this way."

"We have overstayed our welcome. Helm, make course 110 and depth four hundred. Ahead half."

Turning, the giant steel killer slid slowly away into safer waters.

As her depth increased and she exited the danger area, the captain ordered a new course of 118 degrees and two-thirds speed.

On board the approaching aircraft, technicians were monitoring the signals coming back from the dropped sonobuoys. These were dropped from the aircraft and would float sending out sonar pings and also listening for ship noises. The data was streamed back to the aircraft circling overhead. Data from multiple sources would indicate a target as well as position and depth.

After a six-hour flight the pilots of the P-8's and Orion's headed back to Norfolk. Initially, they'd had a very faint return which might have been a possible target or enemy craft, but they'd lost it and couldn't detect it again. They had picked up engine noise - very faint and far too distant to positively classify, but definitely not US, British or French. To make matters worse, there was background whale migration noise partly masking sounds. However, the technicians called it a likely target, origin unknown, but classified as 'highly potential enemy engagement'.

Captain Weimin burst transmitted his report to PLAN Naval Command, Northern Fleet HQ, Qingdao. Two hours later, he received orders to return to Hainan Island via the Pacific instead of crossing the Indian Ocean. Setting course for Cape Horn he ordered speed maintained at two-thirds before passing command to his Executive Officer and returning to his bunk.

18

The Pentagon

The reports flooded back through Norfolk and to Admiral Carter. There had been a potential enemy submarine monitoring US Naval traffic in and out of Norfolk. Origin was unknown but it was assumed to be Russian as it was in the North Atlantic. No international laws had been broken as the submarine had been well outside the internationally recognized 12-mile limit, it had also been outside the enlarged limit of 24 nautical miles the US President had decreed and enforced in 1999. However, none of this mattered to Admiral Carter who despised the thought of anyone snooping on his navy's activities.

Stomping around his office his anger was evident for anyone to see. He ordered the immediate trebling of routine air patrols and active anti-submarine exercises were drastically increased. He also placed calls through diplomatic channels to his equals in both the Russian Navy and the Chinese PLAN, stating both his and the USA's disappointment at their practices and reminding them that any enemy naval ship found within US waters without US permission would be treated as 'hostile' and would be fired on accordingly.

"Vlasy, my old contemporary. We've been chasing a sub snooping off Norfolk today. It better not have been one of yours?" he said, trying to temper his anger.

"Douglas, my friend. What makes you think it would be us doing such a thing to our friends?" The Russian Naval Commander-in-Chief replied. "We've stopped snooping on you and you have stopped on us."

"Hmmh, well some bastard's been hanging around. You're sure it's not one of yours?"

"Douglas, Douglas. We know each other's capabilities, do we not? I can assure you, one Admiral to another, there is no Russian submarine anywhere close to you. Obviously, if there were you wouldn't be able to detect it anyway as Russian technology is far superior to that of the West," the Russian Commander-in-Chief chided.

"Vlasy, when you stop building them like rusty Trabants, you might have a point. I'll take you at your word. Regards to your wife," before hanging up.

"Mitch, no, it's not them. Vlasy's a conniving bastard but I trust him on this one. Get me the Commander-in-Chief of the PLAN," he said after a few moments thought.

After over twenty minutes delay, Mitch finally got put through to the extension of the PLAN Commander-in-Chief. Passing the connection over to the Admiral, Carter picked up the handset and said, "Admiral Zhang?"

Realizing he'd been passed to a secretary didn't go down well.

"I'm Admiral Carter, Chief of Naval Operations in the US of A. I'm waiting for Admiral Zhang. Where is he, young lady?" he asked, his voice becoming angrier the longer he was kept waiting.

"He says he is sorry, Admiral, but he is too busy to take your call today. He said perhaps you could call back tomorrow?" the secretary said.

"TOMORROW?" he shouted before slamming the phone down.

Red-faced with anger building, he called Mitch into his office.

"Lieutenant. I want to know the location of every fucking Chinese piece of shit floating. I wanna know where the fuck it is and what's it up to. And I want it on my desk by midnight tonight. Understood?" he barked.

"In fact, I want to know where every foreign submarine currently is, including our allies."

As Mitch moved quickly away he could hear the Admiral talking to himself. "Tomorrow? TOMORROW? Who the fuck does he think he is, jumped up little cockroach."

Knowing the best thing to do when the Admiral called him Lieutenant instead of by name was to keep out of the way, Mitch made several phones calls to contacts in the NSA and to NORAD to get the latest updates of Chinese ship movements.

Using a mixture of satellite surveillance, data collection and pre-stored information from paid informants, within hours Mitch had assimilated all the data and come to the conclusion the only craft that potentially had the range to approach the US mainland and not be detected was the recently launched Jin-class Chinese submarine, the *Xiangliu*. However, this was believed to be undergoing extensive sea trials close to its home base of Hainan Island. Until it could be proved otherwise, the unknown acoustic signature recorded would be classified as belonging to the *Xiangliu*.

Dubai

It was 09:35 local time on the last but one day of the airshow when Shane Walker's phone chimed again with another text message. The message read - 'Burj K, 148. 18:10'. Checking the source of the text message showed it belonged to a cleaner at the downtown Radisson Hotel.

Heading over to the Burj Khalifa tower, Shane purchased his ticket having arranged for two plain-clothed marines to attend with him. All visitors have to walk through airport-style metal detectors so Shane had made sure he and his colleagues were carrying ceramic knives that wouldn't trigger the alarms.

There are two observation decks in use at the tower. All visitors to the lower observation deck on floor 124 could use either of two elevators and access time there is unlimited. As arranged previously, one of the Marines stood in line and was soon crowded into the elevator with other visitors. However, for those wishing to see more and pay extra there is a higher, but physically smaller lounge, on floor 148 called the 'At the Top' observation deck, where Shane and the other marine headed. Accessed via a separate elevator to a private lounge on floor 125, the guests are provided refreshments before being allowed to proceed by yet another, smaller elevator to floor 148. Moments later, at precisely 18:00, Shane stepped out into the private viewing chamber almost at the top of the highest man-made structure on earth.

Due to the amount of people wanting to visit, and the relatively small viewing area, visitors to the 'At the Top' are only allowed to stay a maximum of thirty minutes before having to move back down to floor 124 where viewing time is unlimited, and every ten minutes a new group arrives. Walking around and standing at the downward sloping windows, he was still impressed with the view. He'd been here before as a tourist and was always amazed at just how much you could see from a height of 1,821 feet, especially in early evening when the lights of the distant cities could be clearly seen, but today he was here working.

It was possible it was still a trap. However this select location made it less likely. His marine colleague had moved away to the other aspect of the viewing platform but kept a discreet eye on Shane as he moved around with the crowd. He spotted Su Ming looking through pedestal binoculars and moved slowly towards her until he was standing close by.

"We meet again," he said just loud enough for her to hear.

Without taking her eyes away from the binoculars, she replied, "So my information was good?"

"It seemed to pan out."

"So as I said before, I want to go to America."

"It would start a diplomatic row. It's not possible."

"Don't waste my time, Captain Shane Walker of the CIA. Tell your superiors I want to come to the USA and I have much more information to provide. Information that your people will happily pay me for. I want a new identity and five-million US dollars in cash for a new life."

"I told you before, Miss. I am Gerald Wagner and I'm a salesman. But when I get back home to Houston I'll call the CIA for you and tell them you're looking to leave. Perhaps one of their people will get in touch."

"Captain Walker, don't take me for a fool. Even meeting you here puts my life in extreme danger. Why do you think I haven't been in contact with your CIA in Hong Kong? Because they are all compromised. Every one of them, all throughout China. If you don't believe me, how do you think I obtained your number? Do you want me to recite your CIA personnel number? How about your IRS number? Maybe your mother's maiden name?"

Not sure what to answer to that revelation, Walker kept quiet as a message came through his earpiece from the marine on floor 124 that a Chinese guy was stood carefully watching everyone who entered and exited the elevators, not looking at the outside views at all.

"I had to wait until I was away from as many eyes as possible," Su Ming continued, "I will check the draft folder of this email address once in four weeks. It will have the name of a contact who is not in your mighty CIA, and I will meet him or her on New Year's Eve in Hong Kong at the lower stern of the 23:30 Star Ferry from Central to Tsim Sha Tsui. Password will be 'Happy New Year, my dear.' My reply will be 'It is the western New Year. Chinese New Year is not until February 16.' Those will be the exact words. If there is no name in the email or those words are not spoken precisely, you will never hear from me again," she said, also giving Walker details of the email address.

Repeating it back to her he said, "How have you slipped your guard today?"

"I told him I'd be perfectly safe up here on my own and I wanted some private time to enjoy the atmosphere and meditate. He wasn't happy but I told him my father pays him and I wished to be alone. He is waiting for me on floor 124. I expect your men will be watching him there," she said with a smile adding, "Stay and enjoy the view," before walking quickly to the down elevator.

19

The White House

An urgent security update meeting was taking place in the Oval Office. With only a few items on the agenda, item number one was concerning a foreign submarine lurking close to Norfolk naval base.

All except POTUS were seated on the two long couches. The President preferred to sit on the edge of his desk known as the *Resolute* desk - a gift from Queen Victoria to President Rutherford Hayes in 1880 and made from the English oak timbers of the British Arctic exploration ship *HMS Resolute*.

"Mr. President, we've covered the area and we're a hundred-percent confident there are no unidentified vessels anywhere near our coastline. We did get a distant possible return on something moving along the Norfolk Canyon, a deep-water channel over sixty miles offshore, but by the time we got closer, it had gone. We've now stationed a couple of sub-hunters to patrol that entire area," Secretary of Department of Defense, General Melvin Tarrant said.

"So you're telling me the fucking Chinese have been sat there monitoring our shipping. For how long?" the President said.

"We, uh, don't know for sure, Mr. President. Less than a week we believe."

"You believe? A week. A whole fucking week? Those bastards have been sat there at least a week and you knew nothing about them? Had you not received a tip-off they'd still be sat there now."

"Uh, yessir, I mean nosir. Fleet replenishment is ongoing so we'd have discovered them then."

"Or they could have sunk our entire fleet? Correct?" the President continued.

"It was a lapse, Mr. President. We have ships and aircraft patrolling as we speak. I've also put our other bases on higher alert and ordered they increase surveillance, sir."

Turning to Secretary of State Bill Casler, the President said, "Bill, get on to China. Tell 'em I do not take kindly to having them snoop around our coastline and any further intrusions will be taken as aggressive and our response will also be aggressive."

"Sir, we don't know if it was the Chinese and anyway, they were in international waters, Mr. President."

"I don't give a flying fuck. You tell 'em if they want to come and snoop on us we WILL take all measures to make sure they never see the rice paddies back home again. Understand?"

Shaking his head in exasperation, he moved on to item two -- the potential breach of security highlighted with the defection of Lieutenant Junior Grade Zhang Su Ming of the People's Liberation Army Navy.

The President started this section of the meeting, saying, "Gentlemen, if we are to take the report from our Baghdad CIA agent seriously, all of Charles's people in China have been compromised. Correct?"

"Not just China, Mr. President. We need to consider all of the Middle-East and Asia as being compromised. Didn't you say your agent said his details in Baghdad were known, Warwick?" Chief-of-Staff Alex Simpson said to Lt. Gen. Warwick Dreiberg - Director of National Intelligence.

Nodding, Dreiberg said, "We really don't know how far this extends." Turning to face the Director of the CIA, he said, "It seems your tight ship has sprung a leak."

Not sure of what, if anything, to say, a rather embarrassed Charles Ingram merely nodded. The President, used to the day-to-day language of normal business and always keen to speak his mind, directed his next comment directly to the CIA Director.

"Instead of sitting there and nodding like a fucking duck, maybe you should be working on how those bastards gained access to our most sensitive data, how far it extends, and what you're going to do about it?"

Suitably chastised, Ingram replied, "Yessir, Mr. President. We already have our technical teams looking into it."

"Your department gets a budget of fifteen billion goddam dollars a year, and our enemies know more than you do. I wanna know how this has happened, how much those bastards know, and what are you gonna do to stop it happening again? Understood?"

"Yessir, Mr. President, sir."

"And let me tell you right now, heads are going to roll. Heads are going to fucking roll. Whoever has compromised our security will answer to me. Directly! Understood?" POTUS continued, his face showing red with anger.

"Mr. President," DNI Dreiberg said, "As a safety measure we have disabled our entire Asia and Middle-East networks until we know more about this infiltration, how far it extends, and what's been compromised. I've gotten the NSA and the FBI technical forensics department involved, as well as the CIA technicians. As soon as we get answers . . ."

"Keep me informed," the President said. "OK, item three. This defection - tell me more."

Pleased to have moved on from the embarrassment of the potential departmental security breach under his command, DNI Dreiberg continued, "Zhang Su Ming is the only surviving child of Admiral Zhang Hu, senior member of the Politburo and senior advisor to President Xiaodong. Any defection by her would be extremely embarrassing to the Chinese government and devastating to the career of Admiral Zhang. I've spoken with Bill at State and he's advised we keep this under wraps at least for now until we know more. Especially as you, Mr. President, have been pushing for improved trade deals with China. The publicity over this and the associated embarrassment to their government would be particularly harmful to those talks. Ideally, we want to have nothing to do with this but the opportunity presenting itself is too big to walk away from. The information Su Ming gave Agent Walker about the *Xiangliu* was, we believe, just the tip of the iceberg. Her current role is involved with supplies and equipment heading to the Spratly Islands. The department head is a Captain Gao. This could give us insight into the thoughts and plans of Admiral Zhang himself and what they have planned for that region, so this really is a top priority. Especially as China keeps saber-rattling in the South China Sea."

The President put his hand up to halt the conversation. It was a rude gesture, but by now the senior staff was accustomed to his ways.

After almost a full minute of thought, the President turned to General Tarrant and said, "Melvin, where have I heard this name of Zhang before? The Admiral, I mean."

"Mr. President, sir. If you remember prior to your inauguration, we discussed past history involving the southeast region. His name came up in connection with the failed attempt to trigger the volcanos back in 2012. We think he was involved in shipping the nuke to Hawaii.

The FBI investigated but could never prove anything. He was on our watch list anyway but more so since."

"So what's he been doing since?"

"He's been playing the political game, sir. As you know, China has been pursuing the nine-dash line in the South China Sea for years. They invaded and took control of the Paracel Islands after their war over them with Vietnam back in '74 and took control of a number of the Spratly Islands back in the late '80s and early '90s. Since then they've been steadily building up their defenses on them and actually building up the islands themselves. Some of them now are fairly large and consist of ninety-percent or more of reclaimed land."

"So was this all his doing?"

"He was the main advocate for it, Mr. President. He sold the other Politburo members on the idea and was given free rein and an unlimited budget to pursue it. He also oversaw the expansion and completion of their submarine base on Hainan Island. He seems pretty well respected and is a close confidant to President Xiaodong. Their army has gone through some modernization but, as you know, their air force and navy have been radically upgraded. We believe Zhang has been the main driving force behind their expansions."

"So where do I know the name of Hanging Island from?"

"Hainan Island, Mr. President. It's a large island at the southern-most part of mainland China. It's about one-hundred-fifty miles off the northern Vietnam coast. The PLAN have one of their largest naval bases there at Yulin. Same sort of size as San Diego or Pearl. Always masses of their surface fleet there. But a couple of miles east they have built Longpo naval base. It's an underground submarine base with underwater tunnel access and a demagnetizing facility to demagnetize ships and subs. It's actually been built under a large mountain and, we believe, it's built stronger than NORAD at Cheyenne Mountain."

"Yeah, yeah, I remember now. Didn't one of our spy planes land there?"

"Correct, Mr. President. In '01 one of our navy EP-3's on a routine surveillance mission was buzzed by a couple of Chinese fighters out over international waters. One got too close and collided with us taking a large part of the wing. They claimed it was an accident, but we've always thought it was deliberate. We had no choice but to make an emergency landing. Unfortunately, it was at one of their airfields. Nobody on our side was injured seriously, although their pilot that crashed into us was killed. We finally got everyone back eleven or so days later. It became a big international incident, though. One of the first major ones for President Bush to have to deal with. We eventually also got the 'plane back and the crew had managed to destroy what data they could before it landed, but the bastards got access to our latest gear and methods. We think that one little incident took ten years or more off our lead."

"So what do we know of this girl, Zhang Su Ming?" the president asked, turning to CIA Director Ingram.

"Not very much, Mr. President. She's never shown up on our radar before. We knew Admiral Zhang had a son first and then a daughter. He'd be thirty-two now, and she's twenty-eight. Both followed him into the services. The son became a fighter pilot in their navy. Quite good, as well, we believe, until he died just under eighteen months' ago when they started practicing carrier take-offs and landings. As you know, they can be pretty risky and there was an accelerated learning program in time for the PLAN's launch of the purchased Russian aircraft carrier, the *Varyag*, now revamped and renamed the *Liaoning*.

Reports after the event showed his aircraft was experiencing power surges as he came into land and he overshot the landing area. Tried to regain height but crashed into the bridge structure. Killed on impact. Zhang, the father, was affected quite badly, we believe."

"They were close?"

"Very, him being the only son. Took him a long while to get over it. Then, to make matters worse, his wife became ill and died unexpectedly. Left just Zhang and his daughter."

"How is he with her?"

"All information indicates he now dotes on her, sir. Never used to, but does now. She is clever in her own right and been promoted on her merit, but as always, I guess having a senior member of the Politburo as her father always helps. Education was initially in China, then Switzerland but she also attended the London School of Economics before heading over here to Stanford where she studied International Development and Global Studies. Quite a bit of family money involved and it seems it was Zhang's insistence she received education abroad."

"So do we know why she wants to defect? It would seem she has a pretty cushy life planned out for her. Why would she want to embarrass the family?" the Secretary of Defense added.

"That," Warwick Dreiberg said, "is the sixty-four-thousand-dollar question. It could just be a trap, but as she already knows Agent Walker's details, I can't see what she or they would have to gain unless it's to make us expose the rest of our network getting her out. She wants to meet again on New Year's Eve in Hong Kong."

"So do you mean maybe our Asia network isn't compromised?" POTUS said.

"That could well be the case, Mr. President. It could just be Walker's details have somehow been exposed and this is just a trap to find out more. Or, of course, it could be genuine. She may have fallen in love with the California lifestyle and want more. At this stage, we really don't know. Either way, I think we need to tread very carefully with this one."

"And if we do bring her over, we can't be seen aiding her defection," Dreiberg continued.

"What about using the FBI?" Simon Clark, the Director of the FBI, asked.

"It's an option, but we need to be absolutely sure nothing can be traced. If any of your people were captured aiding and abetting her escape . . . Well, I'm sure I don't need to remind everyone what it could do for US - Chinese relationships," Tarrant said, "as well as being a monumental coup for China on the world-stage if this administration were implicated."

The President always liked a moment or two of silence whilst he pondered decisions. Woe betides anyone who interrupted his thoughts. Finally, after what seemed an age to the other senior staff members in the room, the President announced, "No, until we can ascertain exactly why she wants to defect and how far this intel leak extends, I think we need to use someone completely isolated from us."

"What about involving the British?" Charles Ingram suggested. "They're pretty good at this sort of thing. They brought out countless of our Russian friends back in the day."

"That's a potential solution," Warwick Dreiberg replied, "but this Su Ming character deliberately sought out our help knowing our agents were compromised. I wonder why she didn't approach the Brits first unless it's a trap. And we really don't want to be washing our dirty laundry in public and admitting to the damn Brits we have a security breach. No, I agree with the President and think at this stage we should keep it 'in-house', but under wraps. Thoughts?"

After receiving nods and approving gestures, he continued, "So if we are to keep this in-house, but under wraps, who do we involve?"

After a few seconds delay, the President said, "I think we have just the man."

20

The Indian Ocean

Eleven days later the *USS Bradenton*, a nuclear-powered, Los Angeles-class, fast-attack submarine was on patrol in the southern Indian Ocean. Away from its home base for two months at a time, it patrolled and listened. Sleek, silent and deadly, it was one of the US Navy's first lines of defense.

In mid-November, it was on patrol southeast of Madagascar, slowly cruising northwards at fifteen knots.

The South Atlantic

As the *Xiangliu* approached the Falkland Islands, Captain Yin Weimin was on duty in the control room when a call came over the internal Tannoy system.

"Captain, sonar."

Picking up the handset, he replied, "Sonar, Captain."

"Captain, I am picking up the sounds of a diesel-electric submarine at maximum distance."

"Range?"

"Sixty-five thousand meters, sir."

Pushing crew out of the way, Weimin rushed into the sonar room. The submarine was already running very quietly. The crew wore soft-soled shoes, and all walkways were carpeted. The outside of the craft was coated in thick sound absorbent rubber, and all extraneous noise was limited. The *Xiangliu* was already an extremely silent boat, but that didn't stop Weimin from quietly issuing the

Chinese equivalent of 'Action Stations' and demanding silent running.

All meals were stopped, and all stations were manned ready. The boat, already quiet, became like a tomb as it sailed on towards the south. Thirty minutes later the sound signals from the unknown submarine were becoming clear. The signature confirmed it as a diesel-electric submarine, country of origin unknown. Mechanical noises could be heard, and it was assumed there were problems aboard. Sonar reported it had blown tanks and risen to periscope and radio depth, and made a radio call before dropping back down to two hundred feet. The water on the surface was being churned as a heavy thunderstorm, common in these parts of the world in the winter months, slowly moved away overhead.

Plotting its course and that of the *Xiangliu*, Weimin knew they would pass only five miles to the east of it and ordered they turn hard to port and proceed with caution.

That was when the first mistake happened. The crew on the *Xiangliu* were experienced submariners but still new to this boat. The helmsman, He Guan, used to operating on slower responding submarines, turned the rudder sharp left. The *Xiangliu*, traveling at just over twenty knots, responded immediately and the sudden sharp turn caused her to heel over almost forty degrees before righting herself.

The second mistake was the steel toolbox that should have been strapped down. It slid along the shelf before dropping off the end, its contents of spanners and hammers clattering down towards the keel.

Captain Weimin was never sure what caused the unidentified submarine to start its active sonar. It should have just listened and monitored. Passive sonar is listening to noises and detecting other ships from their sounds and signatures. Active sonar is the sending out of high energy sound 'pings' to detect another craft. A submarine, although capable, would never normally resort to active sonar as it immediately gives away its exact position to a potential enemy. But the unidentified submarine fired a series of sonar 'pings', and one of them struck the *Xiangliu*.

The effect on the crew of the *Xiangliu* was as if a giant hammer had slammed into the steel hull. The sound reverberated around the hull, and the shock wave broke plates and cups, a number of computer screens and glass partitions. Many of the crew clasped their hands over their ears to reduce the pain in their heads, and the petty officer on Sonar watch felt both his eardrums explode.

Knowing they'd been detected and their boat's envelope displayed on the unidentified submarine's screen, Captain Weimin made his first, but overall, the third mistake. He ordered the immediate firing of a YU-6 torpedo. The torpedo was ejected with a rush of compressed air before its electric motor started and it headed towards its prey at 30 knots, guided by wire and control from the *Xiangliu*. For the next few minutes there was nothing but silence. The unknown target submarine would have known it had given away its position and would be running the envelope of the unknown sonar return signature through its computers trying to find a match, trying to identify if it was friend or foe. But it would fail to find one because the *Xiangliu* was too new to have been previously recorded. In peacetime and with an unknown target just a few miles away the captain had little choice other than move away or attempt to follow at a safe distance. He certainly wouldn't expect to be attacked close to his own shoreline.

At 1,000 meters to target, Weimin on board the *Xiangliu* ordered the cutting of the control cable and the silent running torpedo switched to automatic homing mode, initiated its own active hunting sonar, accelerated to 65 knots and continued heading to its target.

Twenty-nine seconds later, before the crew of the other submarine had time to react or release an emergency beacon, and as the warhead was one meter away from the hull, it exploded. On detonation, a large amount of sodium powder was released which reacted with seawater to produce, within fractions of a second, large amounts of super-heated hydrogen. The now boiling seawater of over 2000 degrees Centigrade caused the hull to immediately implode.

At a depth of two hundred feet, most particles were compressed beyond recognition and immediately sank. The few items that gradually floated to the surface were soon washed away in the storm raging above.

21

The Indian Ocean

Captain Ken Betley of the USS Bradenton called his Executive Officer, Lieutenant Joanna Gordon, to the bridge.

"Lieutenant, I want you to hear what I've just heard and see if you come to the same conclusion as I have. Sonar, play the recordings again and explain to the XO what you heard and what you think."

Moving away so as not to influence the outcome, Captain Betley watched and listened as the Chief Sonar Operator, Dave (Wolf) Forrester played back the recordings on the screen and through the headphones.

"Lieutenant, if you look at this transient it was a sudden bang. It's at extreme range, well over 5,000 miles but sounds like something metal being dropped. Less than a minute later, there are a series of acoustic pings. See here the individual transients?" Dave Forrester said while playing back the audio recording he'd also made.

Nicknamed 'Wolf' during training because he could hear and identify noises others couldn't even hear, like the superhero Wolverine. The name had stuck, much to everyone's, apart from Dave Forrester's, amusement.

"They're too regular to be anything other than active sonar. Then one of them gets a response. Here," he said, pointing to a new transient on the screen, before continuing, "Then here a minute later - the faintest sound I missed the first time around. Only heard it on playback. So faint it's almost lost in background noise."

"What do you think it is?" the Lieutenant asked.

"I think it's the sound of a torpedo being fired. The compressed air expelling it. Then eight minutes later there's the sound of an explosion followed almost immediately by a second explosion and two subsequent smaller explosions a few seconds later."

"Play it all again," she commanded.

After listening to it a further four times while examining the sonar screen, she turned to the operator and asked, "So what do you make of it?"

"I think there were two subs and one made a noise. That's the initial bang. The other sub went active on sonar, but I'd say it was the first one that fired a torpedo. The alignments are different, even at extreme range. Only fractionally, but these two were close together. Maybe six or seven miles apart. Eight minutes later the torpedo hit the other sub and exploded causing an immediate implosion. That's the two loud bangs close together and showing transients here. Finally, as the damaged sub sank, two more compartments imploded. I think we witnessed the hostile takedown of a sub somewhere north of the Falklands. At this distance, I can't be exact as to location and can only pinpoint it to within a 30-mile radius or almost 3,000 square miles."

Lieutenant Gordon examined the data and listened to the recordings another three times before entirely concurring with her Chief Sonar Operator.

"Captain," she said, "I believe, as does Wolf, that we witnessed two submarines attacking each other and the demise of one of them. Wolf's analyzed the sonar pings and believes it came from the German-built Atlas Elektronik CSU 3/4 system. In that region of the world, that system is currently only fitted to two Argentinian subs, the ARA San Sebastian and the ARA Santa Cruz. We don't know the origin of the other submarine involved or its fate."

112

"Lieutenant, your conclusion matches mine. That will be the Flash-Traffic report I'm sending.

<><><>

The Pentagon
Lieutenant Mitch Stringer knocked on the Admiral's door and walked in.

"Sir, Flash-Traffic from the Bradenton via COMSUBPAC. *(Commander, Submarine Force Pacific)*."

"Summarize," the Admiral commanded without looking up.

"Um, possibly sinking of an Argentinian sub by hostile sub unknown."

"WHAT? . . . Gimme!" the Admiral said, suddenly alert and with his hand extended.

Mitch stood there in silence while the Admiral read and re-read the one-page report. Trying to hold back a smile as the Admiral umm'd and ahhh'd quietly to himself before suddenly grabbing a pencil and a ruler before heading over to the large world chart on the opposite wall.

"Mmmm, 24 hours a day . . . say 22 or 23 knots average . . . about 550 a day give-or-take . . . 11 days . . . about 6,000 thousand miles . . . puts them about -- " he muttered quietly while quickly drawing a series of lines down south from Norfolk Naval Base.

"Here!" he said, drawing a circle in pencil.

Scratching his chin, he looked around at Mitch and said, "Mitch, my boy. If it was those fuckers off Norfolk last week and they're heading home, they'd be just about here," he said thumping the wall chart, "about now!"

Even from the other side of the room, Mitch could see the black circle the Admiral had drawn was off the coast of Argentina and north of the Falklands.

"Get COMNAVSURFLANT (*Commander, Naval Surface Forces Atlantic*) on the phone now. I want anything we have in the area in pursuit. Top priority. Also, get Pearl on the horn. If it is the Chinese and they're heading home, they'll pass south of Pearl. Get everything we have that floats out listening in . . ." he said looking again at the world chart and making some basic measurements, ". . . in about seven days' time," he ordered.

<><><>

Later that afternoon reports from CNN started being broadcast stating the suspected loss of the Argentinian submarine, the ARA San Sebastian.

Soon after, offers of assistance to search for the suspected missing submarine flooded in from the USA, France, Germany, Chile, and Peru. For historical reasons and with the memories of the 1982 Falklands War still fresh in many peoples' minds, offers for assistance from the UK, however, were rejected.

Over the following two weeks, even after extensive search and rescue attempts, no trace of the submarine was found.

In the Argentinian press, rumors started circulating that a British submarine had sunk the ARA San Sebastian.

<><><>

Nine days after the USS Bradenton filed her report, distant engine noises were recorded from US Naval ships monitoring the South Pacific. The signals were too faint for 100% positive identification, but the computerized systems placed a 95% probability of the engine noises belonging to the *Xiangliu*.

In the Pentagon, Admiral Carter realized he didn't have conclusive proof about what exactly had occurred off the Falklands, but he had very strong suspicions. Looking at the grainy satellite photos taken of the *Xiangliu* as she'd entered the Yulin Naval Base, the strengthened underground submarine base and workshop located on Hainan Island, he muttered, "You might have gotten away with it for now, but your card is marked, you bastard, your card is marked."

22

Hong Kong

Su Ming swiped her Octopus Travel Card on the MTR barrier and walked out into the cold winter drizzle. Her apartment was less than a hundred yards away, and she was glad to be home. Today she'd been at the Ngong Shuen Chau Naval Base on Stonecutters Island. She had a little Daihatsu car stored in the allocated parking spot underneath her apartment but rarely used it. Traffic in Hong Kong was so busy, and parking so limited it made far more sense to use the public transport system. But today, just two days before Christmas, the crowds were even heavier and she felt she'd been jostled about more than usual on the busy trains. Today, she thought, she would have welcomed the chance to sit and drive even through the heavy traffic, safe in her own space with some quiet music playing. Usually stationed at the PLAN Headquarters building just off Connaught Road, a mere twenty-minute walk away, for the last week she'd been working at the naval base checking on loading. However, the weekend was her own and a lazy bath followed by a glass or two of wine was exactly what she was looking forward to.

Three days previously she'd stopped on the way home at an internet cafe and checked the email account. The message had read, *'Donald Duck 23:30'*. She'd immediately deleted the draft message and the browsing history before spending the next fifteen minutes looking at random pages. She'd also deliberately left the browser open when she'd left so that the shop manager would need to delete and reset the system before the next user arrived.

Humming to herself as she fitted the key to the door lock she walked in and froze. The lamp was on. She knew it hadn't been on this morning. She remembered turning it off as she'd left. Slipping her hand into her coat pocket, she flicked the cover off the small pepper-spray aerosol as she pulled it clear. Raising her hand up she was ready to spray while her free hand pulled her phone out and she silently thumbed in '999' -- the emergency number for the police and a hangover from the days of British rule, when a shadow appeared in the doorway.

"Daughter, you are here!"

"Father, you frightened me. I didn't know you were coming," Su Ming gasped, visibly relaxing.

"Did you not see my car downstairs?" the Admiral said.

"No father. My mind was elsewhere, and it was raining. I must have walked straight past it," she said, wishing she'd been more observant. Checking her phone, she saw she hadn't pressed 'Send' so the call hadn't connected, saving her an embarrassing explanation to the emergency operator.

"Tonight we celebrate. I want to take my favorite daughter out for a meal," he said, hugging her.

"I am your ONLY daughter, father, so I hope I am also your favorite," she said smiling. "So what are we celebrating?" she said, trying not to appear cold to his touch, as she gently pulled away.

"A project I have been working on for over ten years has just finished. It enables my next project to complete and is worthy of celebrations. I was in Longpo and decided to drop in and see you before I return to Beijing. I haven't seen you since the funeral."

"Actually, father, I am quite tired. I've had a busy week and was looking forward to a bath--"

"Nonsense," her father said. "We are going out to celebrate. I insist! Go and freshen yourself up. I've already booked us a table, and my driver is waiting," he said, his voice growing stern leaving no chance for discussion.

Realizing it was an argument she couldn't win Su Ming reluctantly moved to her bedroom and quickly changed her outfit. Walking back into the lounge a few minutes later she said, "I didn't realize you had a key?"

Seeing his satisfied smile, she wondered what else he knew about her routine.

Two hours later after a delicious meal she hadn't really wanted she finally asked, "So father, what is this new project you are excited about?"

Relaxed after finishing almost the entire bottle of wine and over half a bottle of whiskey, the Admiral looked around to make sure he wasn't being overheard before answering.

"My child, your life might be changing soon. Now she's back we can soon block the seas and impose taxes," he slurred.

"What do you mean, father? Who's back? And block what seas?"

"Sshhhh!," he said, putting a finger to his lips. "People might hear."

"Father, look around. We're alone. I think you're drunk and talking rubbish."

"You wait, my girl. Things are going to change. Soon my name will be famous," he said between hiccups and belching.

"You're drunk. I'm going home," Su Ming said, pushing back her chair to stand up.

"Our baby, she sunk them. They never even saw her . . . and she'll do the same to the Americans," he slurred.

Deciding she'd had enough, she asked the waiter for her coat, walked outside and flagged down a cab.

On the journey back home she knew he'd said something important but she couldn't work out what was genuine and what was just the drink talking.

In the meantime, her father continued drinking, finishing the contents of the whiskey bottle, before staggering to the doorway and gently sliding down the door frame while his worried driver tried to half-walk, half-carry him to the comfort of his waiting limousine.

He was completely asleep for the drive back to his waiting jet and didn't feel himself being manhandled up the aircraft steps and placed across two of the leather seats before being strapped in.

Admiral Zhang's private jet landed at Xijiao in northwest Beijing slightly ahead of schedule. The waiting limousine sped him quickly to the Zhongnanhai, a former imperial garden in the Imperial City, immediately adjacent to the Forbidden City. Zhongnanhai houses the office of the General Secretary of the Communist Party of China, who simultaneously also serves as Chairman of the Central Military Commission and President of China.

The guards ushered him in, and he stood waiting. His head still felt woolly from the previous evening's alcohol even after plentiful cups of sweet tea, water and paracetamol tablets.

Eventually, the large double doors were opened, and the figure of President Xiaodong Wang entered.

"Hu, my dear friend. It is good to see you. You bring good news?" the President asked.

"Zhao Zhuxi, it is my greatest honor to meet you again," Zhang said, choosing to use the popular and intimate expression *Zhao Zhuxi* meaning 'President'. "I bring excellent news, my leader," he continued.

Indicating they should sit, Xiaodong Wang led the way to the waiting sofas. "Come sit and tell me," he instructed, after clapping his hands to summon tea.

"Zhao Zhuxi, our submarine, the *Xiangliu,* has returned from her initial sea trials successfully. She spent over a week at each US naval base monitoring and recording without being detected. When heading home she came across an Argentinian submarine that tried to engage her. She sunk it without trace an--"

"That was the one on the international news?" he interrupted.

"Yes, my leader. Even the Americans have tried to find her remains but have failed. These new sodium powder torpedoes burn with such intensity they leave much less wreckage for anyone to find."

"I hear the British are being blamed," he said.

"An unforeseen benefit," Zhang said smiling before continuing and reciting the ancient Chinese proverb "Every smile makes you a day younger, Zhao Zhuxi,"

"What is your next step?"

"First, the *Xiangliu* will need a complete maintenance check. Once we confirm she is fully seaworthy, she will move into our active fleet. This will take up to eight weeks. Then, Zhao Zhuxi, we can begin phase two. She will be stationed in the South China Sea, and we can impose sanctions for passage. She will support the surface fleet, and the Americans will have no choice but to concede and retreat. Then, with your permission, we can finalize our plans for phase three; the retaking and reintroduction of Taiwan."

With smiles all around Admiral Zhang knew he'd done well. Unlike the 'West', the People's Republic of China had longer timescales for projects. He'd been taught in university the famous reply the Chinese premier, Zhou Enlai, said during Richard Nixon's visit to Beijing in 1972. When asked about the impact of the French Revolution, an event that happened nearly two centuries previously, Zhou famously commented that it was 'too early to say'. This was taken by reporters and academics alike as emphasizing China's ability to take the long view in history.

The governments in the West usually changed every four or five years. In the USA the President could only run two terms, meaning most long-term plans had to see fulfillment within just a few years or likely be shelved by each new government.

In China, however, a leader could stay in power almost indefinitely. President Xiaodong had already hinted he would change and amend their constitution to allow him to remain President for life. This allowed plans with very long lifecycles to become a reality under this scheme.

China had been the greatest nation on earth many hundreds of years ago. With the rapid growth and expansion China had been achieving over the past twenty years and the build-up of their Army, Navy and Air Force, China was set to again become the largest and most important world power.

And Admiral Zhang wanted to ensure he was right at the very pinnacle of its influence.

<><><>

After spending the evening with her father, it would be a number of weeks before she heard from him again. With the 25th and 26th of December being public holidays, Su Ming spent the next few days relaxing with friends and attending the many shows and events celebrating the festive season. Although Han Chinese and of Taoist religion, she, like many other Chinese nationals joined in and enjoyed the Christmas Christian festivities being held throughout Hong Kong.

23

Hong Kong - New Year's Eve

The heavily overcast sky offered a threat of drizzle, and the cold wind blew gently in off the sea. Late December was always stormy and tonight was no exception. Deacon finished his meal at the small seafood restaurant, paid, and made his way along Douglas Lane to Douglas Street. Many of the shops were still open and the streets as crowded as ever, even at ten o'clock at night. Heading over the various underpasses overshadowed by the massive high-rises, he quickly reached the pier area known as Central. He'd been staying locally in the Four Seasons Hotel on Hong Kong Island, but the walk to the restaurant and back had allowed him time to check if he was being followed. Twice he thought he'd seen the same person but after changing direction yet again, he'd either lost them or he may have been mistaken. Now he was blending in along with all the other locals and tourists keen to welcome in the New Year.

Everywhere was busy in Hong Kong at all hours of the day and night. The person that first said New York was the city that never sleeps had not experienced Hong Kong, Deacon thought. Tonight, being New Year's Eve was busier than ever.

Pulling his collar up higher to ward off the chill, and glad he'd chosen to bring a winter coat with him, Deacon thought about the request he'd received almost three weeks ago from Admiral Carter. Go to Hong Kong on New Year's Eve and make contact with a Chinese lieutenant who may or may not be a genuine defector.

With little additional information to base his decision on, he chose to couple this request with a pre-planned business trip to the Middle East. The previous night he'd arrived from Ras al-Khaimah, via Dubai, having spent two days in the company of their royal family. He felt good and was pretty confident the extra effort he'd put into the meetings and social gatherings would have earned him prime position for the forthcoming bid for Phylax to supply close-quarter protection services. He already had two ex-marines in mind to fill the role. Both had excellent service records, were polite, good-tempered and both were seeking long-term overseas contracts.

Landing at Chek Lap Kok Airport just before midnight, he'd caught the excellent high-speed shuttle, finally checking into his hotel room at a little after 01:30. Things had changed a lot since the old days of flying low over the city and landing at Kai Tak Airport's single runway, jutting out into Victoria Harbor from Kowloon right in the very heart of the city, he thought. He'd then gone for a walk just to stretch tired muscles and even at 02:30, the place was teeming with people. Come daylight it was incredible. Looking down from the window on the twenty-seventh floor, the people going about their business reminded him of a colony of ants all rushing and running about in chaotic order.

Tonight was no different. Only westerners stood in line. The locals just pushed forward en masse, and Deacon had learned long ago the best way to blend in with the locals was to act like a local, so he just pushed along with the rest of them.

The entrance to the Star Ferry to Kowloon was packed. Jammed in the crowd and moving along with them he managed to get to the ticket barrier. After paying his HK$3.2 fare for access to the lower deck jokingly called Second Class, he pushed and squeezed his way towards the stern rail. As the ferry eased away from its berth and began its fifteen-minute journey across the choppy waters, the breeze picked up, and even the thickness of his coat couldn't stop him from shivering. Wedged shoulder to shoulder he didn't see her arrive. Slim-built, wearing a thick Puffer jacket that hid her shape, and with most of her face hidden by a wrap-around scarf, she had managed to squeeze past others, all wearing thick overcoats against the chill, before ending up stood in front of him, facing away. Trying to see her face over her scarf, he thought he recognized her from the photos he'd been given.

Feeling a little stupid, he bent slightly, smiled and said, "Happy New Year, my dear."

She glanced up at him then quickly looked away, ignoring him.

Deacon was confused. Had he approached the wrong person? The ferry was so crowded it was possible she hadn't managed to board, or maybe something else had stopped her from getting to the rendezvous. However, this girl looked similar to the one in the photos. At least, what he could see of her appeared to.

A few minutes later the ferry docked at Tsim Sha Tsui pier, and the mass of people began to surge forward.

The girl in front of him adjusted her handbag and, in doing so, nudged him with it. She moved back fractionally and stood on his foot. Then she walked away.

Most of the crowd was heading towards Tsim Sha Tsui Promenade, a few hundred meters along the shore. Almost sixty-thousand people were already there, some queuing since early that morning, guaranteeing a front row position. When Hong Kong does fireworks, it does them bigger and brighter than anyone else. The thirty-minute show would commence shortly as midnight arrived. It was staged on a large barge positioned in the middle of Victoria Harbor and the most favored location to view them was from the south banks of Kowloon with Hong Kong Island as a backdrop.

Momentarily losing sight of the girl amongst the throng of people, he suddenly felt a nudge to his arm and heard her quietly say, "It is the western New Year. Chinese New Year is not until February 16."

She then stepped in front and across his path, moving to another part of the massive crowd already there. There were so many people milling about, most crammed towards the seafront, it was impossible to see clearly who was with whom. But this also made it easier for Deacon to try to follow Su Ming without it appearing obvious to anyone watching.

Standing in front of a grassed garden area, Su Ming stood behind him on the small wall surrounding it, bringing her up to Deacon's height.

With a slight tilt of her head, she said, just loud enough for him to hear, "Sky Terrace Observation Deck, tomorrow 2:00 p.m."

Half turning his head he saw her disappear into the crowds.

With contact made and a full stomach, he did the same as every other person there. He waited and enjoyed thirty minutes of the incredible fireworks display.

It was sunny but very cold as he strolled along Nathan Road in Kowloon the next morning. It was still the best place to see the heart of Hong Kong as it has been for most of the last century. He'd stated on his visa that he was here for a couple of days to celebrate New Year before heading on to India for business meetings. So today he played the role of the tourist and headed to the main shopping tourist area.

After wasting three hours aimlessly browsing in shop windows, doubling back and changing direction many times to confuse anyone following him, he walked through an alley, hailed a taxicab slowly cruising by, and leaped in almost before it had stopped. Five minutes later, he paid and exited the cab near the same Star Ferry pier as he'd caught over that morning. Walking on and paying his fare, he wasn't surprised that this ferry was still busy but luckily not quite so crowded as the previous night, and he enjoyed the open deck area near the stern for the crossing back to HK Island.

Victoria Harbor was bustling as usual with shipping, ranging from large, international container vessels; massive white cruise ships with decks lined with passengers; to smaller junks and sampans moving all matter of goods. Fast hydrofoil ferries to the outer islands and Macau sped by, churning the water. But still, the antique Star Ferry plowed on. Fifteen minutes later, he walked up the ramp at Central, through as many side roads and alleyways as possible, before arriving at the entrance to the Peak Tram funicular railway. He knew even if he had been followed that he'd shaken them off by now. The tram was full of locals, tourists and kids all excited to be heading to the Peak, so it was easy for him to play the part of a single person on vacation.

The incline was steep and he laughed as he saw kids letting go of the handholds and sliding along the bench seats until they were all crushed up together, and received smiles from their parents in return. Exiting at the top, he allowed himself to be transported along with the crowds and spent a half-hour just admiring the view.

Walking over to one of two cafes overlooking Victoria Harbor and Kowloon Bay eighteen hundred feet below, he chose a table, sat, ordered a sandwich and coffee and waited.

Part of the time since he'd opened Phylax had been spent with the CIA at Camp Peary in Virginia, known locally as *'The Farm'*, and with the FBI at Quantico, learning their tradecraft.

Deacon was SEAL trained, a near perfect shot, superbly fit and excellent at unarmed combat. But he wasn't a spy. He'd never received training in how to spot a covert tail nor in how to follow someone covertly. The equipment he'd used as a SEAL had been some of the latest technology and robustly built - but both the FBI and CIA had access to equipment he'd only vaguely heard off. Whenever going into action he and his men had carried head cams allowing HQ to see in real-time what was happening. But these were an inch or so across and strapped to his helmet. Not quite the same as cameras small enough to replace a shirt button or skin sensors that would allow limited communication back to HQ merely by moving a finger or thumb.

But today he had no need for any of that. He was traveling 'clean'. No gadgets, no weapons, just sunglasses, and a unique smartphone.

And his wits.

He just hoped that was enough.

24

Su Ming chewed her fingernail as she looked around. Her father's position entitled her to many luxuries although living in Hong Kong was exciting enough for now. Hong Kong had been handed back to the Chinese in 1997 after 156 years of British rule, and since then many areas of freedom had been removed or tightened under Chinese authority. However, it was still far more open than similar places in mainland China. Being the daughter of a senior advisor to the President of China as well as the highest Admiral in the Chinese Navy had opened many doors for her. But she was good at her job. Very good, in fact. No one else that young had achieved the same levels of success as she had.

However, with those privileges came responsibility and accountability. Her father was always concerned, like many fathers around the world, about the type of male suitor his only daughter might attract. Zhang had the power, however, to monitor and check. Su Ming had been assigned a day-to-day male assistant who helped her in all her private matters. He acted as her butler opening doors for her, as well as walking with her, usually just one-step behind. His scowl had stopped many a would-be suitor approaching her, and he reported daily back to the Admiral.

However, as had been noted during her recent trip to the Dubai Air Show, there were limitations on where a male guard was allowed to go, particularly in Muslim countries. Therefore he'd been reassigned and an older female guard, Wu Wei, had replaced him.

Slipping out of her apartment and getting away from Wu Wei hadn't been easy. Last night she'd said she wanted to see the fireworks and losing Wei had been simple in the crowds of people. She'd waited until they were crossing a busy road and had ducked down and hidden amongst the moving crowd in the darkness, before turning and heading the other way. When they'd met again, much later after returning to her apartment, Su Ming had said she'd lost sight of her and gone on alone. She couldn't wait as the fireworks had been due to start.

Today was different. Wei was still annoyed and brooding over the fact that she'd lost sight of her charge last evening and was sticking to Su Ming like glue.

Although busy, Victoria Peak would be nowhere near as crowded as the seafront last evening, so getting away from Wu Wei would be hard. Any suspicious activity would be reported back.

Before they'd left the apartment in the Mid-Level district, Su Ming had made Chinese tea for both of them. Wu Wei had been both surprised and annoyed as preparing beverages was her role. However, Su Ming had merely said she often liked to do things herself and wanted to cheer Wu Wei up a little. Wu, being far lower in the class system, nodded her thanks and wisely chose not to say anything about the bitter taste of her drink.

Waiting in the queue for the next tram and the seven-minute journey to the peak, Wu Wei felt her stomach tighten and cramp. The eye drops Su Ming had put in her drink had begun to work. A few minutes later, she felt her bowels loosen and knew she only had moments to save her embarrassment. Excusing herself, she rushed over to the ladies' bathroom, just making it in time. As she'd rushed away, she heard Su Ming shout out that she would carry on up and they would meet again later.

As the tram carriage pulled away, its slow rise taunting her, Su Ming began to sweat with anxiety even in the cold. On a funicular system, both carriages travel on a single trackway, connected to the same heavy cable. They use a single track, one heading downward and the other upward. As they approach the middle of the journey, the track splits and both carriages move apart and pass each other with mere inches to spare, before rejoining the single track and continuing. Moving to the front of her carriage and past some of the older, slower passengers, Su Ming was eager to be one of the first to alight when they finally arrived. She was desperate to find Deacon quickly because in seventeen minutes, the trip would repeat and the next carriage would arrive with an angry Wu Wei on board.

Heading over to the observation deck, she could see many heads but couldn't recognize anyone from the previous evening. Glancing at her watch, it was already three minutes after two.

Without trying to rush or draw attention to herself, she paraded up and down the area around the observation deck. Still her contact was not to be found.

Her watch now showed ten minutes after two.

She walked the entire length of the deck once more, panic now beginning to set in. She had no other way to contact him. Had he already left? Had he been compromised? Was he now under arrest and being held in police cells, close to where she lived? Since China had taken over control, there were many stories of dissidents and anyone who shouted too loudly against Beijing, its leaders or the Politburo, being taken to Police Headquarters.

Few ever seemed to be released.

131

With her breathing increased she began to consider her options. Had she ever given her name to the man last evening? No, she was certain of that. Would the CIA have told him her name? Quite possibly. Would he be able to identify her from photos? Most likely. Had he already been handed over to MSS, the Ministry of State Security?

Glancing at her watch again she saw it was now fifteen minutes after two. In her panicking state, other visitors to the Peak were beginning to look at her. Looking around wildly she could see police officers milling about. Two of them were walking towards her purposefully. One was even pointing at her. Turning to look away and feeling faint from over breathing her next thought was were MSS agents waiting and watching her even now? Were they about to arrest her?

In danger of hyperventilating and panicking about what to do next, she was looking around frantically when she suddenly felt a hand grip her arm, and she gasped.

25

"Relax," the voice said, "you're acting suspicious, and people will see. You'll draw attention to yourself."

Keeping hold of her arm, he maneuvered her quietly but quickly away from the lookout deck towards one of the many tree-lined walkways as the pair of policemen walked past.

"Keep walking and just relax."

"But I thought you'd been captured?"

"Were you followed? Is that why you're panicking?"

"My guard. . . I gave her the slip at the tram station at the bottom, but she'll be here soon. She can't see me talking with you," she gasped.

Moving more rapidly, Deacon ushered her along various pathways until they reached a grassed area with distant views towards the eastern part of the city. There were other people here, but it wasn't crowded, and it was easy to lean against the barriers close enough together to hear each other, but far enough apart to appear as separate individuals to the casual eye.

From the angle they stood, Su Ming could see beyond the trees and back along the path and began to relax when she realized she wasn't being followed.

"Right, we've played your game a number of times. Now let's get down to business. My colleagues in the US are not interested in your coming over. They said 'Thanks, but no thanks'," Deacon said.

Turning her head slightly, she eyed him up and down.

"I asked for a man, and they sent a stupid messenger boy. Go back to your masters and tell them my demands remain if they want me and my information," she sneered.

Grabbing her sleeve, Deacon looked her in the eye and said quietly but firmly, "I don't think you realize what you've started here. First, I'm not some dumb messenger boy. If they did want you, I'm the guy they'd trust to get you safely out of the country. Secondly, before they'd even consider that, we need some more information. If it pans out, maybe we'll see about getting you away. If it doesn't, you're on your own."

Realizing she'd overstepped the mark, she quietened and apologized, "I'm sorry, I am very nervous. They will kill me if they capture me. But if I am to come to America, I must disappear. My father is a powerful man and will send people to hunt me down and take me back."

"We know exactly who your father is and how powerful he is. If you help us, we will help you."

Glancing around to make sure they weren't being watched, Su Ming moved a little closer.

"What do you want me to do?"

"Give me some more information that we can check out. Like you did to Gerald Wagner in Dubai. He passed the information on, and my superiors in Washington sent me to meet with you."

"We both know Gerald Wagner is Shane Walker and he is the Baghdad station chief," she said, smiling for the first time. "So how do you propose to get me out? Hong Kong is now the same as China. You can't just walk me to the airport here. And your CIA are all known to us. As are your safe-houses. What is your name?"

"Call me Donald Duck. Now tell me, Su Ming, why do you want to leave? You have a very good life here. Favored status. Early promotion prospects. I understand your father is being tipped at being a possible future President and leader of the People's Republic. Your career is already mapped out. If you leave, you will harm your father's prospects. So why do it?" Deacon said while looking around. He and the powers-that-be in Washington still weren't totally sure this whole escapade wasn't a set-up and Deacon was keeping an eye out for anyone watching. He'd deliberately moved Su Ming away from where they'd planned to meet in case of hidden microphones located in the barriers. His smartphone was also a jamming device generating signals that would scramble any cell phone radio transmission coming from Su Ming as well as stopping any hidden recording device she might be carrying. It also generated sub-audio sounds that Deacon couldn't hear but would scramble any long-range listening device.

"That is my business," she said, turning suddenly very frosty. "I want to leave."

"Give me some details. If they check out and my superiors order it, I'll arrange to get you out."

"How? This is China. My name and face will be in the system. I can't just catch a flight without permission."

"Don't worry about that. We'll find a way. Do you have any more planned foreign trips arranged? It's always easier when you are away from home."

Thinking for a few moments, she finally answered, "Maybe. So you want more information? OK, Surmi Reef. More troops will be arriving next week, increasing the garrison from 150 to over 250 men. With armored equipment. My office will announce troops being replaced and sent home, but none will be. The next stage will be even more troops."

"Ok, so more troops deployed on Surmi. But why," he said.

"I tell you that when you get me out. I'll use the same email account two weeks from today to confirm where we meet next," she said, moving away just as she saw through the trees Wu Wei walking urgently along the path searching for her.

Deacon was already over a dozen feet away looking out at the scenery as Wu Wei came around the corner.

"Where have you been, child?" Wu said in frantic Chinese.

"Don't 'child' me you old hag. Just because your bowels are shot, and you can't help shitting yourself, don't expect me to care. Now come, I've seen enough scenery. I'm cold, and I'm leaving," she said, walking briskly back towards the tram station with Wu Wei following.

26

The Pentagon, Washington

Mitch knocked on the Admiral's door, waited for the usually loud grunt and then walked in.

"Morning sir," he said as he placed the coffee on the Admiral's desk.

"Hmm, so what news on Surmi? Anything from Deacon's tip-off?"

"Certainly is, sir. The NSA (National Security Agency) picked this up and deciphered it," Mitch said, passing a folder over to the Admiral. "It seems to corroborate what Su Ming told Deacon."

"Summary!" the Admiral demanded.

"It says PLAN Southern Theater Command announced troop replenishment for a number of garrisons throughout the Spratlys. Meant to be three months on, three off. Shipment of personnel starts later today. It was in orders posted to the transport division. The full text and translation is in here, sir, but that's the gist of it," Mitch said. "The rest just contains figures and also includes stores and water quantities being shipped. The amounts have increased which would seem to confirm John's information, sir."

The Admiral flicked briefly through the pages noting areas Mitch had already highlighted in yellow.

"Little bastards," he said, shaking his head.

"Sir? We've got normal satellite passes every six hours. Do you want the NRO (National Reconnaissance Office) to reposition a couple more?"

Scratching his chin he thought for a moment or two before replying, "No, China's aware of our satellite schedule. If we increase them they'll wonder why. Let's just keep this low-key for now. But I want the troops on these islands counted."

Saluting, Mitch turned and left the office. He made the call to his contact at the NRO asking for a personnel count over the following seventy-two hours for the twenty or so islands China inhabited, but in particular for Surmi Reef. Mitch and the Admiral both knew the quality of the imagery the NRO had access to was second to none. They also knew the staff at the NRO were past masters at analyzing data, and the request for troop numbers would be child's play for them.

Three days later Mitch printed off the report emailed to him from the NRO, read it, marked certain areas in yellow highlighter and carried it into the Admiral.

Lieutenant Mitchell Stringer, or 'Mitch' as everyone called him, was friendly, extremely intelligent, and had a knack for finding needles in haystacks. He also had the ability to speak with senior officers and explain things simply, when required. Soon after he had joined Naval Intelligence, Mitch had made a presentation to some senior officers, including Admiral Carter. His ability to explain a technical matter clearly, without being intimidated by the audience, had impressed the Admiral who had a well-known reputation for not suffering fools lightly and of demanding his subordinates come to the point quickly. Time was too precious to waste with waffle, and word padding, he always said. 'Tell me what you are going to tell me, and tell it to me quickly' was his motto, and Stringer's fresh-faced approach had gone down well with him. Too many people in Washington were just interested in playing politics, the Admiral always said, and because he didn't, Stringer stood out from the crowd.

Mitch was on the mailing list for various daily and weekly reports from the NSA in Fort Meade. Raw intelligence is collected at NSA Headquarters, Fort Meade, from various sources and examined. Using this data reports are generated and passed to the relevant agencies and departments, however since 9-11, there had been more emphasis on the sharing of data and closer interworking between agencies. The raw data is also passed on to the relevant departments and agencies for their specialists to examine. Stringer received this data on behalf of the Chief of Naval Operations. As was normal for the Admiral, he ordered the Lieutenant to provide the summary. He would look through the notes and detail later if it interested him.

"Sir, prior to the replenishment the NRO counted a total of just over 7,000 individuals across all islands, with a ratio of 72%, or just over 5,000, being military personnel. On Surmi Reef in particular, there were 272 individuals of which 150, or 55% were military."

"Why a lower ratio there?"

"There is still a lot of dredger activity on Surmi, sir, so the 272 number included a large number of merchant seamen and civilian engineers."

"And now?"

"Not good, sir. Overall, total individuals has risen to just under 10,000 with the military ratio climbing to 83%. On Surmi, the total has risen to 400 with 270 being military, the remainder mainly manning the dredgers. Work has increased and the island is still growing daily."

"Ok, set up a video conference for this afternoon at 14:00 with Generals' Dreiberg, Tarrant, and Mansfield.

Get on to Alex Simpson -- I want the President on it as well. I also want you on it. I want a five-minute overview of the current position with the Spratlys to make sure we're all on the same page."

<><><>

Not one to make small talk, as the conference screen came alive Admiral Carter waited until everyone was in attendance then turned to Mitch and said, "Lieutenant, summarize. Go!"

Never one to be caught on the hop, Mitch knew exactly what he planned to say and had also prepared a couple of PowerPoint slides.

"Mr. President, Generals, Admiral. As you know, the Spratly and Paracel islands dispute has been going on for decades. The Republic of China (ROC), or Taiwan as it's known, claims to have discovered these islands during the Han dynasty in 2 BC. They claim their fishermen have been regularly fishing around these islands since 200 BC. In the late nineteenth century, Britain laid claim in 1877 and Germany in 1883 resulting in China protesting. Finally, in 1902 and again in 1907 China placed flags and markers on the islands, claiming both the Spratly and Paracel islands under the jurisdiction of Hainan.

During World War II, Japan occupied the entire region, and the islands were handed back to China after Japan's surrender under the terms of the Cairo Declaration. In 1947 the ROC drew up their first 'U' shaped map encompassing all of the South China Sea as their own. Taiwan garrison forces actively fended off Philippine efforts to build on the Spratlys during 1971. After the UN vote to recognize the People's Republic of China, the ROC government in Taiwan was no longer in a position to defend its rights. The Philippines and Vietnam took this opportunity to establish outposts in the Spratlys. It then appeared that the Cairo Declaration was in error and that both the Spratlys and Paracel islands had not been included under those terms. However, the PRC then claimed all of them as their own and drew up what has since been called the Nine-Dash-Line which encompasses all of them.

In 1974 South Vietnam and China came to blows over the Paracel islands, with South Vietnam losing. China has since remained the sole occupiers of them.

As to the recognized islands known as the Spratlys, China currently occupies 8 of the 45 of them; Taiwan claims ownership of 1, Malaysia 5, Brunei 1, Philippines 9, and Vietnam 21. But only China is militarizing theirs. One of the smallest but strategically placed is Surmi Reef. Originally, it was just a tiny rocky outcrop with two small islands linked at low water. Vietnam had always claimed it as their own. Total land mass was a little over ten acres, and it was basically uninhabited. We think a few fishermen may have lived there at one time. China took control of it back in 1991 and slowly started building on it. Dredgers have increased its size, and it's now almost fifty acres. It even has a 2,000 plus-meter long runway - amply long enough to support their Su-30 multirole fighters and their short-range bomber fleet."

"Hasn't China done that to a number of islands?" the President asked.

"They have, Mr. President, sir, but most of the others are closer towards the Philippines. Surmi Reef is in the middle of the deepest water around there, roughly equal distance from the rest of the Spratlys and Vietnam. Right slap bang in the middle of one of the world's busiest shipping channels, the Kitty Hawk Seamount as it's called. Satellite photos show new installations, including high-frequency monitoring arrays, for gathering radar and radio intelligence. With this capability, coupled with its location, anything traversing the South China Sea will be able to be detected, tracked, and liable to be attacked by fighters or bombers located there.

"As you know, gentlemen, we regularly send our Navy through this area under FONOP rules, but Beijing always complains. China repeatedly states we are breaking international law by entering their waters within the internationally agreed 12-nautical-mile limit to its seven man-made islands. State keeps reminding Beijing that a ruling from the international tribunal in The Hague summarized China had no historic title over its waters and just because China is reimagining the area it claims to own under their 'Nine-Dash Line', this has no standing in an international court of law. Our ships traverse within seven or eight nautical miles to any of these islands," Mitch said, receiving a nod from Admiral Carter to continue.

"The latest intel from the potential defector, Zhang Su Ming, stated the troops on these islands were going to be increased, and the NRO has confirmed this has happened. We don't know what Beijing's next step will be. Su Ming has also said she will provide more intel regarding the plans around the Spratlys but not until she is safely in the US."

"And we believe she has access to this information?"

"We do, sirs. So far what she has told us is 100% accurate."

"So, Mr. President, we just need to decide whether we want her out or not, sir?" Dreiberg asked.

Admiral Carter beckoned for Mitch to sit down.

"Gentlemen," the President said, "the issue isn't whether we want her out or not. It's how she can best provide us the information we need and whether this is a trap. I assume our agent is aware that all the local CIA assets are possibly compromised, maybe some of the Asian FBI people as well, Admiral?" the President continued.

"I instructed him to decide himself how to get her out if authorized. I also told him not to put anything in emails or writing to anyone else but Lieutenant Stringer here. The fewer people that know his escape plan, the fewer can leak it, until we have more information on the level of compromise that we are operating under. Until we know more, we have to assume it's extreme," Admiral Carter said.

General Tarrant hadn't spoken much during the discussion but now took over the screen.

"I don't think we can rely on this Su Ming. She may not come over, or she may be captured, or the information she claims to have may be worthless. However, what is beyond doubt is the build-up of military personnel on those islands, particularly Surmi Reef. I think we'd all like to know more about what our little Asian friends have planned. We need eyes on the ground. We need a first-level report. I suggest we consider sending in a SEAL team to reconnoiter and report back."

"No, General, we can't risk an international incident should one of them get injured or god-forbid, captured. It would be the equivalent of a declaration of war. We'd be knowingly invading a foreign sovereign territory," the Chief of Staff stated.

"I don't give a fuck about upsetting the little bastards," the Secretary of Defense, General Melvin Tarrant said, "I just want to know what the fuckers are doing."

The President continued, "I agree. We need to know what they are doing and what's in store for us, but we can't risk sending our own troops in." He then switched screens until Admiral Carter was full and front. "Douglas, we need you to get your man to go in covertly. We can assist a little, but we can't be seen to be involved. And if anything goes wrong . . . well, he's on his own."

27

South China Sea

The USS Chancer steered 030 degrees and away from the receding storm. This depression had come up quickly, as was common at this time of the year, but was now fading and the Arleigh-Burke-class destroyer rode the choppy waves well. Her maximum speed was over 30 knots, and she could easily have maintained that speed but the short, sharp swell made for an uncomfortable passage, so she cruised at 22. It also provided a maximum range between refueling stops.

At 507 feet long and with a crew of 276, she was fitted with some of the very latest Aegis radar and sonar and housed a full complement of weapons, including surface-to-air missiles, anti-submarine rockets, Tomahawk cruise missiles, and an Anti-Submarine-Warfare helicopter. Based out of Pearl Harbor, she was three weeks into a two-month deployment.

Her current course took her within six miles of Surmi Reef, well inside the disputed 12-mile territorial limit China had placed on these islands. Both the radar and electronic countermeasures watch officers' reported the Chancer was being tracked by land-based radar, located on Surmi Reef. Two Chinese fighter aircraft had been scrambled and were heading out towards the Chancer and messages broadcast in English were being transmitted on channel 16, the international distress channel, stating that the warship was in Chinese waters.

The captain on the Chancer, Captain David Shankley, however, chose to ignore the messages. As he'd done four times previously over the last 12 months, he was operating what was called a Freedom of Passage Operation, or FONOP. This is a principle of international maritime law that states a ship flying a flag of any sovereign state shall not suffer interference or impediment of passage from other states while it is in international waters. Only a couple of the Spratly Islands had been granted territorial status with their own 12-mile limits, and Surmi Reef was not one of them.

"Bridge, comms."

"Comms, bridge. Go ahead."

"All frequencies demanding we alter course immediately and head out of Chinese waters, sir."

"Bridge, radar."

"Radar, bridge. What have you got?"

"Getting target lock-on radar from the two fighters scrambled and heading this way, sir."

The Captain had his orders, and he intended to follow them exactly. He knew a message was already being drafted by the Chinese and would be delivered to the US Secretary of State later today, demanding the American Navy desist from these continued infringements of Chinese international and territorial waters. He also knew the SecStates' reply would basically be to clarify that the US Navy had stayed in international waters at all times and he had GPS coordinates to prove it.

Looking out of the rain-soaked bridge windows all he could see was the reflective glow of his instruments and navigation lights. Turning to his Executive Officer, he ordered all weapons systems to be activated, but in quiescent mode, meaning radars would track the incoming aircraft and lock onto them, but the missiles wouldn't be aimed. He also ordered a two-mile total exclusion zone around the Chancer, and this was transmitted on all channels in English and Chinese. Any aircraft straying within the two-mile zone would immediately be shot down. Although this seemed extreme, it was normal practice on military vessels, and he knew unless the Chinese were actually planning to attack the Chancer, they would observe the exclusion limit. The rules of engagement in peacetime were clear - he could only return fire if fired upon first.

He also knew that the time taken from tracking the aircraft on radar to activating his defenses should the aircraft enter the zone, or fire missiles at the Chancer, was mere seconds. On top of certain destruction of the aircraft, the Chancer's countermeasures also had a very good chance of intercepting and destroying any missiles the aircraft might fire at it.

The next few minutes were tense, but radar watch reported the incoming Chinese fighters had turned at the last possible moment and were flying circular patterns around the Chancer just outside the exclusion zone. The Chancer's and the aircraft's exact positions were being continually transmitted back to Pacific Fleet Command in Hawaii.

Fairly convinced it was just normal 'saber-rattling', he passed the word to his XO to slow the ship and allow deployment.

Deacon had joined the Chancer two days previously. He'd flown to Singapore before being picked up by one of the Chancer's choppers and was brought on board. Wearing civilian clothes the crew had assumed him to be CIA or similar, and they had been ordered not to disturb him. The Chief Engineer had managed to find him a spare bunk with some privacy. Deacon had brought two large carryalls full of equipment and a collapsible matt-black kayak with him. He's spent some time both with Captain Shankley and Lieutenant Chris Dowler, the Executive

Officer of the Chancer, but had kept away from the main crew.

Now dressed from head to foot in black non-reflective Nomex, he stored two bags inside the kayak, one in the rear section, the other in the front under his knees. Wearing a close-fitting helmet with night vision goggles already attached, he sat in the kayak on the Chancer's stern in the diminishing rain. He made a final check of the waterproof spray skirt, gripped the Kevlar paddle and gave a thumbs-up ready-to-go command.

On the XO's instruction, and once the Chancer had slowed, a small crane lifted the fabric sling holding the kayak with Deacon inside it and swung him out over the rear of the ship. It was quickly lowered until a mere three feet above the churning wake at the stern. Deacon waited until the swinging had ceased and he was pointing away from the ship. Pulling the release rope allowed the bow of the kayak to drop slightly and as gravity took over, the kayak slipped gently forward out of the sling and headed bow-first towards the ship's frothy wake.

This was one of the most dangerous parts of his mission. If the entry angle was wrong or the ship wasn't traveling fast enough, there was a high chance the pull of the wake would suck the kayak back up towards the spinning propellers. However, if the ship was traveling too fast, the wake would be much stronger, and its undercurrent would pull Deacon and his kayak down fifty, sixty, or even seventy feet making it impossible to get back to the surface safely. But today it operated in text-book fashion. The highly buoyant kayak nose-dived down to almost thirty feet through the tumbling wake, the buoyancy of the seawater greatly reduced by the ships spinning propellers. After what seemed age and after furious paddling to bring the craft back to the surface, the kayak finally bobbed back up, and Deacon shook the water away from his facemask as he saw the stern light of the Chancer already two-hundred yards away and accelerating fast through the gloom.

Dipping the paddle in the still bubbling wake, he began regular firm strokes as he turned the kayak to the new heading of 094 degrees and moved into solid water.

Deacon normally would have motored in using a darkened inflatable RIB and a near-silent outboard motor, but the sensitivity of the island's radar made approaching in this manner unfeasible. The only solution was a fiberglass-framed kayak and with as little made of metal as possible. The only radar reflecting items Deacon was carrying was a handgun with suppressor and a small camera. Both were wrapped in copper mesh cloth and stowed low down in the boat. The copper mesh would absorb the radar pulses and energy and not return any form of signal. It was a basic form of stealth covering, but it worked well. Everything else was Kevlar and non-reflective to radar pulses.

Six miles kayaking was easy in a calm sea and would normally take around two hours, but in a choppy sea still dying down from an aggressive tropical storm, it took nearer to five. Deacon had chosen to be dropped both up wind and up tide making progress a little easier, and over four hours later with numbness setting into his arms and with shoulder muscles burning with effort, the wind and rain began to finally subside, and he could just make out the lights of some of the floodlit buildings.

Keeping at least a half-mile offshore to make sure the loom of the lights from the island wouldn't illuminate him he turned to run parallel to the shore. With one eye open for any roving searchlights, he checked his pale-green GPS display sewn into his forearm sleeve. Not all the reef was floodlit - only the areas near the main buildings. He'd checked and rechecked the satellite

149

images previously and had chosen his landing spot with care, close to one of many areas filled with palm trees. While the reefs had been mainly underwater, parts only breaking the surf at low tide, very little had grown on them - hardly enough to maintain a few people living there. However, with the advent of being built up to twenty or more feet above high sea-level, stray seeds and coconuts had washed up and quickly began growing and now the island had an abundance of greenery and palm trees sprouting between the buildings, with many of these areas overgrown and unkempt.

The tide was high tonight, making less beach to traverse. Aside from two lookout towers, guards regularly patrolled the beaches. Floating over a half-mile offshore, Deacon could clearly see the guards' routine through the NVG's. It took them twelve minutes to walk between towers and they walked in pairs. Although armed with automatic rifles, the obvious boredom of guarding and patrolling a rock in the middle of the ocean had allowed complacency to sink in. Happily for Deacon, they were not patrolling with dogs. He gently paddled staying in position and watched them make three complete circuits. Twelve minutes tower to tower. Then eight minutes in the shelter of the tower's legs for a cigarette before turning around and marching back. Twenty minutes complete, three trips per hour.

Suddenly the searchlight on the western tower nearest him lit up and began sweeping towards his exact location.

The choice was mover further out or go for broke and get lost close in amongst the surf.

He waited a few seconds to see exactly where the searchlight was focused. The guards were playing it along the water from a few hundred feet off the beach out to sea.

Hoping he'd made the right choice, otherwise he would be easily in range of the guard's rifles, he plunged the paddle furiously kicking the small craft forward as fast as he could manage.

Praying he wasn't leaving an effervescence trail, he maneuvered the craft in towards the breaking surf. Usually, waves hitting this outer ring of the reef were two to three feet high, but the storm had caused these to grow to nearer five or six. Although dying back, the winds and tide still had enough power to make the last few hundred yards tough. Especially after almost five hours of intense paddling.

Just as he came to within the last twenty feet in front of the beach, a rogue wave turned him sideways, and the next breaker rolled him right over. The seabed was hard coral, sharp and jagged with a thin layer of sand on top and he felt himself being dragged along by the waves, his upper body being forced back. Unable to right himself in the shallows, the paddle was wrenched from his grasp, and he gagged as he swallowed mouthfuls of seawater. Not able to release himself from the upturned kayak and trapped between it and the hard shoal he coughed and vomited as a roaring sound grew louder in his ears as he began to pass out.

28

Surmi Reef

Deacon's head and shoulders scraped along the shale and rocky shore as the surf battered the small craft relentlessly. The razor-sharp coral edges sliced through his waterproof covering and he felt warm blood beginning to flow from his shoulders. With his night vision goggles ripped off his helmet and desperate for air, Deacon pulled the quick release of the spray skirt and tried to kick himself free. Normally it's not an issue as the kayaker merely slides down lower into the water until their feet are free and then bobs to the surface. However, Deacon was already in shallow water alternating between being wedged hard against a rocky seabed and being scrapped along it, while waves tossed and tumbled the upside-down kayak above him. Finally, after what seemed to take ages, Deacon's fingertips managed to grab some of the rocky seabed, and he held himself firm as the kayak was ripped away from him.

Eventually, he bobbed back to the surface gasping for air in between vomiting up mouthfuls of seawater.
Now the rush was on. If he didn't manage to grab the upturned kayak, it would either drift away entirely or likely wash up in front of the guards. Twice he seized the stern, but in his weakened state each time the next wave pushed it away and ripped the grab handle from his grasp. Finally, in a lull between waves, he managed to reach further along the hull and get his hand to the cockpit rim. The in-built buoyancy would keep the kayak floating even when completely filled with water as it was

now, but the added weight of the water made it too heavy for him to lift and carry it ashore.

In the distance, he could see the guards starting their next patrol. He was roughly in the middle of their path, so he had less than four minutes.

Hauling and pulling, he dragged the craft into the shallows and turned it over. As the water washed down his legs, he thought at least the fading storm would help mask his noise. As soon as he felt the weight lighten enough, he began to drag the craft up the short sand and shingle beach and into the cover of the palm trees and foliage.

Pulling it in through the thick undergrowth, he quickly slid the kayak out of sight. It would need further camouflaging but would pass a quick glance.

Looking back towards the approaching guards on patrol, he could see them clearly in silhouette, being brightly backlit against one of the distant floodlights. Glancing down he realized, in horror, he could see the line in the sand from the trailing edge of the kayak and his footprints leading from the shore towards him and the trees.

With only moments to spare before the guards would be on him, he crawled on all fours back down the beach scuffing and wiping the sand with a palm frond as he went, any noise he made masked by the crashing of the waves. With no time to hide, he slid further into the surf staying as low as he could, his dark protective suit blending in perfectly between the waves. Slipping his K-Bar knife from its sheath, its blade painted matt-black to reduce any reflections, he held it ready to use if the shout went up.

Hardly daring to breathe, he finally sighed as the guards walked past, engrossed in some meaningless chat most likely about women, sex, or both.

153

He spent the following five-minutes staying low but gently moving up and down along the surf looking for his paddle. It had been ripped from his grasp when the kayak had turned over, and without it, his method of escape was useless. He'd also lost his NVG's having been ripped from his head by the rough seabed.

Moving further out into slightly deeper water where it was easier to hide, he searched further along the water's edge. The matt-black of the Kevlar paddle didn't make detection easy, but it also didn't make chance discovery by the guards likely. However, if washed ashore, in daylight it would be easily identified. It took almost another thirty minutes in the water and yet another guard patrol passing before he felt it brush against his shoulder. With only his head visible out of the water, and entirely covered in black non-reflective Nomex, he was invisible against the blackness of the sea. He was now far enough out from the beach to reduce the chance of accidental discovery, so grabbing the paddle, he half swam, half walked back towards the shore.

Keeping low and after checking he wasn't being observed, he staggered up the beach checking his footprints weren't being left behind before collapsing down amongst the undergrowth. He pushed the kayak further through bushes and foliage. The black boat blended in well with the darker greenery and, unless stumbled on, from a few feet away it was barely noticeable. Finally, he crawled behind two trees close together with undergrowth hanging from them. Climbing in close to the tree trunks gave him a good position entirely undetectable from more than ten feet away. His only worry now was if any of the guards had patrol dogs.

He lay there for almost an hour not asleep but in a meditative state. He was awake and aware of his surroundings, but barely breathing and concentrating on getting his energy back. His tight-fitting Nomex suit was badly ripped, but it had protected him as designed. The seawater would have cleaned the cuts, and the suit held tight against his skin thereby reducing blood loss. Now he needed food and drink, partly to flush out the seawater he'd swallowed. Slowly sitting up, he looked around to make sure he was alone before crawling over to the kayak and reaching into the cockpit, before silently cursing when he found one of the bags missing. Both had been held down with elastic ties, but the one in the front section was gone.

All he could assume was he must have snagged that one with his feet when he was struggling to get free from the overturned kayak. In the darkness, he hadn't seen it and could only hope by now it had been taken out with the receding tide and hopefully had sunk. With all his reserves gone, including water, food, his suppressed handgun, radio, and, more importantly, his camera, he knew the mission had already gone to shit. Even the screen on the GPS on his left forearm was cracked and scratched, but the display itself seemed undamaged.

Reaching into the rear hull section, he found the second bag he'd stowed was still in place. Pulling it free, he removed a full set of a Chinese PLAN guard's uniform from the waterproof bag, showing the rank of Major. Deacon knew he didn't look Chinese nor did he speak the language and with no intention of interacting with anyone he hoped that his uniform rank would deter questions in the first instance if anyone spotted him.

He had no illusions. He knew very well if they captured him, he was on his own. He carried no identification and would be treated as a spy. If lucky, he might escape execution, but he would likely serve many years in jail. He'd prefer to go down fighting than chance forty years in a labor camp, though. Daybreak was a little over three hours away, so with his strength recovering, he decided to carry out a walking tour of the island. Nothing suspicious, just distantly observing what was happening.

Dressing quickly in the Major's uniform, he silently walked through the trees as close as he could towards the buildings before stepping out onto the pathways. Some of the paths were lit, but he kept to the darkened areas as much as possible. He found if he varied the speed of his walking he could manage to pass other groups of people when the furthest between lights. Twice he approached a group of armed guards and merely saluted with them quickly saluting back before hurrying on through the light rain.

Within the hour he'd scouted the main areas. While still at the Pentagon he'd examined aerial and satellite photographs of the reef in great detail. The quality of the optics in the KH-11 satellites was astounding. Easily able to identify anything larger than a cigarette pack, Deacon had spent hours looking at every aspect of the reef. By the time he arrived, he felt as if he knew the small island intimately. The canteen and extended barracks were easy enough to identify over on the eastern edge, as were the wind turbines for power and observation buildings. Two large radomes and a satellite communications building complete with radio and multiple antenna arrays were the tallest buildings and looked to be well-lit and well-guarded.

Further along, covering the man-made harbor area and hidden under a false roof and walls, Deacon could make out a large twin-barrel naval gun. It appeared to be the 100 mm dual barrel weapon able to provide rapid-fire against would-be invaders. This hadn't been totally clear from the aerial photos, although the outline had been detected. It reminded Deacon of the Q-ships used in World War II when many an innocent merchant ship had allowed a seemingly innocent merchant or transport ship to come close alongside before the approaching craft would drop its wooden superstructure revealing fully armed and manned deck guns.

The man-made piers jutting out into the sea had a number of large craft docked against them including two troop transport ships. Most of the dredgers were anchored off in the lagoon. It would have been pointless trying to dredge in the storm, but he could see activity on board so it was likely they'd be in full operational mode again shortly now the storm had passed. The airfield at the far end of the island looked conventional. There were large hangers and two aircraft that Deacon identified as Chengdu J-17 fighters were parked outside ready for instant deployment. These were likely the pair that had buzzed the USS Chancer earlier in the evening. The amount of fuel storage containers Deacon observed would indicate quite a few more aircraft hidden in the hangers.

Surrounding the airfield were three sets of short-range ground-to-air missile batteries.

There was one building especially of interest that the experts in the Pentagon hadn't been able to identify. It was sunken and appeared half-buried, located close to what would normally be thought of as a helicopter landing pad, but the island had one of those a few hundred yards away. This unusual landing pad was near to the physical center of the island and was also on the highest piece of land, albeit still only around fifty-feet above sea level.

With the sky in the east beginning to lighten and not willing to chance discovery, Deacon headed back to the palm trees to wait until the following night. He would have four hours of darkness for exploration before having to leave the same way he'd arrived by kayak, with just enough hours to get out into the USS Chancer's return course.

<>↔<>

The day dragged slowly. Deacon was aware he stood out far too much to risk walking around in daylight. He was six-two – far taller than most Chinese – with western European features, but at night time he was willing to risk it. Instead, he stayed hidden amongst the foliage observing everything he could on the small reef, observing guard movements and timings, as well as any other motions of people. He also took the opportunity to catch up on sleep. Although he had lost his food and water stores, the previous day's rain had left enough water trapped on plants for him to quench his thirst.

Storms and rain were common at this time of the year, and as the sun finally set behind rain-filled clouds and the edge of darkness crept slowly across the sky, he readied himself. The wind was already picking up, and the next weather depression was bearing down on the small reef. Dressing again in the Major's uniform, he slowly moved towards the path before brushing himself off and fitting his cap. In the dark, he hoped he would pass muster again, as long as he wasn't spoken to. He had a few words of Chinese, just basics, but any prolonged conversation would expose him.

Creeping over to the sunken building he waited in the shadows as the rain started falling. The entrance door was locked with swipe-card access, and the display showed a red light. He would have to wait until someone entered or left and hope he could bluff his way inside. Moving more closely towards the concrete pad in front of him, he realized it wasn't a landing pad, more a set of reinforced concrete doors. Shifting back towards the shadows he became aware of two guards walking towards him, and his luck ran out.

The guard slightly in front said, "Nǐ zài zuò shénme, Zhòngdà de?" -- *'What are you doing, Major?'*

29

Using one of the few phrases he knew, Deacon answered, "Wǒ hěn máng. Bùyào máfan wǒ. Nǐ bèi jiěgùle." -- *'I am busy. Don't trouble me. You are dismissed.'*

The guard looked at him and said, "Xiānshēng, wǒ xūyào kàn nǐ de bàozhǐ ," -- *'I need to see your papers, sir.'*

Unfortunately, that's when Deacon's little knowledge of Chinese let him down. Instead of replying in a stern voice, "Nǐ zěnme gǎn gēn nàyàng de jūnguān shuōhuà?" -- *'How dare you speak to an officer like that'*, the words he said came out as, *'How dare you treat me as an office'*.

At that moment, a bright flash of lightning lit up the area, followed by an enormous crack of thunder. The stunned look on the two soldier's faces alerted Deacon that he'd made a mistake. Any hope he'd had of being able to bluff his way out was gone when the lightning had exposed his face and realizing the game was up he had only one choice left. As a US Navy SEAL, he was a trained killer. He'd never kept count of how many individuals he'd killed - it didn't matter to him. But as a human being, he never enjoyed killing. Some sadists take pleasure in hurting or ending someone's life, but to Deacon, it was just something he would do if he had no other option.

In this situation, he knew that was the case.

If he were captured there would be no escape. He was an unauthorized civilian on a foreign military base. At best, execution. At worst, months or years of torture before execution.

He stiff-finger punched the front guard in the solar plexus as the second started to slip his Type 81 assault rifle off his shoulder. As the lead guard went down, gasping for breath, Deacon spun on his right foot and elbowed the second one under the chin. Before he fell, Deacon kicked hard into the guard's neck, just below the ear, hearing the vertebrae snap.

With one dead and the other failing, Deacon grabbed the first guard's head from behind, slipped his arms around his neck and with a quick but violent jerk snapped his neck.

Thankful this had happened in the shadows, he quickly dragged both bodies around the side of the half-buried building. This was also in shadow and the only place to hide them. Leaving them laying there, he bent and took one of the dead guard's ID. He also relieved one of them of his Makarov pistol.

Searching their pockets, he found both were carrying cell phones. Smiling to himself as he picked up the newest looking one, he wondered if there was anyone left on the planet without one. Switching it on he found it was screen locked and showing the symbol of a fingerprint. Trying each of the guard's fingers until one opened up the screen, he found the apps were all in Chinese, but it was clear which were for messages and which was for the camera.

With a quick flick of his Ka-Bar, he removed and pocketed the dead guard's finger. Opening the camera app, he switched off the flash before moving back over to the concrete pad. Circling it twice he took as many photos as he could. He didn't expect any to come out or show any more detail than the satellite images but knew he had to try.

Over by the door he tried swiping the stolen ID, but the red light remained on. Running back, he grabbed the

161

other guard's ID and tried that. This time there was a distinctive click and the red light turned to green.

Carefully opening the door, he peered around the edge. The hall was empty. Slipping inside and closing the door behind him he kept the guard's pistol down at his side as he edged forward. The corridor was dimly lit and he could already see from the glass panels in the doors leading off it that all the rooms seemed unlit. Listening, he could hear a faint hum of machinery and there was a slight vibration through his feet. And then it stopped.

At the far end of the corridor was an elevator and next to it a door leading to a dimly-lit open stairway snaking down a number of floors. Although the elevator would be quicker, it would be far too easy to become trapped in it, so he chose the stairs and edged slowly down two flights, weapon in his hand.

The elevator suddenly started up, and he heard it move down past him. As the doors opened and then closed, he heard voices of two or three people as they got in. Then the whine of the motors started again, and he heard the elevator heading back up to the entrance.

Creeping down the last flight, he gently opened the adjoining door a crack. There was an armed guard standing with his back to him less than three feet away. In front of the guard, the double swing doors breezed open as two technicians wearing lab coats wandered out and into a side room. For the few seconds, both doors were open, Deacon could see what was positioned under the reinforced concrete doors above.

It looked to be a rack of six missiles, each approximately twelve feet long and eight or nine inches in diameter, all located on a circular mount, connected to hydraulic rams.

There was no way he could get a photo from where he was, and he knew he was running out of time. He gently scraped the back of the stairway door with his fingertips. Three seconds later, he did it again a little stronger while also making a mewing sound.

As expected, the guard turned, opened the door and stepped in through the doorway while looking down towards the floor.

Glancing up, the guard saw what he thought was a Major and was about to speak and salute when Deacon grabbed him by the jacket front, pulled him towards him and head-butted full force across the bridge of his nose. The guard was unconscious before Deacon even relaxed his grip. He'd be out cold for a good hour and likely suffer severe headaches for a week or two. Even Deacon's head ached with the force he'd used, but the forehead is one of the toughest bones in the human body, and he'd soon recover.

With the stolen phone in his hand, he moved up to the double swing doors. Looking through the glass porthole-type windows, he could see these missiles clearly. He managed four photographs before the side room door opened and the two technicians walked out.

"Hēi, nǐ zài zuò shénme?" -- 'Hey, what are you doing?'

Shaking his head side-to-side slightly, he murmured, "Fuck it, not again," as he pulled the Makarov pistol out of his jacket and ushered both technicians back into the side room, happy to knock both unconscious, but that's when his luck ran out.

A warning shriek sounded, and a red lamp began flashing as the second technician's hand moved away from the emergency switch.

Slugging both of them once each, Deacon turned and ran for the stairway.

The three flights took him moments only, and he crashed out into the corridor to see a guard rushing toward him. The surprised look on the guard's face gave Deacon the extra tenth of a second to react first. Head down, he head-butted him in the midriff before jerking his head up into the guard's chin. With a crunch of teeth, the dazed and winded guard staggered back, and Deacon finished the fight with a rabbit punch to the side of his head.

The outer door didn't open on Deacon's push, and he wasted a half-second looking for the release. Seeing a row of buttons on the wall, he pressed them all, and the door lock finally clicked open, and he was off and running.

The sounding alarm was still confined to this building, but Deacon could see people rushing towards it. He was spotted just as he rounded the end of the building heading into the darkness. First a shout, then a few wildly aimed shots. With more alarms now sounding and klaxon's wailing, the entire atoll seemed to go on alert.

Keeping to the shadows, he rushed on as fast as he could. The rain was falling heavier now, and the wind was blowing the trees, their noise and movement masking his escape. He knew the game was now up. The reef was small and he could only hope to evade capture for an hour at most. If they brought dogs, it would be less.

Running as fast as he could he managed to get back to the large grouping of trees just as three jeeps, lights blazing, came racing around a corner towards him.

Diving into the undergrowth, not sure if he'd been spotted or not, his relief was palpable as the jeeps rushed by without stopping. Knowing even those off-duty would be pulled into the search, he knew he had to get off the island, fast.

Quickly stripping off his uniform he donned his ripped Nomex suit, grabbed his battered headgear, and pulled his kayak towards the beach.

Not sure of who or how many they were searching for the guards were chasing shadows. The searchlights from the two lookout towers were randomly scouring the sea surface while the guards rushed along the beach, still not sure of what they were looking for.

As they moved past him, he began to move forward. He was just a few feet from the edge of the surf when something made one of the guards stop and turn. Whether he'd made a noise, or it was just bad luck, he couldn't be sure, but hearing a shout he looked up to see one guard raising his rifle while the other was using a hand-held radio. Caught on the beach Deacon was perfectly framed and silhouetted against the distant background lights. With no other option, Deacon raised his pistol and shot both of them.

Quickly pushing the kayak the last few feet, the bow began to float and he ran it into deeper water. The breaking waves would keep pushing it back towards shore, so he lay on it like a surfboard and paddled as hard as he could. The noise of the shots had been heard, but the wind had masked their exact location. Twice the searchlight swept over him, each time he tensed expecting the impact of machine-gun rounds to his back, but the black of the kayak and his suit failed to show in the probing searchlight. When he was about a hundred feet from the shore and beyond the breakers, he swung his feet down, sat up and slipped into the craft properly. Laying across it had stopped it shipping too much water, but it was still heavier than it should have been. Sitting up in the seat, though, Deacon could put his powerful shoulders and arm muscles to work and he was soon over four-hundred yards offshore. Five times the machine gunners had fired when their searchlights had illuminated something interesting, but none of it came anywhere close to Deacon.

Glancing back towards the reef he could see soldiers standing on the beach. They had found the slain guard's bodies and were looking out to sea. Some were even firing randomly, but the nearest the rounds landed was over twenty feet away. Even as the searchlight flashed over him once again, the matt black of his suit and headgear along with the kayak failed to show against the dark background of the waves

Turning his head back, he concentrated on deep, steady strokes as he headed out to sea.

He'd rowed another half-mile or so when he heard the throaty roar of twin outboards. Looking right he could see two craft, each approximately thirty-feet-long powering through the chop. Both had a machine gun on a mount in the bow, along with a gunner operating it. Both also had powerful searchlights on the cabin roof sweeping the sea area in front of them.

Turning, one went inshore towards the beach he'd just left. The other headed further out to sea before turning at about a two-mile distance. Both then turned towards each other and began a slow back-and-forth grid pattern search, searchlights probing the seas in front of them, hoping to catch whatever was there between them.

He knew he needed to make headway due west, but his only option now was to paddle as fast as he could due south, away from where he wanted to go.

Paddling hard and fast his shoulders and arm muscles began to burn. But if he didn't get out of this every decreasing grid box, his arms and shoulder ache would be the least of his worries.

Left, right, left, right. Each powerful stroke moving him away from danger but also away from home. With sweat dripping from his face he looked left and right and finally decided he was far enough outside the imaginary lines of the box grid search area. But the launches, lights blazing through the falling rain, approached him yet again. Certain he could be seen in the loom of the piercing lights, and just when he was expecting a shout and the urgent repetition of machine gun rounds across his chest, he saw the bow of one, then the other turn away.

He was safe. At least from them. Now all he had to do was row approximately six miles into the main shipping lanes in strengthening wind and waves, before trying to make contact with a military ship cruising at twenty plus knots without as much as a radio or a torch.

30

The Captain and Executive Officer on the USS Chancer had their orders from PacFltCmd, Hawaii. The orders read: *Proceed, as ordered, on exact reciprocal course to that traveled two days previously ... Be aware you would be monitored and tracked with Chinese radar and intercepted by Chinese aircraft ... Weapons systems to be activated but operating in quiescent mode ... Authorized to fire if fired upon ... Use of deadly force authorized in extreme circumstances ...*

Following her orders to the letter, the USS Chancer was now steaming at 22 knots on a course of 210 degrees when Captain Shankley received an urgent call from the control room.

"Radar - Bridge."

"Bridge, go ahead."

"Captain, we've picked up a tail. Sonar has identified it as the *Yuncheng*, a Chinese type 54 guided missile frigate following us."

"Distance?"

"Fifteen miles and closing, sir."

"Comms - Bridge"

"Bridge, go ahead."

"Captain, the Chinese frigate *Yuncheng* is calling us, demanding we leave the area immediately. Stating we are in Chinese waters and insisting we leave."

"Comms, message the *Yuncheng* captain and state we are in International waters and undertaking a Freedom of Navigation Operation. Thank him and then state 'Out'."

Keeping the crew on full alert and ordering the control room to update him if anything changed, he ordered the Chancer to proceed as planned.

Deacon was paddling as hard and as fast as he could. Without a radio, he knew his only chance of pickup was to get in close to the Chancer's course and try to attract their attention. The wind has risen initially, but had now dropped back a little, making progress easier. He was clear of the reef and their chase boats and was able to make reasonable progress through the choppy sea, the falling rain making observation and detection less likely.

"Radar - Bridge."

"Bridge, Radar."

"Captain, we have two Chinese fighters scrambled and approaching, sir."

"Comms, issue the same statement as two days ago. Remind the pilots there is a two-mile total exclusion zone around the Chancer and any aircraft entering that airspace will be immediately shot down. Restate that we are in international waters and any aggressive act by the PLA Airforce will be met with overwhelming force. Transmit it now and keep resending. In the meantime, anything from our colleague?"

"Yes sir, I mean no sir. Sir, orders understood but no sir, nothing from our pickup."

Turning to his Executive Officer, Shankley ordered him to post lookouts on the bridge with Night Vision Binoculars. He spent two minutes monitoring the sea state before saying, "It's possible, Chris, that he has technical problems. We're not going to be able to hang around so let's have everyone available looking out. Slow to 14 knots and prepare to launch the Zodiac."

As the bow wave began to diminish and the engine note dropped, members of the rescue team donned their lifejackets and climbed aboard the twenty-two-foot inflatable Zodiac before being hoisted and held a few feet above the water, engine ticking over.

With the current sea conditions, Shankley had estimated 14 knots to be the fastest speed possible for safe launching and recovery of the Zodiac.

"Comms - Bridge."

"Bridge, go ahead."

"Captain, the *Yuncheng* is demanding to know why we have slowed."

"Comms, tell him we are sightseeing and remind him we are in international waters."

"Radar, how long before the *Yuncheng* catches us?" the Captain said.

"Captain, at ours and their current speed, a little over eleven minutes."

Turning to his XO, Lt. Chris Dowler, he said, "Let's hope we spot him soon."

Dripping in sweat Deacon watched the small GPS unit display his current coordinates. As the last digits changed, he knew he was less than one-hundred yards off the planned route of the USS Chancer. What he didn't know was whether he was too late and how he would attract their attention in the pitch black.

After subsiding a little, the wind was beginning to whip up again, and he had problems trying to keep the bow of the kayak head-to-wave. In this short chop, if the kayak turned side-on, he realized it would likely overturn and capsize.

Straining to see in the darkness in the direction it was due to come from he thought he saw a glimpse of red, but he wasn't sure. Were those stars moving? Looking again he suddenly felt a wave of relief when he realized he could just make out a red light over the waves. This was the port steaming light of a vessel approaching him almost head-on. The moving stars were the masthead white steaming lights. Grabbing the stolen phone from the waterproof pocket inside his suit and praying it hadn't gotten wet, while hoping it was the Chancer approaching and not any other ship, he pulled the severed finger out and wiped it across the screen before resetting the camera app and took photo after photo in the general direction of the advancing light.

On board the Chancer near the bow, Able Seaman Leroy Jackson had been staring out into the darkness. Suddenly a faint flash caught his eye. Taking a quick bearing, he radioed, "Captain, a light flash bearing five degrees port."

Within seconds, every pair of eyes on the Chancer were pointed in the same direction, just as another flash lit the sea around it.

Lieutenant Dowler ordered the immediate launch on the Zodiac that dropped the last few feet into the water before racing off towards the light.

Grabbing the intercom, Captain Shankley barked, "Radar, where's the *Yuncheng*?"

"Captain, four minutes until abeam starboard."

Looking through his night vision binoculars, Shankley could see the Zodiac racing away and swiftly approaching a dark shape in the water. Within a minute it was alongside, and he could see the dark outline of a man climbing aboard. Moments later, the Zodiac turned and headed back towards his ship.

Thirty-seconds later the Zodiac turned sharply again and came close alongside the rear port quarter of the Chancer. The crew tried to attach the strop cables while the coxswain steering did his best to keep the small craft stable but the bow wave kept tossing them around. Twice they almost managed to secure the strops before the waves rushing along the flanks of the Chancer pushed them away. Finally after what seemed an age but in reality was less than a minute the shackles clicked closed, and with a whine of powerful motors, the Zodiac lifted clear of the water and rapidly rose before swinging back over the railings onto the deck. Lieutenant Dowler watching from the bridge wing shouted 'Clear' as the Zodiac began to rise and Captain Shankley ordered the immediate speed increase back to twenty-two knots.

Five minutes later, a very tired but very relieved John Deacon climbed the steps to the bridge, saluted and thanked the Captain before handing the phone's memory card over and asking for the immediate transmission of its contents to Admiral Carter.

31

The White House Oval Office

As Mitch walked the last few feet towards the door of the Oval Office, Alex Simpson, the White House Chief-of-Staff, opened the door and stepped out before speaking with the President's secretary, Angela. Mitch actually relaxed slightly because he could hear the booming voice of Admiral Carter from somewhere behind him and knew he wasn't last to arrive.

Waiting to be announced as was protocol, Mitch and Admiral Carter were led by Alex Simpson into the inner sanctum of the White House just as the President walked along the West Colonnade and entered from the Rose Garden before taking his seat at the *Resolute* desk.

Already present on the two sofas were Warwick Dreiberg, Melvin Tarrant and Ulysses Mansfield being served coffee by a Navy steward. Moments later, Bill Casler walked in and apologized for only being five minutes early.

After the laughter had died down, the President waved the steward away and began the meeting.

"Melvin, what's the latest on this reef?"

"Mr. President, Douglas's and your man did a great job. Pretty close call too, I believe. We knew the island had radar and aircraft based there with the airfield protected by ground-to-air missiles, but he uncovered other types of missiles hidden away. They appear to be the new Chinese YJ-18 'Over-The-Horizon' anti-ship cruise missiles. With a range of over 290 miles and supersonic speed, they pose a deadly threat to all shipping in the area and a major threat to future FONOPs. These are shore-based, each ten feet long by just under 1 foot in diameter. We believe they are fitted with Destex high-explosive - the same as we have fitted in our AGM-84 Harpoons. They are self-seeking and fly at just over ten feet above the ocean. They're damn near impossible to stop. At that height, by the time they are detected they are usually too close to intercept. The damage is done by the initial explosion and the kinetic energy of the missile blasting through armor before ignition of the internal structure is caused by both the explosion and the burning rocket motor. Intelligence has already nicknamed them the 'ship killer'. The PLAN has been deploying them along the coast of the Taiwanese Strait. Surmi reef is the most westerly of the Spratlys occupied by China and we believe now the most heavily armed."

"Why is this the first we're hearing of this?"

"The NRO had already identified those along the Taiwan coast, but these were hidden below ground in a bunker. From the photos, it looks like they are mounted on a rotating system that can be raised up through bomb-proof doors by hydraulics. With the location of the bunker being on the highest part of the reef, it gives them almost a full three-sixty degree target view."

"And we'd missed this bunker?" asked POTUS incredulously.

"No, sir. The circular concrete bunker had already been identified by the NRO and they had marked it as a helicopter landing pad. When our man was close-up he could see that it opened. We also hadn't fully identified the building next to it which is mostly underground. We thought it was local fuel storage for the chopper pad."

"So this presents a clear and present danger to the region?"

"Yes, Mr. President, it does," Admiral Carter admitted. "If the Chicoms want to play it tough, between those reefs and their Navy, they could effectively block the entire South China Sea to all traffic."

"But surely we're better equipped than they are?"

"We are, sir, and taking out any of those islands would be pretty straightforward ... but China would see it as the start of war, sir. Those weapons ... they only need to threaten merchant shipping. World trading markets would collapse. They could easily stop all traffic or start charging a passage tax."

Turning to his Secretary of State, Bill Casler, the President continued, "Bill, you need to find a diplomatic solution to this. We need those islands demilitarized, and we need those YJ-18's gone. Find out what's it gonna take."

Turning to his Secretary of Defense, he instructed, "Melvin, I want a plan to get rid of those missiles. If Bill fails with the diplomatic approach, I want options. Understood?"

"Moving on," the President said, without waiting for a reply, and turning to his Director of National Intelligence, "What's the latest on our security breach?"

Coughing once to clear his throat, Warwick Dreiberg said, "Mr. President. We believe we've identified the leak. It looks like it was down to a lack of judgment by a staff member from State. Bill?"

"Mr. President," Bill Casler said, "Warwick had alerted me to what the FBI had found. One of my female Human Resources staff who visited our Consulate in Shanghai has confirmed she had a memory stick in her purse with some staffs' contact and address details on it. The memory stick was on her key ring with her home and car keys. She didn't think anything of it and left her purse in the room safe while dining in the hotel restaurant downstairs. She was only down there less than an hour. The rest of the time her purse was in her possession. We believe that's when the data was likely copied but as Warwick will attest to, there is no evidence of network penetration. We believe only 15-20% of our total Asia staff have been compromised and they have been put on alert, with some being redeployed."

Going red in the face with anger, he snapped back, "If she was only out of her room for less than an hour, how the fuck did the Chinese know?"

"We're not one-hundred-percent sure, sir, but her hotel room was booked from reception at the Consulate. Probably the hotel staff just guessed and informed their Ministry of State Security who were keeping watch on her. We know the MSS follow and watch a huge number of visitors. Maybe they just got lucky this time or might have had her name on some database and chanced it. There's no evidence our employee did this deliberately. The FBI have scoured her bank details, and there's no evidence of any monies being received. We think it was just a stupid mistake. On a positive note, the data on the stick concerned two dozen staff, some in Beijing, some in Shanghai and a couple in Hong Kong. It also included three from the UAE of which two had already retired from service. Unfortunately, Shane Walker's details were there as he used to be located in Dubai. It wouldn't have taken much effort to track where he's now located. All the staff affected in China have since been relocated or repatriated back to the US."

"What's happened to the employee?"

"She's at work awaiting review. She's a good employee. A hard worker. I plan to move her down a grade and remove some of her security clearance."

"I want her tried for treason."

Looking around the room at his fellow colleagues, Bill could see their look of surprise on their faces.

"Uh, treason, Mr. President? With respect, don't you feel that's going a bit over the top?"

"No, I goddam don't. I'm fed up with you all covering up for each other. I want the bitch tried for treason and jailed."

After a few seconds of stunned silence, the Director of National Intelligence stood and looked the President directly in the face.

"Mr. President. That would be a mistake. Her error was a mistake, albeit a major one. However, a mistake none-the-less. It wasn't malicious. Trying her in court would raise public awareness and alert the Chinese. The damage has already been done. If you really must seek vengeance, my suggestion would be to let her clear her desk with immediate effect with loss of pay and benefits. Bill?" Warwick Dreiberg said, turning his head to Bill Casler to silently urge a supportive response.

"Mr. President, I agree with Warwick," Bill said reluctantly, "I'll get security to walk her out."

A silently-fuming, angry looking President, realizing he'd been outvoted but also understanding if he pushed too hard he would likely lose what little support his executive team had for him, merely stood then strutted out, stating the meeting was over.

32

Washington

Deacon woke up early, stretched and lay there staring at the ceiling. Even as a Navy SEAL, he'd always found it unsettling how he could be on the front line fighting an enemy thousands of miles away under serious danger of death, yet a mere twelve hour or so flight would put him back in the comfort and total safety of home. He still found it hard to accept how on one day you could be dodging bullets in the desert, under attack from mortars and facing an enemy who was willing to sacrifice themselves to kill you; while the next day, your biggest choice was whether you wore the blue shirt or the green.

Thirty hours ago he'd been wet and shivering as he climbed the steps to the bridge on the USS Chancer, having escaped death from sharks, drowning, or execution by Chinese forces. An hour later, he had showered and was on board a Sea Stallion helicopter en route to the small U.S. military facility at the Philippine Air Force base in Pampanga, north of Manila. A thirty-mile cab ride had him in the business lounge of American Airlines before a nineteen-hour flight back home. A cab ride, a quick shower, then sleep.

And here he was now, under clean sheets, relaxed and rested in his apartment in Palisades, Washington D.C. He'd chosen this area well. It was far enough away from the hubbub of central Washington to be quiet, but close enough when it suited him. The parks and countryside along the Potomac allowed for easy morning runs, and he would often jog the entire way to the office before showering and changing there. The apartment wasn't large - it didn't need to be. Two bedrooms, a good-sized lounge, and a well-equipped kitchen. He wasn't a bad cook but often couldn't be bothered and ate out. He still didn't have many possessions having been in the Navy since leaving university, where everything tangible had been provided. What with that, and continuously moving bases, he'd never felt the need to accumulate the standard weight of possessions owned by most people of his age.

Powering up his laptop he quickly scanned for new messages. Of one-hundred-and-seventeen of them, most were junk or, if ignored for long enough, the sender would send again still requiring a response. A couple of them needed urgent attention, and he forwarded them on to Gina with instructions of how to proceed. Phylax had won the tender for the supply of protection services in Ras al-Khaimah, and the cover was due to commence shortly. Five of his team had volunteered to go for the two-year contract, and it had been a tough choice to whittle it down to two. Gina and Sean had both been involved in the selection process, but the final decision had been Deacons. The pair would fly out in a few days' time to start work. Emailing Gina, he asked her to get both of them in the office today for a briefing.

Twenty minutes later dressed in running shorts and a T-shirt he set out on the easy five-mile run. It was a typical February day - cold, biting wind, with sunny blue skies. He was at the office before 07:30 am and walked in to find Gina already there. She was an early starter as well and always seemed to get to work before Deacon, whatever time he turned up.

"Morning, Gina. What's on for today?"

"David and Liam will be here for your ten o'clock with them. Paperwork on your desk to clear. Apart from that, your day is clear. Phew, you need a shower!" she said, wrinkling her nose in disgust.

Laughing at her Deacon headed towards the bathroom and then on to his private room where he kept a complete change of clothes.

Twenty minutes later, showered, shaved and feeling good he walked back into her office carrying two coffees and a couple of toasted bagels before sitting on the edge of Gina's desk and sharing breakfast.

Together they discussed the latest work bookings and, as always, Deacon was content to leave all the day-to-day organization to her. As both she and Martock had security clearance, Deacon also provided a run-down of what had occurred on Surmi.

The morning came and went quickly. David and Liam - the two heading over to Ras al-Khaimah - met with Deacon and Gina. Together they discussed what the contract included, what was expected of them and what to do in an emergency. Gina would be their 24-hour US point of contact, and the meeting concluded with her handing over two business-class tickets to Dubai.

Just before lunch Deacon's cell rang. It was Mitch asking him to come to the Admiral's office that afternoon.

Following an enjoyable discussion with Petty Officer Sandra Teasman, as he was accompanied to the Admiral's office, Deacon saw Mitch leaning against the door frame watching him, with a smile on his face.

"What?" he said, also beginning to smile.

"Yes, Petty Officer ... no, Petty Officer ... You don't hang around, pal," Mitch said, his smile growing wider and they both watched the Petty Officer walk away, her backside framed beautifully in her tight black skirt.

"Gotta prove I've still got it!"

"Ha! Anyway, brains out of your pants, pal. Business awaits," Mitch said, leading him into the Admiral's office.

After saluting and shaking hands with the Admiral, Deacon took one of the comfy chairs and spent the next hour covering his recent trip to Surmi Reef. The overall response he received back was of a job well done and with some excellent intel gathered. Finally, the Admiral came to the point.

"Mitch has been checking the email address Su Ming used, and we have a response," he said. "Here, read it for yourself," he added, passing over a typed piece of paper.

The email message was short and simple. Deacon read 'Jordan, Amman. March 9, 17:00 Roman Theatre, Third row down, ten seats north of center.'

"Is that it?" he asked.

"That's it," Mitch replied, before adding, "I've checked what's happening in Jordan and it's --"

"Sofex!" Deacon said, interrupting. "It's already in my diary, and I was attending anyway."

"Sofex? The exhibition?" the Admiral asked.

"Yes sir. The conference and exhibition of Special Operations Forces, held biennially. Hosted by King Hussein of Jordan, it's held at old the King Abdullah I airport, now known as Marka International. Global weapons and surveillance companies will be there showing off their gear to assist Special Forces. Ranging from handheld pistols to surveillance drones, comms gear, clothing, directional microphones, lasers, night vision equipment; the lot. I attended once while on local leave when stationed in Iraq. I'm attending to keep up to date with what's new and meet some old friends. Over the years I worked with so many different groups - British SAS and SBS, the French, German, Polish and Spanish, and others of course. They won't all be there, but most

181

will send one or two along just to check it out. Hopefully, there'll be some people I know."

"So what about Chinese companies? Do they exhibit?"

"They've started to, sir. As we know, a lot of Chinese stuff is just straight copies of ours, but some of it is pretty good, although I can't see them exhibiting that. As you know, the only thing we really have in common with the Chinese is the overall fight against international terrorism."

"I wonder why Su Ming will be at that show?" Mitch asked.

"I don't know. It says in her file she likes to travel. She's already been to Dubai. Maybe as a favor from her father? Perhaps he's pulled a few strings?" Deacon said.

"Or it could be a trap?" the Admiral added. "When you meet her you need to uncover why she wants to defect. After listening to advice, the President has decided not to proceed officially with Su Ming's defection. It would cause far too much embarrassment to the Chinese government if it became public, especially at these times of increased tension, more so because of the position her father holds. The West needs China's help in persuading North Korea's Kim Jong-un to cancel his country's nuclear weapons program. Taking that into account and current and planned trade talks between the U.S. and China ... Let's just say now is not a good time. The view is it would be better for all concerned if Su Ming were to stay as an informant, quietly passing us information in the background."

Stroking his chin, Deacon said, "How do we go about doing that, sir?"

"The President already has the FBI and CIA working on a plan. Your job will be to sell it to her."

33

Jordan

Alighting from the United Airlines aircraft at the new Queen Alia International Airport in Amman, Deacon was surprised at how busy the airport was. He waited in line at the visa desk before paying his JD 40 and receiving a two-month visitors' visa, before passing through passport control and customs. He wasn't carrying anything unusual beyond the conventional electronics most business people carry nowadays, namely a smartphone, a laptop, and an iPad, but still, his bags were searched, and he was electronically 'wanded' before being allowed to proceed. Six years previously he had flown into Jordan on a two-day weekend pass, but that had been through the old, smaller airport. This new state-of-the-art building was equally as impressive as any he'd seen - clean, large and full of floor-to-ceiling glass. The air-conditioning kept the temperature comfortable meaning, the sudden blast of heat from the late afternoon sun hit him as he walked outside, quickly donning sunglasses against its glare, to wait for a taxicab.

To make things easier for passengers and travelers, the airport ran an approved taxicab service where only suitable clean and upmarket cabs were allowed to pick up passengers and, surprising for a Middle Eastern country, there was no pushing or shoving as airport security staff deftly allocated vehicles.

After less than a two-minute wait, he was sitting in the rear of a Mercedes enjoying the forty-five-minute journey into the city and to the Four Seasons hotel. The driver, a local and quite friendly, introduced himself as Ahmed and struck up a conversation, providing a free sightseeing and tour overview as they drove along the dusty highway. Arriving at the hotel, he happily gave over a good-sized tip and took Ahmed's cell number, promising to use his services for the duration of his stay.

Wanting to grow his companies' client database, he'd also arranged meetings with various heads of companies located in the King Hussein Business Park. The park, still being built when he'd last visited, and previously the home of Jordan's Armed Forces Headquarters was now complete and housed many international firms including Microsoft, Dell, and Oracle.

Deacon wanted to ensure Phylax would be the first company any of those senior executives would call on when traveling internationally.

Two days later, after numerous successful business meetings, Deacon climbed into Ahmed's cab for the short ride to the city center and the Roman Theatre, a near-perfect amphitheater in the center of the older part of Amman. Open to the public, this magnificent structure dates back to the 2nd-century and is still one of Jordan's major tourist attractions, along with the Dead Sea and Petra.

He got out the cab, checked his watch and walked the two-hundred feet across the bright paved area to the entry gate where he paid his entry fee to the official. Sitting in the shadows under a large sun umbrella were two policemen. Casually glancing at them, it was evident this was just a routine daily duty to make sure no one tried to damage any part of the priceless structure. Moving slowly around the site he read and examined the information posters while keeping a careful eye open as he scanned the other visitors.

No one was paying him any attention. Most visitors appeared to be tourists from a group of coaches parked outside. Walking up the first fourteen rows of seats to the top of the lower arena, known as the *cavea*, he stood silently and just enjoyed being a tourist for once. The weekend break he'd enjoyed here years previously had included visiting Sofex in the daytime and then partying and drinking with colleagues, leaving little time to enjoy the sights.

The middle arena was a further fourteen rows higher, and even Deacon was a little breathless in the warm afternoon sun as he reached the top of the steep steps. Casually standing dead center facing the main auditorium at the top of the final sixteen rows of the area known as the *gods*, he could only marvel at the history and ambience of the place. For eighteen hundred years, man had been seated on these very seats listening to leaders and philosophers conveying their messages. Since Roman times, up to 6,000 people at once had marveled at the teachings and wisdom of their peers and masters.

Even now, eighteen centuries later, whispered conversations in the auditorium could be heard clearly where Deacon stood, and he listened to the excited chatting of the tourists down below him.

Walking back down three rows and then moving to his right, Deacon silently counted out ten small depressions in the stone slabs before seating himself on the eleventh. There were no formal seats, just slight indentations made over the years from thousands of bodies that had sat and fidgeted, the clothing gently abrading the shiny stone surface a fraction at a time.

Relaxing, Deacon felt completely at peace. It would be easy to drift off to sleep, to relax in the shade of the warm afternoon sun, but he had a job to do.

He waited as the time ticked by and at 16:45 he saw Zhang Su Ming enter the theatre. But she wasn't alone. Two men were talking with her, and the same female guard he'd seen in Hong Kong was walking just behind her. Deacon saw one of the men approach the entry gate, hand over some notes, and return to the others with tickets and the other various pamphlets handed out to visitors.

Together they walked around the theatre talking to each other and reading the information posters, much as Deacon had done. They looked like tourists, but it would be impossible for her to make contact with him without arousing suspicion. Finally, at precisely 17:00, Su Ming ran up the first few rows, laughing and squealing with delight, as she shouted at her colleagues to play-act in the middle of the stage while she photographed them.

As she took their photographs, she appeared to stumble slightly and lose her footing and sat down quickly on one of the lower stone steps. Her three colleagues stopped smiling and rushed towards her to help, but she put up a hand to stop them, smiling again she said she'd just stumbled and was fine. As she stood, she quickly scanned the theatre, her eyes locking onto Deacon's for a few seconds as her head turned. Moving back down to the lower area she spent the next fifteen minutes or so with her colleagues before finally, they all walked out together.

Deacon had stayed put throughout the performance. Any approach would have quickly been seen, and it was apparent her plans had changed. He eventually stood and wandered along various rows before walking towards where she had stumbled. Sitting down, he saw a small piece of crumpled paper pushed towards the rear where the stone base met the seat area. Ignoring it, he glanced around casually, but no-one was taking any notice of him.

Leaning back it was easy to slip his hand over the paper and palm it. He stayed a further ten minutes looking around some of the other areas before eventually exiting. Three hundred yards away from the entrance was a small coffee shack with tables and chairs laid outside. Strolling over casually, like the tourist he was that afternoon, he ordered an Arabic coffee.

A non-smoker, he often carried a pack of cigarettes and a book of matches as cover. Anyone watching would pay little attention to his hands as he opened them, and anyway, the vast majority of the population in the Middle East smoked. What anyone watching wouldn't see was the unraveled piece of paper pulled tight across the pack front and the scrawled writing on it.

He covered the packet with his hand as the waiter placed the sweet, strong Arabic coffee and the obligatory glass of water on the table in front of him. Passing a five-dinar note to the server and a polite "Shukraan", he was soon alone again.

He re-read the note twice, then ripped it into small pieces, placed it in the metal table ashtray and set light to it. Using the stub of the match, he rubbed the burned paper until it was almost dust.

Two hours later, he was in the inner sanctum of the Umayyad Monumental Gateway at the ancient Citadel overlooking the city. Open late into the evenings, the Citadel often hosts outdoor orchestral events but this evening it was just open for tourists. Standing quietly in the shadows he waited as the time approached seven-thirty. Su Ming arrived on her own a few minutes later, nervously glancing around. Moving forward out of the dark shadow, he walked close past her saying, "Follow me."

Together they moved to the ruins of the Umayyad Residence thirty yards or so away. Here in the shadows of the collapsed walls and maze of broken buildings, they could finally talk.

"Were you followed?" she asked, nervously.

"No. You?"

"I don't think so," she said. "When can you get me to America?"

"Not so fast, Su Ming. What happened earlier and who were those two men?"

"I planned to be alone, but Wu Wei arranged for the men to come with me. Both are agents from the MSS with our delegation. I know them quite well, but I couldn't get away. I managed to write the note when I was in the ladies bathroom."

"So are they with you tonight and who is Wu Wei?" he asked.

"No, I managed to slip out unnoticed. Wu Wei is my constant guard. She follows me everywhere and reports back everything I do. She's a real pain."

"You speak good English, and you seem to have a very privileged life in China. Tell me, why do you want to leave?"

"That is my business."

"Well, that's as may be, but moving to America will cause major embarrassment to your father. He might even lose his job."

"Good, I want him ruined. Like he has ruined my life."

"Su Ming, your life is far better than many or even most of your fellow countrymen. I ask again, '*Why do you want to leave*'?"

"I want my father to suffer," she said.

"And what if he doesn't?"

"What do you mean? Why wouldn't he suffer?"

"I don't know. Maybe he will, but he seems to be nicely creeping his way up the political ladder. If China is anything like the West regarding politicians, they are liars and cheats. We have a saying in the U.S., '*They would sell their grandmother for a dollar*'."

Su Ming started giggling, "Sell their grandmother . . . that is so funny!"

"It means most people don't trust politicians. They all promise to help the country or their city or whatever - anything to get elected, but most seem to be in it only for themselves," Deacon said. "I have never met your father, but it takes skill and a lot of cunning to get where he has. I can't see him giving that up willingly. What if he disowns you? What if he claims you are unwell or insane? Or have been brain-washed by the evil U.S.? What if he survives any scandal and lays all the blame on you? Who will have suffered then?" he said.

Pondering her thoughts, Su Ming finally said, "So what do you suggest? I want to hurt him and his evil colleagues. I want all of them to suff--"

"Ssshh!" Deacon said, quickly putting his hand over her mouth. "Quick, this way."

Grabbing her hand, he dragged her around the next wall and deeper into the dark shadows. The moon was bright and cast a pale yellow glow over the entire Citadel. Arc lamps lit parts of the ancient monument site as bright as sunlight with their vivid beams but also caused shadows no light could penetrate.

With his hand still clasped over her mouth and hidden deep into the shadow, the pair of them watched as her two male guards from earlier that afternoon at the theatre came into view. One was talking over a walkie-talkie radio, and the other was carrying a pistol with what looked like a suppressor attached. They stopped near the

189

edge of the shadows and spoke over the radio and then to each other before moving on.

Deacon waited a full minute after they'd left before moving his hand away from Su Ming's mouth.

"You were followed," he hissed, "Why are they after you?"

"They're not," Su Ming whispered back. "When they just stopped I heard what they said to each other and over the radio to Wu Wei. She must have seen you in Hong Kong, up at The Peak. She said she thought she saw you again at the Theatre. Tonight at the hotel the old hag must have heard me tell the doorman."

"What do you mean? What doorman?"

"The doorman asked me if I wanted a taxi. I said yes, and he asked me where I wanted to go. He spoke to the taxi driver. She must have seen me leave and asked the doorman where I'd gone. She'd have told them about seeing you today. They were here hunting you! They think you are trying to kidnap me."

Giggling, Su Ming continued, "It's funny really. I want you to kidnap me and take me to America."

"Well, I can't. My government won't help at this time. You want to hurt your father? You need to stay with him and report back what he says and does. You need to provide us with far more information about what the PLAN are doing and help us stop them. That'll hurt him and his colleagues far more than running away. You do that for a few more years, and then I'll help you come to America safely," Deacon said.

"But he never tells me anything, and I want to come to America now?" she said, beginning to cry.

"That isn't going to happen, Su Ming. You need to decide. Stay a few more years and help us first with information or you're on your own," Deacon said.

Sniffling, she said, "If I should choose to do that, how will I get the information to you? I don't even know your name?"

"I don't know yet. Check your draft folder email in seven days. In the meantime, go back to the Gateway where we met and act surprised when you see your tail. If asked, say you've spoken to no one. If they ask you about me, act dumb. It's safer for you if you don't know who I am. I told you, I'm just Donald Duck. Say you don't know what they are talking about."

"What if I have more information now?"

"What do you mean, Su Ming? What information?"

"I was going to tell you when I was safe in America, but my father became drunk at Christmas before you and I met the first time. He said something I didn't understand..."

Trying not to show his impatience, he counted to five and took a slow breath before saying, "What Su Ming? What did he say?"

"He said *'Our baby, she sunk them. They never even saw her . . . and she'll do the same to the Americans.'* That's what he said. His exact words. But I don't know what was sunk. What does it mean?"

Annoyed that she'd never disclosed this before, he glanced around the head-height crumbled walls, before taking her hand.

"OK, thank you, but I don't understand it either. Go now and do as I say. Stay safe and don't look back," he said, ushering her forward.

She walked quickly back towards the main Gateway but couldn't resist glancing behind her once.

All she could see was dust gently swirling in the shadows as she heard her name being called and turned to see her two male colleagues rushing towards her, the one on the left holstering his weapon, while the other spoke rapidly into his radio.

34

Ningbo, Eastern China

Early the following morning Su Ming, accompanied by her two male colleagues and Wu Wei, boarded the early Emirates flight to Dubai. Two hours later, they were escorted onto the first-class section of the AirChina flight to Shanghai.

Just over seven hours flying time later, Su Ming and her protection detail walked down the hastily placed steps at the front of the aircraft. The waiting black limousine skirted Customs before whisking them off for the three-hour drive to the PLAN East Seas Fleet Headquarters at Ningbo.

The guards manning the security barriers at Ningbo had been alerted to their arrival and after scrutinizing their identification cards, waved them on in. As their car pulled up at the steps in front of the main building, Admiral Zhang Hu walked out to greet them.

Climbing out of the car, Su Ming placed both hands together, bowed slightly, and addressed her father, "Honorable father, it makes my heart swell with joy to see you again."

"Mine too, my daughter, mine too. Come let's eat," Zhang said as he led her by the hand towards his office.

After an enjoyable meal together her father discussed his worries. He was concerned her open lifestyle gave encouragement to the West to try to lure her away.

"Hong Kong is full of radicals who may try to influence you. I am concerned you might even be kidnapped and taken from me. That would be too much for me to bear," he said.

"No father, I would never leave you," she said, "I have many friends in Hong Kong, and my work keeps me busy. I am perfectly safe there."

"It is possible, my child, that foreign agents were following you in Jordan. Wu Wei believes she saw a man there who she also believes she saw following you in Hong Kong. I think it is safer if you no longer travel outside of China for now."

"But father, I love to travel and see the world."

"That is as may be, but it is safer if you stay here. To that end, I have arranged for your immediate transfer from Southern Theatre Command. You will be working here at Fleet Headquarters on our forthcoming plans for the liberation of Taiwan Province."

"But father, my life is in Hong Kong. My friends are there. My apartment is there. No, I don't want to move here," she said, her eyes filling with tears.

"You are a Junior Grade Lieutenant of the People's Liberation Army Navy. You will go where you are ordered! I, as your commanding officer order you to Fleet Headquarters, here in Ningbo," the Admiral exclaimed sternly.

Mellowing his voice a little, he continued, "As your father, I have arranged for you to be here for your own safety. You will remain here, and I will arrange for all your possessions to join you. In the meantime, there is a car outside waiting to take you to view three apartments I have chosen. Decide which you like best. Wu Wei will be moving in with you. You will see, my child, it is for the best. Now go, I have meetings to attend."

And with that, their discussion was over.

Su Ming still had tears in her eyes as she walked out to the waiting car. All she wanted was a little freedom, but now she would be monitored closer than ever. She also knew any further argument with her father was pointless. Either he would overrule her as her commanding officer or as her father. Either way, she couldn't win.

As they drove towards the center of Ningbo, her hatred for her father intensified.

While Su Ming and her colleagues were boarding their aircraft to Dubai, Deacon was busy packing his bags. He was booked on the mid-morning flight by Royal Jordanian to Paris then the early-afternoon direct Air France service on to Dulles International, Washington. The previous evening he'd kept to the shadows and easily outfoxed Su Ming's two guards. He'd waited until he saw them leave before he walked to the other end of the Citadel and exited through the back streets towards the bus station, where he hailed Ahmed.

What he didn't see, though, was Wu Wei standing in the shadows with a camera taking a photograph of him as he left.

On her return to her hotel, she spent the next hour on a secure phone to MSS headquarters in Beijing.

In the privacy of his hotel room, he'd typed up and sent to Mitch an overview of what had transpired earlier in the evening, including Su Ming's latest revelation. Deciding he'd earned a beer or two, he spent a few minutes booking his flights home before walking down to the hotel bar.

Sixteen hours after leaving Amman, Deacon cleared customs and immigration at Dulles and caught the free courtesy bus to the long-term car park and to his truck. He'd traveled business class and enjoyed the long flight. The in-flight entertainment, the quality of the food, and the wine on offer from Air France made up for the disappointment of the meeting. He hadn't received Su Ming's commitment to stay in China while working for the Americans, and he also hadn't found out anything more about her reason to leave China except she now, for some reason, hated her father and wanted to hurt him. He had forwarded on the information her father had mentioned while drunk but thought it might have just been gibberish. Turning his phone on it chimed with messages. The first one he listened to was from Mitch requesting him to come to the Pentagon on his arrival back in Washington.

Preferring to have driven home for a shower and a beer, he sighed, started his truck, paid at the booth and drove to the Pentagon.

35

The Pentagon, Washington

"Hiya pal, sorry to have dragged you in here after your recent trip but the Admiral was pretty insistent," Mitch said, shaking Deacon's hand and back-slapping him. Leading him into the Admiral's inner sanctum, Deacon was pleased to see coffee and cookies were already waiting.

Admiral Carter finished the call he was on, slammed the phone down, exhaled noisily, rose from his desk, smiled and walked over to Deacon, hand extended, and sat down, all in one smooth movement.

"Deacon, my boy, tell me about your trip," he commanded after shaking hands.

For the next forty minutes, Deacon talked about everything that had happened in Jordan, including casual conversations he's overheard while mingling near the exhibition stands. Some were either just gossip or typical salesman bluster, but he'd come away with the literature on over a dozen or more new electronic surveillance gadgets to help Special Forces and SWAT teams. He'd already planned to copy and distribute to his former colleagues in Coronado, as well as to his peers in the Green Berets, Army Rangers and Delta Force. Although the rivalry between these groups was very high and each would insist their group was the best, toughest, or worst; in practice, the special forces often worked together, and all regularly put their lives on the line usually for little gratitude or acknowledgment.

He could tell the Admiral was interested in what he was saying, but he was only verbally covering everything he'd written in his reports and sensed some other reason for the Admiral's attention.

Eventually, it was mentioned. After a throat-clearing cough, the Admiral said, "And what of Su Ming?"

Again, Deacon covered everything that had happened, including the evening encounter with her guards at the Citadel, before finishing with the comments her father had made.

"Are you sure those were the exact words?"

"Yes, sir. She said her father was drunk and said to her *'Our baby, she sunk them. They never even saw her . . . and she'll do the same to the Americans.'*."

Slamming his fist down on the table and making the cups rattle startled Deacon. Then a smile rapidly spread across the Admiral's face and he half-shouted, "Got you, you little bastard. Got you!"

"Sir?" Deacon asked in surprise, also seeing a smile on Mitch's face.

"John, we have intelligence reports that Admiral Zhang Hu, Su Ming's father, was the driving force behind the construction of their latest Jin-class sub, the *Xiangliu*. It's been a ten-year project, and it's believed to have some of their very latest sonar and weapons systems on board. It's cost them well over a billion dollars. We've received a couple reports from some other sources and in a few of them he and his immediate group of engineers and technicians referred to it as 'our baby'. We believe the *Xiangliu* was involved in the disappearance of the Argentinian sub, the San Sebastian, near the Falklands late last year. Couldn't prove anything and no wreckage has ever been found, but your message clinches it," Mitch explained. "I passed on your report to the Admiral, but we wanted to hear it from you directly," he continued.

"So will you go public with this against Zhang?" Deacon asked.

Putting his arm around Deacon's shoulder, the Admiral smiled again and said, "That, my boy, is up to the President, but they can't be allowed to get away with what they've done."

Five days later the Director of the FBI, Simon Clark, arrived at Phylax offices. Deacon and Clark knew each other well having worked together against the Florida terrorist plot eighteen months or so previously. Deacon had also gone undercover against a White Supremacist group in Montana wanting to harm the U.S. after Clark had lost a couple of agents trying to penetrate their organization. Clark had been instrumental in advising the previous and current Presidents about the advantages of having a private company such as Phylax 'available', and had become a keen supporter of Deacon for that role.

Welcoming him into his office, the two of them shook hands warmly.

"Director, my pleasure."

"Simon, please John. No need for formalities. So I understand Su Ming has reluctantly agreed to stay in China and work for us?"

"It appears so. She wasn't happy, and I still don't know why she wants to leave, but her father has done something to really upset her. I think she won't be happy until she ruins him."

"I'd like you to make contact with her again and introduce a new contact," the Director said. "Our technical people, working closely with our colleagues at the CIA, have come up with some malware to put on the Admiral's Mac and his cell. It's extremely sophisticated stuff. Totally undetectable. Works in conjunction with his cell, so she needs to get access, just once, to both devices," he said, showing a thumb drive and a small plastic gadget roughly the size of two matchbooks.

"A Mac? Wouldn't Zhang be using a Chinese manufactured computer?"

"It's all to do with position and showing off. Zhang loves to show how important he is. He drives a top range BMW, wears a Patek Philippe watch and Gucci shoes. For him using a Mac is just another way of showing how important and untouchable he is."

"And are sure this malware is undetectable? She's a nice kid, and I really don't want anything to happen to her."

"I am! I don't fully understand it myself - that's why we employ technical whizzkids and we've had some of the very best working on this, but what I've been told is that this malware is completely undetectable. It hides itself in the devices' persistent memory. That's the portion of the memory that persists even after the machine is turned off. Stages two and three are far more technical, but essentially this bug passes all the tests because it's not seen to exist. It passes information to us through various cut-outs, but it encodes the data within the standard information that it's meant to transmit."

"You are losing me," Deacon said.

"People usually get caught because either more information is sent than expected, or it's sent at a time it shouldn't be or to some place it shouldn't go, and it gets reported in a data log somewhere. That's very basically how we detect problems. That's how systems detect errors. This malware doesn't work that way. It's only seen to send out data when it should, and to where it should, therefore there's never anything 'wrong' to be detected."

"And what about if they run anti-spyware or anti-virus software? Won't it be picked up?"

"No, not at all. Guaranteed totally undetectable. I'd stake my life on it."

"Well, we'll being doing exactly that to Su Ming, so I hope you're right."

"You need to get in touch with her again. Her local contact will be a new CIA agent, code name Daisy, fresh into Hong Kong," Clark said, passing over a folder. "Let her know her name, and that she will make contact locally to meet her and pass everything over. Just let her know what to expect. This should be your last involvement with Su Ming, and I thank you for what you have done," he finished.

Later that same evening Deacon logged onto the secure email account and opened the Draft folder. Her message read 'Moved to Ningbo, Shanghai. Have news. Must meet - Urgent!'

Cursing as he realized the plan had already changed, he logged out of the account before sending a secure text to Mitch and the Admiral.

36

Shanghai, China

Eight days later, as the eighteen-hour flight from Ronald Reagan Airport, Washington to Pudong Airport, Shanghai touched down at Friday lunchtime, Deacon stretched and worked his tired back and neck muscles. He remembered the many long military flights he'd made into danger over the years, sitting in aluminum-framed-canvas seats with little heating and virtually no noise control, heading towards a situation he might not return from. Every mission had been fraught with danger. Every outing likely to be his last. Never actively thinking this could be 'the one', but silently pondering even cats only have nine lives.

How different traveling the world was encompassed in a reclining leather stretch chair, waited on by attentive stewards being served liberal amounts of excellent food and beverages, before settling back and watching the latest movie. Yes, the Air Canada Signature Class flight was worth every penny, he thought as he wheeled his small case towards immigration.

As with all his trips on behalf of the government, if she could, Gina scheduled him genuine Phylax business meetings to offset some of the cost. Today, after checking in to his hotel with time for a shower to freshen up, he was meeting the executive board of a Shanghai-based firm of lawyers based in Huangpu district with offices in New York, Washington, and Los Angeles. Their executives regularly traveled, and Gina had picked up on local news of an incident of one of their people being mugged after leaving a bar in New York late one evening. A personal bodyguarding service that offered complete discretion would seem to be the perfect offering and Deacon was keen to win their business.

The one-hour meeting turned into almost two as references were checked and questions asked and answered. With rates discussed and agreed their next executive due to travel the following week would be protected by Phylax, Deacon happily left the meeting with a smile on his face and signed paperwork in his briefcase.

Arriving back at the Waldorf Astoria hotel, he locked his briefcase in the room safe before changing into casual clothing. Now he looked like every other businessman relaxing in the evening as he headed back downstairs.

The best views in Shanghai have to be along the Bund or Waitan walkway on the western shore of the Huangpu River, just yards from his hotel. With the last gentle rays of the setting sun painting the impressive skyline across the river with its golden hue, even Deacon found it hard not to be impressed.

As the hands on his watch moved to 19:30, he slowly strolled past the line of people waiting at the western entrance to the Bund Sightseeing Tunnel - a pedestrian-only, illuminated train ride under the river - before casually walking on towards the metal railings nearer the riverbank where he could see Su Ming approaching quickly.

Su Ming was accompanied by her ever-present watchdog, Wu Wei. As they approached along the Bund, she told Wu Wei to fetch her a drink from one of the many stalls. As Wu Wei waited in line, Su Ming moved slowly further away before darting in between the people, down steps, and back through crowds. Within moments she'd left Wu Wei far behind still in line. As she approached the meeting point through the groups, she suddenly saw Deacon standing alone near the railings. Su Ming darted through the dense pack of people until she was also leaning against the railings mere feet from him.

With neither acknowledging the other and keeping both their faces towards the river, he quietly said, "It is good to see you again. Where is your guard?"

"I don't know. Somewhere behind me. I managed to lose her, but only for a minute or two. I have news for you."

"Don't look at me. In fact, look slightly away down the river. Now quickly, what news?"

"My father is making me stay here. At Ningbo Fleet Headquarters. I am to help him prepare for the liberation of Taiwan Province."

"Holy shit! Taiwan!"

"That is what he said. When he was drunk that night in Hong Kong, he said some rubbish about now she's back we can block the seas, and that things were changing and soon his name would be famous, but I assumed it was just the drink talking. But since he's moved me here, I've seen invasion plans for Taiwan. They plan to invade in five weeks' time."

Realizing he had to get this information back to the Pentagon urgently, he whispered, "Tomorrow go to the Super Brand Mall. Be at the ladies restrooms at the east end of the concourse on the 3rd floor at 11:48 exactly. Go into the ladies restroom at precisely that time. OK? Carry a bag because you will be given two small pieces of equipment."

"But Wu Wei will be with me. And what do I do with them?"

"Don't worry - it's all being taken care of. Everything will be explained tomorrow. Now go and don't look back. Don't forget ... 11:48 precisely."

Su Ming turned to find Wu Wei pushing through the last of the crowds towards her, her face full of anger that again her charge had escaped her.

Beckoning her over, Su Ming cried, "Look, look at the sunset reflecting off the buildings. Isn't it wonderful?" waving a hand in the general direction of the river to keep her distracted, as she saw a last glimpse of Deacon, by now already ten feet away, disappearing into the crowds.

Heading through throngs of people, Deacon followed standard evasion techniques before finally stopping at a small bar. Ordering a beer he sat with his back to the wall, facing the entrance. After ten minutes he was sure no one had followed him. Grabbing his cell, he pressed the five-key sequence that placed it in full encrypted mode. Every keystroke he entered now came up as a random digit on the screen. Three minutes later he pressed send, and the fully encrypted message winged its way from Shanghai through four non-traceable dead-ends to finally chime on Mitchell Stringer's phone on his desk in the Pentagon.

Thirty seconds later, a pale-faced Mitch rushed into the Admiral's inner office, their Friday morning coffees forgotten.

Saturday morning dawned bright and clear. Deacon was up early and headed out for his seven-mile morning jog. Running north along the western river bank he felt sure he was being followed. Twice he stopped to adjust his laces, both times noticing two men in dark tracksuits staying a couple of hundred yards behind. When he ran again, so did they. After almost four miles, he swung around and started running back towards his hotel and directly towards them. He smiled to himself as he noticed they both panicked and ran off in different directions.

However, he could soon see in the reflections in some of the glass-fronted buildings that again they were on his tail. Arriving back to his hotel, he ordered a room service breakfast before showering and dressing.

At 10:30 he walked outside the Astoria, hailed a cab, and instructed the driver to take him to the Bank of Shanghai Tower. His meeting with four of the bank executives took until 12:00. He then left, hailed another cab and headed back to his hotel.

For the past hour Su Ming, followed closely by Wu Wei, had been idly window shopping in the Super Brand Mall. She'd tried on various clothes but had only purchased a t-shirt. As the time approached 11:20, they headed up to the third floor.

At 11:45 Su Ming turned to Wu Wei and announced she was going to the bathroom, arriving at the entrance doors at precisely 11:48. As expected, Wu Wei followed her in just as a loud crash sounded outside and people started shouting.

Wu Wei pushed Su Ming further into the bathroom and demanded she stay there before rushing out to see what the commotion was, narrowly missing a large-built dark-haired woman walking in.

The dark-haired woman grabbed Su Ming and pushed and dragged her into one of the cubicles. As Su Ming opened her mouth ready to scream for help, the dark-haired woman hissed, "Donald Duck sent me, Su Ming. We have less than a minute. Here."

Thrusting two small packages at her, the dark-haired woman explained, "This is a thumb drive disguised as a lipstick. You need to plug it into your father's computer. His computer needs to be powered up but only as far as the password. Understand? When the screen flashes pull the thumb drive back out, and you can turn the computer off then. This device is for his cell. You need to connect this to his cell for thirty seconds. Just plug it in and watch the screen. As soon as the bar finishes moving, unplug it. After, dispose of both items in the public trash as soon as possible, but in separate bins. OK?"

"Wha ... Who are you?"

"SU MING! Repeat what I just told you. We haven't time to waste. Come on," the woman said sternly.

Nervously Su Ming confirmed back the instructions, before hiding both small packages amongst her shopping and her handbag.

Opening the booth door, the dark-haired woman checked the bathroom for other people before turning and saying to Su Ming, "Act normal. Finish in here then wash your hands as normal. Stay in this bathroom until your guard comes back. Two last things. What is Donald Duck's wife's name?"

"Wha ... what?"

"Donald Duck's wife. She's called Daisy. Understood? Daisy. In two weeks check your email again. You will have a message from Daisy. She'll arrange to meet you. You won't hear from Donald again, just Daisy."

With that the dark-haired woman pulled the booth door closed behind her, leaving Su Ming inside, before walking back out of the restrooms and disappearing in the gathered crowd.

It was another three minutes before Wu Wei came back into the bathroom.

"Come, we need to go," she said.

"What happened?" Su Ming said, "What was all the commotion?"

"Just a local. He fell over in the entrance of the shop opposite. That was the crash. Suspected heart attack. The Police were called, and the Ambulance is on its way. He smells of beer. Might be drunk," she replied, leading Su Ming away.

37

Since forcing her to move from her beloved Hong Kong to Ningbo, even Admiral Zhang had noticed his daughter was upset. With both his wife and son dead, Su Ming and his mother were the only family he had left, and his mother was already in her late eighties. To try to make amends, he'd decided to arrange as much time as possible to be with her. He would make sure each Saturday evening and Sunday were allocated, work permitting, to spending time with his daughter.

As had happened the previous two weekends, Su Ming arrived with her overnight bag early on Saturday evening at his palatial apartment in the hills of Zhoushan Island. His butler bade her good evening and carried her bag to the guest bedroom while she strode out towards the balcony.

"Father. My heart warms when I see you."

"As does mine, daughter," he said, as he poured her a drink. Guiding her to the table already set for dining, he continued, "We have your favorite meal tonight - I have instructed the chef to prepare it especially."

An hour later, after three courses of excellently prepared food, and already on the second bottle of wine, Su Ming finally giggled and said, "Enough! If I eat any more, I will pop, father."

Zhang Hu, happy at the way the evening had gone and pleased to see his daughter smiling and laughing, felt content. He's already dismissed the staff, and it was just the two of them together. Perhaps, he thought, his daughter had finally forgiven him for moving her this far east. Leaning over and taking her hand, he said, "Daughter. Tomorrow we will do something special together. We will visit the ancient water town of Zhujiajiao. It is full of picturesque waterways and traditional houses. And with its dozens of stone bridges, this wonderful place has been nicknamed the *Venice of Shanghai*. It was one of your mother's favorite places. I am sure you will love it also."

Smiling back, Su Ming thanked her father before making her excuse to visit the bathroom. Standing, she picked up her small handbag and walked towards the stairs.

The guest bedroom, hers for tonight, was next to his master suite. Quickly darting inside his she looked around for his laptop or cell before cursing silently when she realized neither were there. Heading back out to her own room, she quickly popped into the en-suite before washing her hands to keep up appearances.

Walking back out to the balcony, she said, "Father, I am growing cold. Can we move inside?" Settling into one of the many easy chairs in the lounge, Su Ming swung her feet up under her and sat looking very content, holding a refilled glass in one hand.

During the next hour they spoke of many things, but all personal and none relating to work. She finally came to the conclusion her father had been working in his study immediately prior to her arrival, and that is where his laptop would likely be.

Shivering slightly, she said, "Father. I am still a little cold. Would you be kind enough to fetch my stole from my bedroom?"

Keen to comfort her, Zhang slipped his jacket off and placed it around her shoulders before heading up to her room.

As the door closed behind him, Su Ming pulled his cell out of the jacket's inner pocket with one hand, while reaching for her handbag with the other. Quickly grasping the small device the woman had given her, she pulled the short connecting cable clear and plugged it into the bottom of her father's cell. Immediately a pink bar appeared on the screen and began to move across it.

It only took thirty seconds, but each second seemed like a minute to her. Willing the pink bar to move faster she could hear her father's shoes sounding on the marble stairway as he returned.

As his fingers gripped the door handle and opened it, she slipped his phone back into his jacket pocket while sliding the small electronic device down next to her thighs. With it completely hidden from his view, she thanked him as he put the woolen stole around her shoulders and took back his jacket.

They enjoyed another hour relaxing together before she eventually headed off to bed.

Laying there in the darkness, she willed herself to stay awake. Her father had come up to bed shortly after her, and she heard him moving around. When he settled, she could faintly hear his breathing slowly relax until finally, gentle snoring took over. Waiting another ten minutes or so, she put on a dressing gown and slippers and silently opened her door. His breathing and snoring sounded louder out in the hallway, but its rhythm was regular.

Careful not to make a noise, she headed back downstairs, venturing in through the lounge towards his study. Quietly closing the door behind her, she flicked on the light. There on his desk, powered down, was his Apple Mac. Taking the lipstick from her dressing gown pocket, she twisted its base, and the USB connector was exposed. She pressed the computer's power switch and waited as the screen glowed and went through its start-up routine. When it came to the sign-on prompt, she plugged the thumb drive in and waited.

Nothing seemed to happen until suddenly the screen flashed once. Pulling the thumb drive back out, she powered off the device and closed the lid as she heard a click.

With her blood turning to ice in her veins, she stood immobile as the handle of the study door turned.

38

Sitting in the Business Lounge of Air Canada, Deacon enjoyed a long pull on a glass of ice-cold beer. The flight home would be long, but there were a few films he was keen to catch up on and between that, the meals, a glass or two of fine wine, a little light reading and some sleep, the time would pass pleasantly.

"Mind if I join you?" a familiar voice said.

"Sean, is Gina with you?" he said, smiling.

"Shopping in the Duty-Free! She said she'll catch up with us later or meet us on the 'plane. All good?"

"Yup, Mitch reports they are already getting stuff," he said, happy the plan had worked.

Fearful too much contact with Su Ming might lead to her exposure, he'd devised a plan to get the equipment to her quietly. Sean Martock had worn a signet ring with a tiny needle hidden within the jewel, and he carried a small aerosol spray can. All he'd needed was a likely target. That had come in the form of an older Chinese man out shopping with his wife. Sean had patted the guy on the shoulder just as he passed the entrance to a crockery shop while spraying his back from the can. The hidden needle in his ring had injected a small amount of a quick-acting relaxant drug into the man's upper arm. Within a second, it took effect, and he staggered and fell near the doorway, knocking over a display of cookware. The drug also released a pain stimulant, so the guy grasped his arm as he fell.

To anyone watching the old man displayed all the normal actions of a person suffering a heart attack. The smell of stale beer on his clothes also caused momentary confusion. Was the guy drunk and stumbling, or was he suffering from some form of a medical emergency? However, it had the desired effect, and the gathering crowd increased as more people came to see what was happening. Including Wu Wei. The police and medics were called, however, the undetectable drug would wear off by the time the ambulance reached the hospital and the old man would make a full recovery.

In the meantime, Gina Panaterri, dressed in disguise, and carrying a small bag had entered the women's restroom. Minutes later she had left before the crowd around the old man had even begun to disperse.

Meanwhile, anyone watching Deacon would confirm he was in meetings at the Bank of Shanghai Tower all morning.

Su Ming still couldn't believe she'd gotten away without being detected the previous night. After standing there frozen to the spot and terrified of detection, she suddenly snapped out of her reverie and quickly dived under the desk as the night guard came in. She'd forgotten the guard patrolled each hour to ensure the Admiral's safety.

Su Ming's heart was pounding so loudly she was sure the guard would hear the thumping in her chest, but he only gave a cursory glance around before switching off the lights and leaving, closing the door behind him. He was used to the Admiral working late before heading to bed, leaving doors and windows unlocked, and lights blazing, so tonight was no different.

However, to Su Ming, her close escape terrified her. Weeping silently, she hid there for another forty minutes building up the courage to venture out. When she finally heard the guard open and close the front door behind him as he started his next outside inspection, she gently crept out of her hiding place and tiptoed to the doorway.

Opening it just a crack confirmed the hallway and stairs were empty, so she slipped out, quietly closing the door behind her. She then crept back up the marble staircase to her room, passing her father's room to the sound of soft snoring.

Nothing untoward was discussed at breakfast the following morning, and together they spent the remainder of the day enjoying the sights and sounds at Zhujiajiao. Making her excuse to use the restroom, Su Ming dropped both devices into the trash bins as the updated software in her father's cell and laptop continued its secret work.

39

The White House Oval Office

"Gentlemen," the President said, "I apologize for the short notice for this meeting, but information of the highest importance has recently come to light. Warwick, please continue."

The Director of National Intelligence smiled before looking around the Oval Office at his colleagues.

"Thank you, Mr. President. As you know, Douglas's man has been in contact with Zhang Su Ming, the daughter of the Chinese Admiral Zhang Hu. We have had a few meetings with Su Ming as she is keen to defect. We still don't understand her reasons, but she met with our agent again last Friday. Douglas, would you like to continue?"

Admiral Carter briefly cleared his throat before speaking.

"Thank you, Warwick. The meeting went well, and she has reluctantly agreed to remain in China and pass us information. She also agreed to plant a software bug on her father's cell and laptop. She then came out with a statement saying she recently saw plans for the imminent invasion of Taiwan. The timescale she referred to was five weeks."

"Five weeks? Why are we only hearing about this now?" Bill Casler almost shouted.

"We needed to verify," the Admiral said. "So far, her information has been one-hundred-percent correct, but we could still be being played. As soon as I was informed, I raised this to Melvin and Warwick and called the

216

President. We agreed to use the weekend to verify, and Melvin immediately ordered the redeployment of our NROL-47 satellite covering North Korea to the Straits of Taiwan."

"But aren't we normally monitoring that area anyway?"

"We are, but the '47' has the latest infra-red and ground-penetrating radar. She can detect things the others can't. And she's already proved her worth. All our satellites there are showing a definite build-up of armed forces along the Chinese mainland coastline. They are using heavy camouflage and are in the process of moving a large number of shore-based rockets closer to the strait. More fighters and bombers have been redeployed towards the coastline airbases from further north. We are also seeing naval movement towards their forward operating bases."

"But could this just be routine movement or exercise planning?" the Secretary of State asked.

"It could if it wasn't for some other details we've received," Warwick Dreiberg interrupted. "The software loaded onto Zhang's laptop has already come up trumps. The NSA has intercepted emails covering the first stages of the attack. Dates, deployment details, personnel and equipment strengths - even a complete copy of their battle strategy."

"Fuck! So this is real? But every year since 1949 China has been threatening to retake Taiwan back into the Chinese fold. Why now?" Casler said.

"It certainly looks that way. Bear in mind, 2021 is an important milestone for the PRC. July 2021 will be the 100-year anniversary of the forming of the Chinese Communist party. To have the country reunified by then ... well, that's the dream of the PRC high command and President Xiaodong personally."

"There's a number of reasons why the PRC may believe now is the correct time," the Secretary of Defense, General Melvin Tarrant said. "The U.S. military is already stretched and fighting wars and conflicts around the world, from ongoing insurgency raids in Iraq and Afghanistan to conflicts in Africa and the Middle East. Let alone the potential outbreak North Korea keeps promising. Any one of these could escalate and tie up more men and machinery. But it's more than that. As we've recently found out, Surmi Reef is due to come online in defense of the South China Sea with those damned missiles. Surmi is the last piece in their current puzzle. The PRC can very effectively block all shipping using the SCS. Or they can impose tariffs. That's all part of their battle strategy document."

"Would they really do that?"

"The South China Sea holds billions of dollars of natural resources, fish and fossil fuels. Underground it also holds some of the largest sources of rare-earth elements. Add to that some of the busiest shipping lanes and all of this will be under Chinese control. What do you think?" Warwick answered.

Turning to his Secretary of State, the President said, "Bill, I ordered you to get China to remove those missiles. Why haven't they?"

"Uhh, Mr. President, the PRC refuses to answer questions about their plans for the Spratlys or about what weapons and forces they have on them. They insist they are part of sovereign China and any attempt to invade, damage or destroy the islands would be classed as an act of war. The instigators would suffer the wrath of the People's Republic."

"Goddamn fuckers. OK, can't we just run a few more FONOP's through the area to make them keep their heads down? Just flood the area with our Navy?" the President asked.

"We could try, Mr. President, but their battle plan also indicates how they will use a fleet of subs in and around the SCS, headed by their latest, the *Xiangliu*, to defend any aggressive acts from outside forces. With their increased naval fleet, any conflict with the PRC needs to be avoided at all costs."

"At all costs?" the President said.

"Well, maybe that's the wrong phrase, Mr. President. Maybe not at all costs, but certainly to be avoided if possible. Our ships would be a long way from home."

"I don't agree," the President said. "The PRC has grown because we've let them. My predecessors did nothing to stop them. Nothing. They were allowed to grow and harbor anti-American views. Their new wealth has given them the ability to outgrow and out equip us. We need to make it clear to them there is a line and if they cross it ..."

"Going back to the present threat, Mr. President, how far are you prepared to go to defend Taiwan?"

"The Taiwan Relations Act says we will come to the aid of Taiwan, if need be," POTUS replied.

"Correct, Mr. President. But how many Americans will support yet another military conflict? Especially protecting a country's people who are related to their aggressor almost 8,000 miles away? How many body bags will it take on the nightly news for the people to turn against you? There's not even a worthwhile win of oil at the end. To many Americans, if you ask them the difference between the People's Republic of China and the Republic of China, they will say they're the same. Most wouldn't understand that while both the Republic of China and the People's Republic of China are both technically Chinese, the term 'Chinese' only means the communist People's Republic of China. "

"But we can't just turn our backs and allow them to retake Taiwan? We'd become a laughing stock and no other country would believe our military promises or commitments?"

"What we could do is move the Fifth Fleet down to Taiwan and run an exercise with the Taiwanese Navy that has been in planning for over a year," Melvin Tarrant added. "With both ours and the Taiwanese forces at exercise level, they wouldn't dare try to invade. That would buy us time while we push for a diplomatic solution."

"Do we have such an exercise, Melvin?"

"We always have contingency plans, Mr. President. The next full exercise with Taiwan isn't for another three years, but all we need do is backdate it to now, and announce it's a surprise joint exercise to determine both sides alertness and 'ready-for-battle' preparedness. Bill needs to get onto his equivalent over there, and both countries announce it together."

"Can we do it in time?"

"Already drawn up orders for your signing, sir. The Ronald Reagan battle group can be ready within days. The Carl Vinson and her group are on liberty in Pearl, but she can be back at sea within the week, and on station within two," the Secretary of Defense said.

Looking around the room POTUS smiled. He knew any military action would initially raise his profile and he could do with a win before the next elections. Dead soldiers and body bags would lose him support, but straightforward military action was great for news and great for votes.

Addressing his Secretary of State, he said, "Bill, get onto your equivalent in Taiwan. Tell him both governments will be making a joint statement in two days' time to announce military exercises starting in three weeks. Get them up to speed."

Turning to Melvin Tarrant, the President said, "Melvin, I want plans drawn up for a raid on Surmi. I want those fucking missiles gone, but it's got to be done quietly. I'm not going to be known as the President that instigated World War III with China."

40

Zhongnanhai, Beijing

Admiral Zhang was waiting in the president's inner sanctum. He'd been there almost thirty minutes before the double doors opened suddenly, and President Xiaodong Wang strode swiftly in.

"Zhao Zhuxi, it is my honor meeting with you today," Zhang said, bowing. "I have excellent news of our preparations."

Instead of suggesting they should sit, Xiaodong Wang kept Admiral Zhang standing while two aids brought him a high backed chair to sit on.

"Tell me," he instructed as he eased his frame down.

Surprised by the sudden lack of friendliness and courtesy, Zhang was momentarily taken aback.

"My leader, I am pleased to announce our preparations are almost complete, and our movements of troops and equipment are going to plan. We will have everyone in position in twenty days' time, ready to commence action after the *Xiangliu* inauguration."

"That is very interesting, Zhang, but while you work and plan your attack the Gweilo are one step ahead," the President hissed angrily.

Shaken by his use of the derogatory word for westerners Zhang replied quickly, again using the popular and intimate expression *Zhao Zhuxi*, meaning 'President'.

"Zhao Zhuxi, you are displeased. Somehow I have wronged you?"

"I am not displeased, Zhang. I am furious and demand answers. It appears our plans have leaked to the fucking Americans. Foreign Secretary Wang Liu has just gotten off the phone with the US Secretary Bill Casler, having been told of an imminent planned naval exercise between the US Navy and the Forces of Taiwan, due to commence in two weeks' time."

"WHAT? There was no exercise planned?"

"Well, there is now. The Gweilo have outsmarted you."

"How is that possible, Zhao Zhuxi? Our security is tight. No one would talk."

"SOMEBODY HAS!" an enraged President shouted so loudly two security staff rushed in.

Waving them away, he continued in a quieter voice filled with venom, "You will find the person or persons responsible and bring them to me. Do you understand?"

Shocked by the prospect of what he'd heard, Zhang could only nod acceptance.

Trying to think of a way to keep within the President's good books, and knowing what fate might otherwise await him, he quickly added, "The inauguration of the *Xiangliu*, Mr. President. Will you still attend? It is planned for the next spring tide next week."

Zhang knew the way the politics in China worked. Officially, mainland China was a socialist republic run by the Communist Party, and headed by the General Secretary. There is also a President of China, a titular head of state, serving as the ceremonial figurehead under the National People's Congress. Finally, there is the Premier of China who is the head of government, presiding over the State Council composed of four vice-premiers and the heads of ministries and commissions.

However, as a one-party state, the General Secretary of the Communist Party of China holds the ultimate power and authority over state and government. What were individual roles were merged. Since 1993, the offices of President, General Secretary, and Chairman of the Central Military Commission have been held simultaneously by one individual, granting him de jure and de facto power over the country and of every individual person.

Zhang knew President Xiaodong Wang could offer great riches, prospects and comfort to those who pleased him, but also knew the President had the power to make Zhang and his family disappear.

After almost two minutes of silence, President Wang nodded before standing and leaving the room. The lack of pleasantries and politeness offered to Zhang confirmed the anger seething within the President.

Saluting before turning and heading towards the double doors, Zhang breathed a sigh of relief to find the door opened on his approach and with no armed guards waiting to escort him away.

Walking rapidly to his waiting limousine he shouted at the driver to get him back to the airport at Xijiao as quickly as possible, before calling ahead and ordering his jet prepared for immediate take-off.

With preferential flight clearance already approved, his Gulfstream G550 had its engines already spinning and warmed up as his car sped towards it. Mere seconds after he climbed the stairs, the female attendant pressed the button, and the stairs started their fold-up routine as the pilot eased off the brakes and the sleek aircraft started rolling forward.

By the time the Admiral had strapped himself in, the nose wheel was already approaching the main runway, and with a sudden thrust as the engines spun up to full power, Zhang felt himself hurtling along the runway.

One hour and forty minutes later the aircraft was on final approach to Ningbo Zhangqiao airbase. The waiting car whisked him to Fleet Headquarters where his staff was gathered and waiting for an afternoon and evening of intense meetings.

On the agenda the final details of the forthcoming inauguration were waiting to be confirmed before being emailed the garrison commander on Surmi Reef, Captain Zu Qian; the captain of the *Xiangliu*, Captain Weimin Yin; and to the department of the General Secretary, President Xiaodong Wang.

As the emails were being transmitted, the software virus program embedded in the Admiral's computer continued its task.

41

Airborne over the Pacific

Deacon stretched and felt his lower back click. Four hours into the seventeen-hour flight on the C-5 Super Galaxy - one of the largest military transport aircraft ever built - and he was already bored. The aluminum frame and webbing seat was reasonably comfortable, and he'd already configured a hammock option, but there was little room left. Every spare inch was filled by either equipment or people, all heading over to Taiwan for the forthcoming military exercises.

Dressed in casual clothes he was something of an oddity to the others. He was obviously security cleared to be on board, but his dress code hinted at spy.

One or two fellow passengers had nodded in his general direction, possibly keen to strike up a conversation and discover if he was CIA or FBI, but the aircraft designers had given little regard for the comfort of its human cargo. With its lack of soundproofing, conversation was difficult, usually resulting in shouting. Deacon had no friends or colleagues on board and no wish to enter into discussions, so with earplugs in place he settled back to get as much sleep as possible.

The meeting two days previously with the Admiral and Mitch had gone well. Admiral Carter had been open and sincere and had made it clear the choice to accept this mission was Deacon's and Deacon's alone. The President had already called for plans to attack Surmi Reef and destroy its missile capability, but apart from using cruise missiles, the highest probability of total success without the PRC knowing where to place blame was coming in at less than sixty percent.

The SEALs had looked at using large or small teams, airborne or seaborne assault, and any number of other combinations, but could not get the success probability factor over sixty.

The main issues were: no easy access to the reef, very little cover when actually there, too many hostiles manning the outcrop, and a requirement for zero chance of discovery. China's foreign minister had made it extremely clear to US Secretary of State, Bill Casler, that any intervention by US Forces into mainland China, or any of its occupied islands in the Spratlys and Paracel chain would be considered an act of war between both nations, and would result in grave consequences. Deacon knew from past experience when nations talk of grave consequence, they usually mean major amounts of blood would be spilled.

So with an attack by SEALs out of the question, the only other option was a one-man attack with no fallback or repercussions if captured. That had been the agenda for the meeting.

The US Navy could assist, in a limited fashion, with ingress and egress, but couldn't be seen to be actively aiding the mission. If captured, the US Government would deny all knowledge and support of Deacon. Any weapons he used needed to be available from sources other than the US. He'd be completely on his own.

Initially, he'd been in two minds. Although he'd faced death many times over the years, he certainly didn't have a death wish. His last escapade to Surmi had been a close call, and he knew from Su Ming the garrison had been expanded since then. What finally convinced him was a copy of the inauguration agenda email, forwarded by the NSA.

Most container ships have a maximum draft of 12.5 meters, and ports and dockyards are dredged to accommodate them. The *Xiangliu* was believed to have a draft of 12 meters, similar to many of the other craft moored at Surmi Reef. With the port being built from dredged coral and rock, and on a firm bed of compacted sand and coral, low water would only provide a bare minimum under her keel. Therefore the timing of the inauguration ceremony was timed for around a 2-meter high water in five days. She would stand off and only enter into the port at 07:28 with the ceremony planned for 11:00 on the quay. By 15:00 she would be on her way again and heading back out of port towards safe deeper water.

With only a day to get everything organized, Deacon had needed to use Mitch and Gina to help with arrangements.

Thirteen hours later the C-5 Super Galaxy was on final approach and landed with a gentle thud at Ching Chuan Kang Air Base, in the heart of Taichung City, in the Republic of China, usually referred to as Taiwan.

Trucks, transporters and a fleet of helicopters were waiting to move men and machinery to the various ships and land bases being used in the imminent joint U.S. and Taiwanese military exercises.

A lone U.S. Navy SH-60 Seahawk stood, engines idling, on the adjacent taxiway. Leaving the others to look after themselves, Deacon grabbed his four bags of kit and manhandled them down the loading ramp to the tarmac.

The aircrewman stepped down from the helicopter, sprinted over and carefully checked Deacon's ID. Then he waved at a group of ensigns who ran over, picked up the bags and loaded them on board as Deacon climbed into his seat. Moments later, before Deacon had even finished strapping his helmet on, the aircrewman slapped the pilot on the shoulder, the engine whine rapidly increased, and with a lurch, the Seahawk quickly rose before continuing to climb as it headed south over the darkened countryside.

A little over forty minutes later, it began to descend towards a jet-black sea. Hovering at roughly twenty feet above the waves, the black of the water suddenly turned white as the conning tower sail of the USS Bradenton broke the surface.

The rest of the deck of the Los Angeles-class nuclear hunter/killer submarine quickly came into view, and before the waters had even cascaded off the black, rubber-covered hull, the pilot deftly hovered the skids of the Seahawk over its surface.

A half-height hatch at the bottom of the sail opened, and three crewmen exited and ran towards the helicopter. By the time Deacon jumped down, two of them had grabbed his bags, and the other crewman waved the 'copter back off.

The helicopter was less than one hundred feet away as the last crewman pulled the hatch closed and hit the green button and Deacon felt the angle of the deck change, and the surge of acceleration as the Bradenton swiftly dove to the safety of the depths below.

Captain Betley was waiting for Deacon as he was escorted to the Captain's Cabin.

"Mr. Deacon, it's a pleasure to meet you. Let me introduce you to my Executive Officer, Lt. Joanna Gordon," he said.

Shaking hands, Deacon smiled and said, "Captain, Lieutenant. It's my pleasure. Thanks for rerouting for me."

Glancing at each other, the XO said, "When an order comes from the CNO it would be a brave sailor to ignore it."

"Our orders are to make you comfortable and drop you off at a specific coordinate. We will then pick you up twenty-four hours later. The Chief has arranged a private cabin for you, and I would ask that you don't interact with the crew. Your mission is on a need-to-know basis, and no one else of the crew have been made aware," the Captain said as the Chief Petty Officer arrived. "Meals can be served in your cabin if you wish," he added, before finishing with, "Your bags have been taken to your cabin, and the other gear is already aboard and is stowed in the forward torpedo room. The Chief will take you to your cabin now."

The walk towards his cabin reminded Deacon how much lack of privacy existed on a submarine. No one spoke to him, as the entire crew had been ordered by the Captain to just ignore their current guest and follow their normal orders. The crew were used to carrying various Special Forces operatives on clandestine missions and knew never to discuss it when ashore, but Deacon knew the rumor mill onboard would be rife with differing opinions and views on who he was and why he was there.

Sixty-three hours later the Chief alerted Deacon that they would be at the drop site in a little over two hours. In the two and a half days Deacon had been on board he'd only spoken occasionally with the Captain, the XO, the Chief, and Able-Seaman McBride who served him his food. He's only been out of his cabin a few times, each time to exercise and check and test gear.

Now it was game-on.

With the time taken on his last visit to Surmi Reef to get from the drop-off point to inshore, and the near capture on his return leg, Deacon had decided on a better method of approach. He also needed more equipment this time.

Grabbing the remainder of his gear he moved everything to the forward torpedo room.

There, already unboxed and fully charged, was the eight-foot-long Underwater Transit Sledge, or UTS. It was a microprocessor-controlled, battery-operated propeller-driven winged sled designed to carry a diver for up to ten miles. It was a standard, commercially-available product, that had been modified and enhanced at the underwater training school in Coronado.

This model had enhanced electronics and more powerful batteries, enabling it to run for up to almost thirty miles. It also contained two air tanks to supplement the diver's own, along with a navigation board, GPS screen (operated from a trailing aerial finer than a fishing line), and modified underwater telephone based on the old and proven 'Gertrude' system used since 1945. The wings of the sled folded and concertinaed in so that the complete unit could be passed through the submarines diver escape and inspection hatch –– a separate small compartment that could be flooded and opened underwater to allow divers to exit and inspect the hull without the need to surface the boat. The only limitation was the submarine had to remain close to the surface at just below periscope depth and moving at no more than three knots while the hatch was in use.

He would be carrying a Makarov PB pistol with a suppressor, 8lbs of Czech manufactured C4 explosives, 100 feet of German-produced PETN detonation cord, 6 waterproof electronic Swiss manufactured timer detonators, 4 Bulgarian hand grenades, a Swiss hunting knife, and a bag of sticky putty. His black Nomex dive gear was of Japanese manufacture, and his air tanks had Malaysian writing on them.

He double-checked again that he was carrying nothing of exclusive U.S. design and that everything he had was internationally available. Admiral Carter had been insistent on this in the event of his capture so nothing would trace back to the United States military.

From one of his last bags, he removed and assembled a fiberglass frame twelve feet by six, covered in a sand-colored sheeting, with webbing straps hanging down. Satisfied everything was complete, he repacked and stowed it all and, with the help of McBride, moved everything to the diver's inspection hatch.

Deacon, Captain Betley and Lt. Gordon had spent the previous afternoon making a final decision on the best drop-off point. The course the Bradenton would take was in a southwest direction, remaining in international waters at the 12-mile disputed territorial limit. It would turn and proceed towards Surmi Reef for 3 miles, before dropping him off, where it would reverse course and head back out into international waters. The following day, at 15:00, the Bradenton would wait at the same coordinates for the pickup. It would wait a maximum of one hour. In the event of a missed pick-up, Deacon was to head further west to a secondary pick-up coordinate and wait for the USS Chancer that would be traversing the area completing a FONOP.

As the Bradenton turned towards Surmi, Captain Betley shook hands with Deacon and wished him luck.

At the drop-off point, the Bradenton gently rose to just below periscope depth and slowed to a mere walking pace. Deacon closed the internal door to the escape hatch, locked it and pressed the button to flood the chamber. When the red light turned green confirming pressure equalization, he pressed the green button to open the outer door. With a soft clunk and a whirring sound, the outer hatch opened, and Deacon was free to leave the Bradenton. As he pulled his cargo out onto the submerged deck, he looked up and could see the dark waves on the surface over one hundred feet above. Looking down into the depths was just darkness, with the seabed almost five thousand feet below.

Unlocking the wings of the sled, he powered up the unit and allowed the GPS aerial to free float towards the surface. It would take a couple of minutes to compute its position, but, once done so, had an accuracy of mere inches.

With everything else already stowed or tied down to the sled, Deacon plugged in his helmet and spoke quietly into the microphone. The Gertrude telephone system connected him immediately with the bridge, and he issued the command, "Sailfish One Away," before pressing the motor switch and silently steering the UTS on its new course at a depth of ninety feet.

The UTS had been built to be undetectable. The Gertrude telephone system was extremely low-powered, with a range of only 1,000 yards. This had been done to make detection by others near impossible. The motor and propeller were low-noise with anti-cavitation channels on the propeller blade tips. Even the most sensitive underwater sonar listening systems couldn't detect the running of the motor at over 200 yards.

The UTS could run for short bursts at its maximum speed of fifteen knots, but at that speed detection by the Chinese listening posts on Surmi became likely, and its range was greatly reduced. Running the motor at half-power reduced progress through the water to a mere six knots but extended the range to over twenty-eight miles. With only nine miles to go Deacon was confident of

enough remaining power to get back to the Bradenton the
following day.

42

Surmi Reef

An hour into his journey the problems started. Suddenly the low-lit display on the control board of the UTS flickered, went out, then came back on slowly. The electric motor also stopped before starting again at lower revs. Toggling through the controls, the battery power gauge suddenly changed from eighty-one percent remaining to under forty. It also showed the drain rate of the batteries was rapidly increasing.

With three miles still to go it would be touch-and-go whether he had enough power to even reach Surmi, let alone get back to the Bradenton. Cursing, he slowed even more to conserve what power he could while running through his options in his mind.

He couldn't return to the Bradenton now because she wouldn't be back until tomorrow. If he kept the speed low, he was hopeful he could reach Surmi with everything intact. The plan had been to leave the sled submerged anchored to a small group of rocks lying a few hundred yards offshore before retrieving it for the journey back home. That idea was obviously now shot, and he needed to find a new way off the reef.

By reducing speed to a little over three knots, the remainder of the journey took another two hours and by the time he approached the rocks the battery gauge was down to two percent. Powering it down completely, he anchored the sled and then gently floated to the surface where he could rest and watch for guards near the beach.

Everything seemed as before with the searchlights from the towers casually scanning the beach. Floating for almost an hour he could see the guards were still patrolling in pairs and still taking twelve minutes to walk between the towers, but the patrols had been doubled. However, they still didn't seem to be using dogs.

Leaving some of his gear stowed with the now-defunct UTS, he made two trips with the remainder and made a new encampment close to his previous one.

As before, he covered his tracks in the sand before collapsing down and hiding in the dense foliage. Although he'd not exerted as much energy on this trip, the sea temperature was noticeably cooler this time of the year and over four hours in the water had both exhausted and chilled him. Pulling out a non-rustle foil blanket, he wrapped himself up in it and quickly went to sleep.

Two hours later, refreshed and reenergized he ate two high energy bars as he sorted out his gear. Removing his Nomex suit, he donned camouflaged fatigues and placed the pistol in his waistband. He put some of the C4 explosives, forty feet of the det cord, the hand grenades, and four timers in a small backpack, before slowly and quietly heading off north.

Captain Zu Qian was in his mid-fifties and heading slowly towards his retirement. He'd joined the navy as a boy and worked hard, gradually gaining promotions and rising through the ranks. Your lineage is still important to success within the PRC, and being the son of a poor farmer his rise had only been on merit. It had also plateaued. He knew the pinnacle of his career was to be in charge of the Surmi Reef garrison and he would not be promoted further. However, he also knew any mistake could easily trigger a significant fall from grace resulting in demotion, expulsion, or even court-martial and prison. Therefore, after a person or persons unknown had gained access to the island some weeks previously, he'd wisely chosen not to report the full matter to his seniors. Instead, knowing rumors were bound to get back, especially as troops were being moved around, he'd recorded the incident as an exercise to test their security and the deaths of the two guards had been an accident. However, he also knew that if enemies of the PRC had come once to his island, they would likely come again, therefore he'd increased patrols.

When the final confirmation had arrived issued by Admiral Zhang himself stating that he, along with the Paramount Leader and associated press entourage, would be arriving by executive jet the following morning for the parade and inauguration ceremony commencing at 10:00, Captain Zu was over the moon.

A photo of him shaking hands with the two most senior people within the People's Republic would be shown in newspapers and on television everywhere. Him. Captain Zu Qian. A poor farmer's son. Adulation and jealousy from his peers and subordinates. He would finally have made it. His wife at home in Wuhan would be so pleased. Her social standing in the town would be heightened so quickly. She'd become a local celebrity and would be on the invite list of all the other senior's wives in the area. She'd be so pleased with him they might even spend some time together in bed on his next leave, he hoped.

Happier than he'd been in a long time and excited about the visit, he'd called his subordinate officers in and read them the riot act. Nothing must be allowed to go wrong the following day, he made clear. Or heads would roll. Smiling, he'd dismissed them, had a glass or two of whiskey, before retiring to bed and having a sleepless night caused by a mixture of excitement and worry.

The increased patrols had hampered Deacon throughout the night. He'd not been detected, but he also hadn't been able to get to the aircraft parked around the airfield. On the third attempt, he had managed to get to the fuel dump, quietly slipping between the barbed wire and the cold metal sheet of the furthest tank.

From there, he'd slowly edged his way across and around to two of the other three tanks, carefully laying det cord along their lower edges before scraping small holes in the ground with his hunting knife. Into these small indentations he connected the timers, set their alarms and buried them. He'd also placed two of the grenades behind access pipes primed to explode when the rest of the tank went up, before quietly scurrying back into the safety of the longer grass and foliage.

The YJ-18 missile bank and offices were too heavily guarded at the moment, and the *Xiangliu* had yet to arrive, so he made his way back to his hideout for the few remaining hours before dawn.

At 05:30 he put on his Nomex wetsuit, grabbed his gear and, after checking the beach was clear, entered the sea and quietly swam out to the rocks. Diving down he found the UTS exactly where he'd left it. Placing the regulator from one of the stowed air tanks in his mouth he took long, slow breaths.

Powering up the sled he saw the battery charge had increased slightly back up to four percent. This often happens when a battery is low, but the discharge is removed. The internal chemical reactions actually help a battery to regain a very small portion of its charge again.

Four percent wouldn't allow Deacon to get away from the reef, but would help him carry out part two of his plan.

Keeping the depth at fifteen feet and the speed at three knots, it took Deacon almost thirty minutes to move the mile north along the coastline towards the man-made harbor entrance. With the batteries now virtually exhausted the sled went slower and slower until finally the panel lights went out for the last time and the UTS sunk to the coral below.

Keeping attached to the air tanks with the long regulator hose, Deacon began clipping together the sprung fiberglass frame before checking the sand-colored sheeting was attached firmly to it.

Slipping some of the remaining C4 into his wetsuit pockets and grabbing what was left of the det cord and one of the timers and the bag of putty, he slipped a Dräger Rebreather onto his back, connected it, looped the webbing straps of the fiberglass frame around his arms and legs and spat out his current regulator. Unconnected now to the UTS, he started swimming in long, slow strokes towards the entrance while the fiberglass frame and sheeting billowed out above his back.

Parts of the harbor had been dredged to a depth of 12.5-meters and were able to accommodate the larger container ships, but most of the harbor was shallower. However, the dredging had removed all natural seabed vegetation, and most of it was just a mixture of sand and/or coral.

From anywhere on a ship, Deacon swimming would have shown up like a bug on a white wall. Even if he'd been wearing a matching color wetsuit, his shadow on the seabed from the sun would have given him away.

By keeping within a foot or so of the seabed and by having a colored shield far larger than he was, he blended in perfectly. The only thing to give him away would be the bubbles coming from his air tanks. However, the Dräger rebreather system doesn't emit any bubbles, feeding the diver's exhaled CO_2 breaths back into itself to be chemically altered and reused. Its limitation, however, is after a while the chemicals became less effective and the quality of the breathable air it reproduces drops.

Keeping clear of the main channel he was only a few hundred yards from the dockside when he saw the shape of the *Xiangliu* pass him. Glancing at his watch, he saw it was just after 7:30 and the submarine was making its approach on the surface ready for the inauguration in a few hours' time.

He continued until he was a little closer to the dockside before stopping and sinking down the last few inches onto the coral. With his rebreather not producing tell-tale bubbles and with the frame and sheeting totally covering him, he was completely invisible.

43

The Xiangliu

At 07:00 Captain Yin Weimin ordered the *Xiangliu* to rise from her depth of four hundred feet to periscope depth. Prior to raising the periscope, sonar had already confirmed there were only two ships within at least ten miles. The ESM, or Electronic Support Mast, went up next. Thinner than the periscope and less likely to be seen, it would detect any local radio or radar transmissions.

The ESM system squawked having picked up 'friendly' signals so having assured himself the US Navy wasn't lying in wait on the surface for him, Yin then instructed the periscope raised for visual clarification. Satisfied the only ships present were the *Hohhot* and the *Changsha*, both Chinese type 52D destroyers, Yin then ordered the course to be 175 magnetic, the speed to be one quarter and to surface the boat.

In the movies, this is usually shown as a time when everyone is rushing around, but in practice, this is just another standard maneuver for a well-trained crew.

With a hissing of vented air, the *Xiangliu* broke the surface five miles north of the entrance to Surmi Reef, the first time the decks had touched fresh air in over six weeks. With the air down below being air-conditioned and recirculated and a stable temperature throughout, to most of the crew busy with their duties the only difference was a slight rolling in the swell. When submerged there was usually no detectable movement.

The Captain stood at the observation wing in the tower looking out through binoculars. Everything looked peaceful and he was pleased to see a tug was standing by in the harbor for the closer maneuvering required. Instructing his helmsman, He Guan, to maintain course, the Xiangliu slowly edged closer and closer to the dockside.

At 07:38 the rubberized hull of the *Xiangliu* passed thirty feet to the right of the prone body of Deacon, still on a course of 175 magnetic but with speed adjusted to Dead Slow.

Yin was confident things would go well today but worried about the lack of full navigation charts for the area. As with all captains, Yin liked to study the passage plan carefully, but the dredging had been completed so recently, paper charts were not yet available. However, the main channel had the IALA buoyage system marked, so for safety, the *Xiangliu* kept right in the middle.

It took them almost thirty minutes to secure the *Xiangliu* to the dockside. Her draft restricted how wide she could turn so she had to maneuver back and forth a couple of times with the aid of the tug, each time getting closer, until finally with bow and stern lines attached ashore, she stopped. With extra lines run ashore to stop her twisting or swaying, and with bunting now strung from her periscope to the bow and stern, she became a hive of activity.

Captain Yin Weimin was making sure everything was perfect. He was extremely proud of the *Xiangliu* and had already received thanks and commendations in private for his round-the-world test sail and in the monitoring of the US naval bases. He'd even received gratitude for the undetected sinking of the Argentinian submarine, the ARA San Sebastian. Today would bring the public adoration he so wanted and the proudest day of his life. To shake hands and be honored by Admiral Zhang Hu and by the leader of the country, the General Secretary of the People's Republic of China himself ... He could think of no greater honor.

The crew had spent the last two days cleaning and polishing everything before cleaning and polishing it again. A stickler for tradition and for his role in running a clean boat, Yin had inspected every conceivable part of the *Xiangliu* while wearing white fabric gloves. The merest smudge of dirt or grime on his gloves after he wiped wherever he could reach would mean the immediate reduction in rank and pay of everyone in that department.

To his surprise, the crew had performed well. His gloves were as clean as when he had removed them from the drawer.

Some of the crew were using brooms and hoses to wash the decks where his esteemed visitors would walk, while the cooks were busy making special celebratory refreshments.

In his eagerness to impress, one young Rating enthusiastically swabbed his broom too far, knocking a bucket over which teetered and rolled, before a gust of wind sent it spiraling off the deck. Before Captain Yin needed to say anything, the Chief Petty Officer had already shouted at the Rating, ordered him to jump in and retrieve it, and he ordered two other Ratings to drop a line to pull him back out.

There was an immense feeling of pride throughout the boat and nothing would be allowed to ruin it. All of the crew would be standing at attention in dress whites, and there would be a band playing on board for the duration of the president's visit.

At the 10:00 ceremony, the reef would be formally decreed operational, and the *Xiangliu* would then be center stage at 11:00 when she would be commissioned into full active service. She would become a significant part of the Surmi Reef Traffic System, a plan to limit unwanted traffic from the South China Sea and to charge a tax for those allowed to pass through.

All the preparations made the crew less vigilant and provided a perfect cover for Deacon.

Remaining just inches off the seabed, Deacon slowly approached the stern of the *Xiangliu*. The dark rubber covered hull appeared above him, blanking out the sun and the sky. As he disappeared under the hull he unclipped the frame and screen and wedged it against the one of the dockside supports.

The space under the *Xiangliu* was less than he'd expected. He'd planned on eight or nine feet clearance, but there was only five, reducing down to about two under the main bulge of the hull.

Rolling over onto his back he edged along the centerline of the keel while pressing balls of the putty against the hull. He then pressed the det cord into the putty, effectively holding it there tight against the hull. If the submarine had been underway, this technique wouldn't have worked as the water movement would have quickly washed it off, but here at the dockside it was perfect.

The other option had been magnetic mines, but to fix these the heavy-duty rubber coating would have to be cut through and scraped off to leave a clean metal surface. There was too much risk the noise of doing this might be detected.

Twice he had partial panic attacks. The seabed was solid, made of rock and coral. Parts of the 11,000 ton *Xiangliu* were floating a mere two feet above this. Deacon was trying to maneuver within that space and a large passing wave would be enough to move the submarine crushing him flat within seconds. Had he been wearing the conventional air tanks he wouldn't have been able to get into the gap -- it was only because the Dräger Rebreather was a slimmer design allowing him the few extra inches he needed. He wasn't claustrophobic but this was really at the limits of his ability, and twice he had to stop, close his eyes and try to slow his breathing to relax.

He was also carrying a miniature Geiger counter. Swimming along on his back he kept checking the hull until the count on the instrument increased before reducing again. This was the approximate location of the small nuclear power plant within the submarine. He made sure the det cord extended to this point. He then molded the C4 into a long sausage shape before pressing it firmly to the hull. He pushed the small detonators into both the det cord and the C4 before connecting the ends of them to the timer.

With the waterproof plugs and sockets all mated he set the timer to trigger at 11:35, and with an enormous feeling of relief headed back to the extra few feet of clearance near the large seven-bladed propeller.

A sudden splash and the body of a person appeared beside him.

Deacon froze.

Had he been detected?

Slipping his dive knife into his hand, he pushed in tight to the propeller. He wouldn't go down without a fight. Just as he was preparing to make the first strike, the swimmer grabbed what looked to be a bucket slowly sinking, pushed back up to the surface, and didn't come down again.

Deacon sat there waiting.

If the submarine moved, he was done for. If the engine was started and propeller turned, it was game over.

Waiting there for over five minutes, hardly breathing, it slowly dawned on him. The guy had been dressed in work clothes minus shoes. He must have been a crewman who'd dropped his bucket and was ordered to dive in after it. Now he'd gone, and it was safe again.

Realizing the cold water had slowed his thinking, Deacon swam back over to the dock support and retrieved the frame and sheeting. Clipping it on his back again, he slowly moved out from under the protection of the boat's hull, again a mere few inches above the barren seabed.

Gently moving at slightly more than a snail's pace, within minutes he was over fifty feet away and able to speed up slightly.

He would never be sure what alerted the guards as he neared the entrance. There were two PLAN helicopters circling overhead. Maybe one of them thought they saw something. Maybe they saw a large fish. But suddenly the water surface was being churned up by two fast-moving patrol boats dropping grenades.

Deacon was almost thirty feet away from their drop zone, but the shockwave of the subsequent explosions almost turned him over. That would have been disastrous as his Nomex suit was dark against the sandy coral seabed.

Dazed and confused with ringing in his ears he righted himself, before kicking and swimming as fast as he could away from the churned up water. The effect of the grenades actually helped his escape, the explosion churning up sand and small pieces of coral until visibility temporarily dropped to mere inches. Swimming rapidly, he was using more air than he wanted and he'd lost his bearings and was going in the wrong direction. Feeling the seabed rising he stopped and drifted while he got his breath back and let his head clear. In the panic, he'd swum across the main channel and was now on the wrong side of the harbor.

Knowing the amount of time he could use the Dräger was limited, he knew he had to get back to the abandoned sled and its supply of good air so had to swim underwater once again out towards the sea before crossing the entrance.

Finally, after another thirty minutes of hard swimming against the current, and with the air from the rebreather system quite heavily polluted by his own CO_2 exhalations, he arrived back at the abandoned sled. His head was pounding, and he felt totally exhausted.

He jammed the regulator into his mouth and almost cried out in relief with the sudden improved air quality from the other tanks. He knew he had to breath slowly -- the regulator automatically tries to limit the amount you can breathe at any one time and gasping too quickly actually stops it working.

It took another ten minutes before he felt well enough to continue. Slipping the tank out from its compartment in the sled and fitting it to his harness, Deacon started a long slow swim back along the coast of the reef towards his hideout.

44

Captain Zu Qian stood looking through his binoculars. Since the last intrusion, he'd arranged for additional sensors and detectors to be located at key points around the reef. This included a series of pressure sensors placed in the harbor channel. These would trigger an alarm when any craft large enough passed through the water over them. The entire garrison stationed on the reef was on heightened security alert for the period of the inauguration and visit by the Admiral and Premier and for the arrival of the *Xiangliu*.

Usually, a diver swimming over sensor number 5 would not have triggered it. However, Deacon was swimming mere inches above the seabed and much closer to the sensor than a diver would normally be. When the alarm triggered, the control room issued immediate orders for the two launches to investigate. With nothing visible on the surface, it was quickly decided a large fish, or bottom feeding shark swimming close by had likely triggered it. Nonetheless, due to tightened security, both launch commanders chose to drop grenades in the local area.

Now, with nothing untoward found and the sea surface covered with dozens of dead or stunned fish, Qian ordered the boat crews to collect the marine bounty and pass them to the kitchens.

Turning away, he checked his watch. The VIP aircraft was due to arrive in a little over an hour, and he still had a lot to inspect before he would head to the airfield to greet his guests.

After a long swim back to the beach, Deacon came ashore unseen and changed into a Chinese guard's uniform again showing the rank of Major. He then collected his remaining explosives and prepared to head out. He knew this was the risky part of the mission as he was taller than most of the personnel on the island and would stand out. However, he'd seen the agenda and knew that apart from the guards in the towers and on the beach, everyone else had been ordered to attend the event.

The main buildings were already looking deserted. In the distance, he could see the motorcade slowly progressing around the airfield as he walked swiftly towards the missile building. The outside of the building was unguarded and not willing to waste time, Deacon pulled out his suppressed Makarov and shot the lock out. Stepping inside, he closed the door behind him and walked quickly to the stairs.

Two floors down he gently opened the door. The guard stood there facing away from him. Deacon was moving forward ready to knock him unconscious when something made the guard turn. Whether it was a sixth sense, or the air pressure that changed slightly as Deacon moved, but the guard turned with one hand going for his weapon while the other went towards the alarm button on the wall.

With no way to get there in time and no other choice, Deacon shot him in the head.

Pushing the double doors open he checked there was no other staff present.

Four missiles were mounted on the launching system, ready to fire, and there were four more missiles located in storage boxes in the adjoining room.

Moving swiftly, he looped the remaining pieces of det cord around the motor section of three of the missiles on the launch frame before connecting a timer. He split the last of the C4 into two before jamming it into the tail exhausts of two of the additional missiles and connected his last electronic timer to them. Setting the alarm times to 11:20 he then turned to look at the steel and concrete roof doors, and an idea came to him.

The silo the missiles were in was not a reinforced launching silo, merely a safe storage area. In a launch scenario, the concrete and steel doors above would be swung open by hydraulics, the complete missile bed would raise, also by hydraulics. The solid concrete doors would then be closed protecting the storage area before the weapon would be aimed and fired.

Looking around, Deacon saw a fire axe in a glass case mounted on the wall. Smashing the glass with his gun butt, he grabbed the axe and checked its edge. Sharp enough, he thought.

Climbing the gantry on one side of the silo, he swung the axe three, four, five times at the strengthened hydraulic rubber hoses connected to the massive hydraulic rams. After multiple swings, the sharpened edge finally did its job, and high-pressure oil sprayed out. Moving to the other side, he did the same until that hose was also severed.

Back at ground level, he attacked the hoses connected to the missile platform until the floor was awash with oil.

With a final few swings, he smashed the computer systems and the fire control panel.

Stepping back outside he checked the dead guard's pockets until he found cigarettes and a lighter. It had been a fairly safe assumption the guard would be a smoker.

Grabbing a pile of paper from one of the desks, he quickly twisted it into a rough tube shape and placed the cigarettes inside, before lighting the complete bundle. Laying the gently burning paper on the floor touching the hydraulic oil, he knew as the paper burned, it would ignite the fluid. Oil takes more effort to ignite than gasoline, but once started, it's very hard to extinguish.

Heading back up and outside he headed over towards the main barracks when two PLAN guards came around the corner and ordered him to stop. He shot the first one center chest but the other dived sideways, and his shot missed. As he turned and ran two more guards joined the remaining one and the three of them opened fire.

Ducking and weaving Deacon managed to keep ahead, but that was when his luck ran out. Racing around another corner, he almost collided with two other guards attracted by the shouting. Before he could change direction, he was suddenly struck by the barbs of two Tasers piercing his skin before being triggered a moment later. His muscles spasmed as 50,000 volts coursed through his body and he collapsed to the ground.

The last image he saw was a raised rifle butt being slammed down towards his head.

As the Premier's Airbus A350 turned towards final approach, Admiral Zhang felt butterflies in his stomach. So far everything was going to plan. As they banked, the weather was clear, and he could see the *Xiangliu* against the dockside. He'd spoken with both Captain Zu and Captain Weimin of the *Xiangliu* and made them both fully aware of what was expected of them, the importance of today, and what would happen to them should anything go wrong.

But still his butterflies wouldn't go away. President Xiaodong was decidedly cool towards him. Nothing Zhang could put his finger on, but some of the warmth of their relationship had definitely cooled.

A wing of six Chengdu J-17 multirole fighter aircraft had escorted the president's flight and took turns landing to refuel, with four remaining aloft at all times for the duration of his visit.

The wheels of the President's plane touched down with barely a bump and the reverse thrusters rapidly slowed the aircraft. President Xiaodong usually used a modified Boeing 747 for official visits, but the runway at Surmi wasn't long enough. For travel within mainland China, the smaller A350 was fine. The normal cabin layout had been upgraded and modified. There was now a separate cabin for the Premier and his VIPs, along with a communications section. The rear half of the aircraft was basically as usual, but with larger and more luxurious seating. Today, this area was filled with security, senior advisors, the press and television crews.

The waiting band was already playing the national anthem as the doors were opened and the stairs were wheeled into place. As was standard, security deplaned first and secured the immediate area. President Xiaodong then stood at the top of the stairs before saluting the waiting military.

Waiting at the bottom of the steps for him was a beaming Captain Zu.

"Honorable leader, my pleasure is immense in meeting you," he said, bowing at the waist.

"Captain, today the pleasure is mine," he replied before offering his hand.

The cameras flashed as the two shook hands. Zu had never felt prouder or more nervous than at that moment.

"Honorable leader, may I have the pleasure of showing you around?"

Receiving a nod of acceptance, together they moved towards the waiting limousine that had been flown in the previous day, especially for the President's visit.

Moments later, Admiral Zhang stepped down the stairs just as the motorcade moved off with a beaming Captain Zu proudly showing the airfield, hangers and aircraft to the President, before heading towards the main barracks. Climbing into one of the waiting jeeps, Zhang ordered the driver to take him to the *Xiangliu*.

Although security had been tightened for the President's visit, Zu had ordered that all personnel except essential military were to be present and in attendance at the official opening ceremony.

After a fifteen minute conducted tour of the facility, the motorcade arrived at the main hub of the island, and the President stepped out of his limousine and walked up the steps of the podium, before turning and welcoming the attendees.

Opening his eyes, the inside of a concrete room slowly swam into view. Deacon's head hurt, and something was stuck to his cheek, which he guessed to be blood. He tried to move, but he was tied to a wooden chair. His arms were cable tied to the armrests, and his ankles to the chair legs. Suddenly a hand grasped his hair, and his head was yanked back until he was looking straight into the face of an extremely angry looking guard.

The guard spat in his face before walking over to the desk and removing his shirt. Approaching Deacon again, he kicked him hard in the shin before delivering four hard punches to his head and stomach.

Feeling at least one tooth loosen and blood in his mouth, Deacon spat a snotty bloody globule to land on the guard's foot before saying in a put on English accent, "I guess we're not going to play Mahjong then?"

Whether the guard understood the comments or not, he replied with more punches to Deacon's face and stomach.

It was then Deacon shivered and realized he was dressed only in his undershorts. His clothes, watch, everything had been removed.

"Who are you?" a voice said.

Deacon just sat there ignoring him. Unfortunately, all that generated was another severe beating.

"I ask again. Who are you?"

Gasping for breath and having vomited, Deacon just kept quiet.

"Who sent you?"

More punches.

"Are you working for the Americans?"

More punches.

Realizing they weren't getting anywhere, the sergeant-in-charge said something to the guard administering the beating. He suddenly grabbed Deacon's left hand and gripped his middle finger.

"Who are you?"

When Deacon didn't reply the guard yanked upwards, and Deacon's finger broke.

With a cry, Deacon cursed, swore, and spat at him.

Five minutes later the guard snapped Deacon's ring finger.

Again, Deacon cursed, but this time as the guard gripped both broken fingers and began to squeeze them, Deacon passed out.

He awoke to cold water being thrown over him before the beatings continued for another ten minutes or so until Deacon was virtually unconscious. He hadn't spoken again after his first reply, and that had angered the Chinese sergeant in charge. His cheeks and lips had split, his eyes were badly swollen, and he was bleeding from at least a dozen cuts. The two fingers on his left hand were agonizingly painful and were jutting upwards at an unnatural angle.

Through his pain, he thought he could hear jet engines being put into reverse and moments later the sergeant's radio crackled to life.

Shouting something to the guard, the sergeant turned and walked out leaving the guard to grab his shirt and follow, before standing to attention outside.

45

Looking around the assembled crowd, President Xiaodong welcomed the applause. After two minutes of intensive clapping and cheering, Xiaodong raised his hands and silence ensued.

"Captain Zu, Officers of the Navy, fellow countrymen, good morning. Let me pay high tribute and express heartfelt thanks for all the work you have put into this project ..." the President began.

As the President continued his address, the sergeant quietly approached Captain Zu, who had already moved to the rear of the podium.

"Sergeant, what of our visitor? Who is he? Who sent him?" Zu asked.

"Honorable Captain, we do not know. He has refused to answer. We have beaten him, but still, he keeps his secrets."

"Where is he now?"

"He is locked up and under guard, my Captain."

"Keep it that way until our VIP guests have left," Zu said, "Then execute him."

Deacon's capture was being kept quiet until Zu knew more. The embarrassment of admitting a spy had landed on the reef was too much for Zu to handle, especially in front of Admiral Zhang and the President himself. Better to break the spy and report a successful capture and interrogation as a fait-accompli than be seen to offer excuses. If the spy remained silent, he would take that silence to the grave, and that would be the end of it, Zu considered.

Zu's thoughts were suddenly interrupted by intense cheering and applause as the President finished his address and reveled in the ensuing adoration.

Zu was there to congratulate him on his speech as the President stepped down from the podium, and taking his arm, started guiding him towards the submarine docked several hundred feet away for the next event.

Deacon's left hand felt like it was on fire. With two fingers sticking up grotesquely at a right angle to the rest, any slight movement caused the broken bones to grind against each other. But he knew he had to escape. He wouldn't be able to take much more and knew the beatings would only get worse. The bonds holding him to the chair were tight. His hands were held to the chair arms with cable ties, while his legs and ankles were bound with cord.

Rocking gently back and forth he surged forward until his naked feet were flat on the floor and he was supporting his weight on them. Bent forward in a crouched position, he bent his legs as far as he could until he suddenly sprang up. As his feet left the floor, he leaned backward, and his entire weight came crashing down on the rear two legs of the chair now hitting the floor at a forty-five-degree angle.

As hoped, the wooden legs splintered under his weight and the chair broke into multiple pieces. Ignoring the pain coursing through his left hand, he shook himself free of the remaining bits of the chair just as the guard, on hearing the crash, rushed back in through the doorway.

The guard stopped, looked Deacon up and down and smiled. Rolling his sleeves up to keep any blood splatter to a minimum, he moved forward grinning.

Deacon was naked except for his undershorts, covered in dried blood and vomit, with bits of the broken chair still attached to his hands with cable ties, and pieces of rope around his ankles. He didn't look much of an opponent.

Moving forward, the guard swung a haymaker of a right hook. Had it connected fully, it would have been game over there and then, but Deacon ducked sideways and took it as a glancing blow across his shoulder. He then swung around and sunk his teeth as hard as he could into the guard's muscular bare arm. As the guard shouted and pulled his arm away, a large chunk of flesh came free and remained in Deacon's mouth.

Spitting the bloody flesh out, Deacon ducked his head and charged at the guard, catching him in the chest. Snapping his head up he gave the guard a heavy blow under the chin and heard his jaw break. He brought his knee up straight into the guard's groin and felt the soft tissues squash as the guard gasped and snot flew out of his nose. As his opponent doubled over, Deacon chopped down on his exposed neck and tried to grab him, but his left hand let him down.

The guard aimed a wild punch that just connected against Deacon's left hand, but with his broken fingers it was enough to make him scream. Staggering back out of reach, Deacon could see a blackness at the edge of his vision and knew he would pass out if he received one more hit like that. Keeping his injured hand behind him he angled around and tried another body punch, but the guard was waiting and threw a heavy blow into Deacon's ribs first. Deacon kicked with the sole of his foot catching the guard's knee in mid-stride, snapping the patella at a backward angle. The guard staggered back, his right leg broken and useless. Deacon rushed forward, feinted with his left and as the guard reached up to block it landed a full power right to his throat crushing his larynx.

As the guard collapsed down on his knees gasping for air, his left hand moved towards his holster. Deacon bent and picked up one of the broken chair legs before leaping forward onto the guard and driving the splintered end directly into the guard's eye with all the force he could muster twisting it as he pushed.

The sharp wooden ends went through the soft tissue of the eye and pushed directly on through the thin eye socket bone before ending up embedded in the brain tissue behind. That should have been enough on its own, but the twisting motion confirmed it. With half the brain ripped apart the guard was dead within a heartbeat.

Deacon stood, dripping in sweat and blood as he pushed the body away. A half-second later and the guard would have had his sidearm in his hand.

Ripping some of the guard's shirt apart, and taking a smaller piece of the broken chair, he wrapped the cloth around the wood and put it between his teeth. Placing his left-hand flat on the table, he took a deep breath and shouted out through clenched teeth as loud as he could while he pushed his broken fingers into place.

Collapsing on the floor and vomiting from the pain he somehow managed to keep from passing out, although it was touch-and-go and his vision dimmed. But at least with his fingers back in their normal position, the pain lessened. Using the piece of wood and cloth he made a simple splint and bandaged all four fingers together. It was crude, but it worked. With his fingers back in line and immobile, the pain was intense but manageable.

His clothes and items were gone, and the guard was too small to use his uniform. If he couldn't find something to wear, he'd have to go as he was.

Just as he bent to retrieve the fallen handgun, there was an enormous explosion, and the whole ground shook.

46

Immediately after Deacon's capture, Captain Zu had instructed his men to check where he might have ventured. By the time Deacon had been stripped and tied to the chair, they had discovered the dead guard at the missile silo. Rushing into the inner room the paper Deacon had lit was ablaze, but the hydraulic fluid hadn't caught, and the paper was easily stamped on and extinguished. The damage to the hoses was discovered as was the det cord, which was quickly removed. Entering the storage room the missile boxes looked undisturbed, although the fluid had leaked under the door. When Zu learned of the damage to the hoses and the time it would take to repair, meaning the missile system couldn't be demonstrated to the President, he decided to keep quiet about the intrusion and delay the President by extending his visit on the *Xiangliu*.

At the submarine, Captain Zu quickly organized refreshments to be served as the President and Admiral Zhang arrived. Their schedule was already very tight and the extra few minutes delay would cancel his need to show the missile system.

With the success of the presentation so far, the President's demeanor had warmed a little towards Zhang. Standing on the podium, Zhang watched as the President inspected the submarine's crew, presented smartly in their dress whites and standing to attention along the clean and shining deck. Each officer and rating was worthy of a salute and handshake.

Moving to the small, recently-built podium, the President took the microphone and started praising the crew and their vessel.

<><><>

In the storage room in the missile silo, the remaining timer tripped over from 11:19 to 11:20 and the small charges of C4 detonated. The tail sections of both rockets exploded, but their warheads remained intact.

The blast instantly killed the guards in the silo but the underground building deadened the explosive noise, and nothing was heard over the band playing loudly for the President.

The heat from the blast triggered one of the missiles' solid propellant to ignite, which started burning fiercely. The small but intense fire quickly melted the storage container leaving the flames to spread to the fluid-laden floor.

Within minutes the flames had raised the temperature of a small section of fluid beyond its critical 500 degrees Fahrenheit threshold, and with a 'whumf', it finally ignited.

The flames spread quickly, and within seconds the entire floor was ablaze. The dividing door between the main silo and storage room was closed, but the oil had seeped through the gap under the door allowing the flames to travel.

The Halon fire-control system would usually have automatically cut in minutes ago and quickly extinguished the flames, along with the triggering of multiple alarms, but Deacon's axe blows had put an end to that.

By 11:30 the temperature inside the silo was approaching 800 degrees. The remaining missiles propellants had also all ignited further raising the temperatures. At 835 degrees the first missile detonated causing an immediate and rapid chain reaction to the other seven. One-hundredth of a second after the first, the other missiles exploded.

Had the concrete and steel doors been open the majority of the blast would have vented upwards, but they were closed, and the heavy rams had no hydraulic pressure left to make them open. With the twenty-ton doors unable to open, the blast from the explosions was redirected within the chamber downwards and outwards. Finally, under enormous pressure, the doors did give way, cracking and breaking into multiple pieces, with deadly concrete shrapnel flying off in all directions.

On the deck of the *Xiangliu* the President was in full swing. The entire crew stood to attention in two lines along the deck, all in their dress whites, rapturously listening to their President.

"... the greatest achievements ... the *Xiangliu* represents the latest and best in weaponry and technology ... far more advanced than anything the West has ... you, my soldiers, have helped make the People's Republic great again ... a great day in history ... " he was saying.

He'd just taken a breath for his next comment when a powerful explosion shook the ground and dock the *Xiangliu* was moored against. The white painted gangway proudly displaying 'Navy Ship Xiangliu' wobbled twice before twisting and sliding down into the water between the hull and the dockside.

As alarms activated and people looked around trying to determine the type of threat, the time changed from 11:34 to 11:35.

Three fuel tanks located near the airstrip blew apart. The force of the blast caused the fourth to buckle and explode. The power of the explosions, along with a strong wind, caused flames to engulf two Chengdu J-17 fighters that had landed to refuel. Both were destroyed, killing one pilot and four support crew.

Seconds later, with a deafening boom, the entire rear of the submarine was lifted clear of the water, snapping its mooring lines like twine. Bodies sprawled everywhere, with many falling off the sloping decks into the sea. As the hull came crashing back down dozens of the sailors in the water were injured.

PETN detonation cord, or Pentaerythritol tetranitrate cord to give it its full name, is a fuse that, once triggered, burns at a rate of 6,400 meters per second. At that rate, it appears to explode instantaneously. Had the depth of water under her keel been greater, she might not have suffered such severe damage as the sea would have absorbed some of the blast. Unfortunately for the submarine, the shallow depth of just a few feet focused the downward blast back up into the hull.

The blast itself tore straight through the steel and titanium hull into the rear torpedo and engine room. The upward thrust and subsequent downward fall bent and twisted the machinery inside, allowing torpedoes to bounce around like kids' toys. The blast from the forward section of cord ripped into the nuclear reactor forcing an automated emergency SCRAM, or shutdown; however, the blast shifted the reactor off its mounts, fractured the connecting pipes and allowed both radioactive and non-radioactive high-pressure water to spray.

As the hull crashed back down, its downward motion caused the lower part of the rudder to bend and shear against the hard coral seabed, allowing the boat's weight to be transferred to the propeller and drive shaft.

Some of the coral crumbled under the sudden intense weight, and the finely-honed propeller blades bore the strain until they too bent and the remaining force was transmitted to the drive shaft. Never designed to withstand those forces, its bearings snapped allowing more seawater to flood in.

By the time the clock hands moved to 11:36, what only sixty seconds before had been a gleaming, fine-tuned weapon of destruction, had become a semi-sunken wreck that would cost hundreds of millions of dollars and months, if not years, to repair, if at all.

To add insult to injury, the confined blast downwards and outwards at the missile silo caused the coral rock base to fracture. Coral reefs are created by millions of tiny polyps forming large carbonate structures over hundreds and thousands of years. The two explosions, close together in both time and distance, caused the coral to split and fracture. When a pane of glass is struck, cracks spread outwards in a spidery pattern. The same happened to the coral. Large fissures opened up heading further inland of the reef and out towards the sea, allowing seawater to rapidly fill its gaps.

It would take many months of heavy reinforcement to make the reef safe enough to build structures on again.

47

Half-falling out of the door, Deacon turned and watched as the silo's roof doors exploded. He was over three hundred yards away but still had to take cover from the shrapnel. As the danger from the concrete and steel rain eased another massive explosion occurred. He couldn't see what was happening but could hear the sounds of impact and the screaming of men.

He knew if he didn't get off the reef within the next few minutes he was a dead man. Running as fast as he could, he circled out behind the buildings and headed towards the far end of the jetty.

Ensign Wah Yin had been sitting cleaning the control console of the thirty-two-foot launch. New to the navy he was proud to show his best effort. He'd celebrated his eighteenth birthday just two weeks previously, had been assigned to Surmi Reef a month ago, and had suffered all the usual ribbing and hazing as a new recruit.

He was standing in the cockpit, mouth open in amazement at the plumes of smoke rising from the explosions when somebody jumped onto his craft. Turning, he was astonished to see a six-foot-tall white man, covered in blood and vomit, with pieces of rope around his ankles, and wearing nothing but undershorts, pointing a pistol at him.

The guy pointing the gun waved the universally understood command with his thumb suggesting Wah Yin jump over the side into the water. Not waiting for a second invitation, he dropped his cleaning cloth, turned to the side of the launch, and did exactly as commanded just as the first shots rang out.

Ignoring the shouts from his pursuers, Deacon quickly untied both fore and aft warps, and jammed the fingers of his good hand on the starter motor buttons. As the still-warm twin Yamaha 350 horsepower outboard motors roared into life, more shots rang out from his pursuers, with two rounds ricocheting off the helmsman's canopy.

Jamming both throttles to their stops, the little craft dug her stern in and raised her bow as the outboards spun up to power. Then, with an almighty thrust, she leaped forward like a racehorse from its gate, throwing Deacon back just as a fusillade of rounds missed him by millimeters and blew the Perspex windshield to smithereens.

A badly shaken President Xiaodong was helped from the deck of the stricken sub. Covered in oil and with cuts and bruises on his hands and face, he was ushered away to safety by his security team. Admiral Zhang was also quickly rescued from where he'd fallen, and both were manhandled into the President's limousine for a rapid drive to the airfield, surrounded by security.

The President's A350 already had its engines running as the security people half-ran, half-carried the President and the Admiral up the waiting aircraft steps. Before they'd even secured their seat belts, the A350 was racing down the runway before a steep ascent.

"Zhang, you will pay for this!" the President seethed, still unable to fully comprehend what had happened.

Admiral Zhang, in the meantime, just sat there almost in a trance. He didn't know how, but knew the Americans were responsible for this. Knowing he would be finished unless he could bring the culprits to trial, he silently swore revenge. He would get to the bottom of this, and someone was going to pay!

By the time the aircraft had reached two thousand feet, assuming he was under personal attack, President Xiaodong had raised the national defense level to 'Severe', causing the immediate 'Battle Stations' to all air, land and sea personnel.

With engines screaming at full power the launch surged forward at almost forty knots. Deacon kept low behind the control console as multiple bullets peppered the superstructure. At first, Deacon running along the dockside had only been observed by one guard, but after he'd opened fire, many others joined in.

As the craft surged out through the harbor entrance, the waves increased causing the small craft to be tossed around. Hanging on as best he could, Deacon kept the throttles jammed open as the boat leaped from crest to crest, with the erratic movements making it harder for the pursuers to hold their aim.

Heading out to sea until the rifle fire ceased he turned the craft westwards just in time to see two Chinese destroyers in the distance turn and head toward him.

Spinning the wheel, he turned back on himself as the second chase launch came hurtling out of the harbor in hot pursuit and opened fire.

48

The White House Oval Office

The effect of the PRC raising its alert level to severe was immediate. Systems monitoring Chinese communications picked up the keyword transmission, and satellites detected increased alertness.

Director of National Intelligence Lt. General Dreiberg and Secretary of Defense General Tarrant demanded immediate access to the President.

As Chief of Staff Alex Simpson ushered the President's previous visitors out, the two generals rushed into the Oval Office and waited until the door had closed.

"Mr. President, China has gone on full alert," Dreiberg blurted out. "President Xiaodong was on Surmi Reef with Admiral Zhang, and our satellite has picked up multiple explosions. Xiaodong and Zhang are airborne now, and we're still monitoring communications putting his entire armed forces on 'severe' alert."

"Do we know what caused the explosions?"

"We can only guess, sir, but it's likely your man may be the cause."

Pressing the intercom button, he commanded, "Angela, get me Bill over at State right now."

Turning to General Tarrant, he said, "Melvin, what do we have in the South China Sea area?"

"Sir, we have a couple of EP-3's in the SCS area monitoring what's going on with half-a-dozen F/A 18's supporting them. The Chancer's about to run a FONOP through the region and the Bradenton is standing by. We also have the joint exercises going on in and around Taiwan."

"Contact the EP-3's and their escorts. Get them to pull back. They are only to fire if fired upon first, understood? I want them to pull back out of harm's way. I want everyone to clearly stay in international waters."

"Sir, we're turning tail and running away?"

"No, Melvin, we're trying to avoid an escalation. The joint exercises continue, but I want to de-escalate tensions down in the South China Sea."

"What about your man?"

"It was his choice to go. He knew the risk." Turning to Alex Simpson, he said, "Set up a direct call to President Xiaodong," just as the phone rang, and Angela said she had Bill Casler on the line.

"Bill, you've heard the PRC has gone on full alert?"

"Yes, Mr. President, I've just been advised now."

"Get onto your counterpart over there. Point out we had nothing to do with the accidents on Surmi, we know they are on full alert, and we've ordered our forces to remain passive as normal. Make it clear to him that any, I repeat ANY, intrusion or aggressive action against US forces in the area will be met with overwhelming response," he said forcibly before slamming the phone down.

"Mr. President. President Xiaodong is out of reach currently, but his advisors have passed on your request for a direct conversation," Simpson said.

With nothing much more to say and knowing all they could do was wait and monitor the situation, the tension in the air was palpable as they moved the meeting down to the Situation Room deep underground beneath the White House.

<><><>

270

USS Chancer

Captain Shankley was enjoying a coffee when his XO, Lt Chris Dowler, stepped quickly onto the bridge.

"Sir, comms is monitoring urgent radio traffic from Surmi and radar has noticed what seems to be an urgent take-off of an Airbus A350. This is the same one that landed just over an hour ago with a flight of J-17's escorting it, but the Airbus climbed rapidly, and the 17's are keeping a really close formation to it. All their targeting radars have been spun up, and we're getting painted. Comms has received transmissions demanding we halt our passage and keep away."

"How many Chicom escorts do we have, Chris?"

"Previously we had two but soon three. One of the two destroyers close in towards Surmi keeping an eye on their President's visit, the *Hohhot,* has turned and is rapidly approaching as well. She'll be close by within twenty minutes on our starboard quarter."

"Class?"

"She's a type 52D, sir. A Luyang III guided missile destroyer. Launched earlier this year."

Having just read his orders to keep within international waters felt he needed to double-check.

"Get the Seventh Fleet Commander on the horn, Chris. These new orders to remain in international waters supersede our previous ones to be available to pick up our man. Clarify how far into international waters we need to be"?

After finally getting through to COMNAVSURFPAC *(Commander, Naval Surface Forces Pacific)* command Lt. Dowler explained the situation to his superiors.

"Sir, we're being tailed with two Chicom destroyers on our starboard beam between him and us and another destroyer on our stern. They are at battle stations, sir. Do we engage?"

After talking with the Commander of the Seventh Fleet for nearly three minutes, Dowler turned to Shankley and said, "Orders are to bear away, sir. Move out of range and bear away and remain clearly in international waters. We are not, repeat, not to proceed to the pick-up point or engage in any hostilities with the Chicom's, sir."

Reluctantly, Captain Shankley ordered a new course a further five degrees west from their current one.

Looking towards Deacon's fast launch just visible in the far distance through his binoculars, he whispered, "Sorry son. You knew the risks. God help you now!" as the Chancer turned away from a potential converging course with Deacon.

Surmi Reef

Deacon had wanted to maintain a course heading westward towards where he hoped he could get rescued. The original plan had been to leave Surmi as he'd arrived, by water sled, and meet up with the Bradenton again just nine miles off the western coast. The destroyer, Chancer, would be making another FONOP and would attract any Chinese craft into tailing them, making it easier for him meet-up with the Bradenton undetected, but that was before the sled had died on him and he had no way to contact the Bradenton.

He'd already resorted to plan B. He'd taken the fast launch to try to get in front of the Chancer and get picked up similar to last time. But he hadn't allowed for the amount of Chinese surface ships. With two destroyers already flanking the Chancer, and another on its way, he'd easily be seen and intercepted speeding towards them. His only remaining option, he thought, would be to head eastwards and head down past the leeward side of the reef before turning and heading west and trying to catch up with the Chancer later.

Keeping an eye on the destroyers heading toward him, he'd already seen one of them turn away and head at flank speed towards the USS Chancer, now heading away from Surmi and fast disappearing through the choppy water.

However, the other destroyer, the *Changsha*, had increased speed and was still approaching him.

The larger waves had caused Deacon to slow but heading eastwards enabled him to increase speed again as he was now traveling with the waves, not into them. However, every mile took him a mile further into Chinese controlled waters and further away from potential rescue.

Gradually the heavier sea swell further from the reef began to take its toll and Deacon had to slow to less than thirty knots. However, the extra size of the pursuing *Changsha* was in their favor. Running at flank speed, she easily maintained thirty-five-knots and began to slowly narrow the distance between them.

The second chase boat was less than two-thousand-yards behind, and Deacon was soon in range of its 20 mm forward cannon.

On board, Deacon was swerving and turning trying to hamper the gunners on the launch from getting a clean shot. He was maintaining speed, but every swerve and turn allowed his pursuers to gain just a little. His overall speed had dropped now to nearer twenty-five knots, but so had his pursuers as they fought the rougher water and swell as they headed further away from the shelter of Surmi. His only hope had been to outrun his pursuers, but the longer the chase lasted, the less likely he would make it. Strapping the wheel with a lanyard to maintain course temporarily, he took a few moments to quickly check what weapons he had on board. He found six automatic rifles, three handguns and a half-empty crate of grenades. In the aft locker, he also found divers masks, swim fins, weights, and two single air tanks. Checking their weight, he estimated one was near empty while the other seemed half full. Just as he turned, he heard and felt the 20 mm cannon shells hitting the stern of the launch. Diving for cover he knew he'd left it too long on a straight course, and the gunner had gotten his range.

Jumping back to the wheel he tugged off the lanyard and spun the wheel to the left. The little launch was leaping from wave top to wave top, its engines screaming at near maximum revs and it slewed violently to port. There were shell holes along the stern, but they had miraculously missed the outboards that were still running sweetly, and the damage seemed to be only superficial.

He was now almost twenty miles off the eastern coast of Surmi Reef, heading south, and had completely lost sight of the Chancer behind the island. The chase launch was gaining very slowly, and it would only be a matter of time before a lucky shot disabled his craft. Even if his luck held and all the shots went wild, the destroyer was still chasing and gaining.

The nearest land westwards was Vietnam and at almost three-hundred miles away, it was over two-hundred miles beyond the range of his launch, especially burning fuel at the rate he was. All other directions were further into Chinese-controlled waters.

With a screaming roar overhead, the first shell from the destroyer landed just twenty feet away to port. Instantly Deacon slammed the launch over to starboard. The second shell was even closer.

The stakes had just been raised, and Deacon knew he had no escape. With radar-controlled firing, the *Changsha* could sit back and shell him as they slowly approached. His luck couldn't hold. And with every evasive turn he made, the second launch with its deadly 20 mm cannon fire came closer.

Not willing to give up and risk execution or a lifetime of torture in a Chinese jail, he smiled and thought 'So be it' just as the gunner on the chase launch seemed to get his eye in again. This time the rounds hit further along his craft, four of them hitting the wheel console itself and shattering the compass and most of the instruments. Hit by flying plastic he shielded his eyes as he heard the engine note of the mighty port Yamahas cough and falter and the revs dropped. Jamming both throttles forward they picked up again, but the port engine wasn't running as smoothly as the other.

Steering one-handed, he kept an eye on the destroyer. With a flash and a distant puff of smoke, the 130 mm cannon on the destroyer's forward deck fired. That shell whistled harmlessly overhead three seconds later. The next, a few seconds after that, landed harmlessly too far to Deacon's right. Yanking the wheel hard to starboard moved his launch towards where the last shell had landed just as the guided-missile destroyer gunners altered their aiming and the next half-dozen shots exploded harmlessly in the sea all to his left. But Deacon knew it couldn't last. One hit from one of these shells, and it would be all over, and the law of averages was against him. He also knew he couldn't outrun them. The destroyer could easily keep at 30+ knots in this sea and Deacon was limited to nearer twenty-five. Turning his craft directly at the approaching chase launch he held the wheel with his injured hand and forced the throttles beyond their stops with the other.

On what remained of the broken wheel console, he balanced one of the automatic rifles, flicked the selector switch to fully automatic, and held the trigger.

Bouncing and careening off one wave to the next and with the plumes of the shells near misses sending up torrents of water and soaking him, he knew the fight was one-sided.

His return fire caused the helmsman of the launch to bear away but the final few rounds from the 20 mm finally hit home.

The starboard outboard coughed, lost revs, misfired, and stopped. The casing of the port one was blown off, but miraculously, it didn't seem to receive any more hits. However it was already down to just 80 percent of its power.

The next shell from the destroyer landed just feet in front of his launch, and the force of the explosion lifted the little craft entirely out of the water. As it crashed back down the port engine faltered again and also stopped.

Having been almost thrown overboard by the near-miss explosion, Deacon struggled to his feet and glanced forward. The bow was split open, and water was pouring in. The launch was already down by the bow.

Looking back at the fast-approaching destroyer, its bow wave churning white in the dark grey sea, he saw one last flash and puff from the forward cannon and knew this was directly on target. He knew this was the one. He had less than three seconds before it landed.

His luck had finally run out.

Rushing for the stern, he yanked open the dive gear locker, grabbed what he could, took a deep breath and half fell, half dived over the rear.

He'd just disappeared under the surface of the water when the shell hit the launch, and the gas tank exploded.

In a flash of light and a dull boom, the launch disappeared entirely.

49

The helmsman on the chase launch turned his craft around and headed towards the blazing wreckage at Deacon's last position, the gunner raking the water with 20 mm cannon fire. The remaining pieces of flotsam, mostly plastic and fiberglass, danced and shattered under the withering fire.

Circling the remnants of wreckage surrounded by the blazing fuel spill, it was obvious nothing had survived. The hull and superstructure had exploded from the impact of the 130 mm high-explosive cannon shell. The two massive outboards engines had cartwheeled off when the fuel tanks had exploded and had already disappeared. Only the seat cushions and lifebelts were still floating in the burning fuel, and they were being shredded by the 20 mm cannon fire.

A short while later the *Changsha* approached and slowed. Standing off a couple of hundred feet away, her starboard rail was full of cheering sailors. She held her position for almost thirty minutes until the remaining fuel had burned off and the only pieces remaining of the once proud launch were no larger than a deck of cards.

As the wind and sea dispersed the small amount of wreckage, the *Changsha* gave two short blasts of her horn before slowly increasing speed. As her wake increased, she turned sharply to port before heading away.

The chase launch followed in her wake before turning and headed back towards Surmi.

<><><>

The flames on the surface illuminated the sea enough to see the heavier bits of the boat slowly sinking beneath him as he swam down to around twenty feet. At over 4,000 meters depth it would take them hours to reach the seabed. The waters around the reefs were shallow in close but shelved to some of the deepest on the planet just a mile or two offshore.

He'd only dived to around eight feet when the shell had landed, and the boat exploded. The shock wave had hurt his ears and spun him over and over. He'd dropped some of what he'd grabbed and he'd almost lost consciousness but had managed to slip the regulator into his mouth and breathe slowly. At that depth, the air in the air tank balanced the weight of his body and kept his buoyancy neutral, and he just floated. Above him, the sea surface was being raked with 20 mm cannon fire, the spent shells and remaining parts of the launch dropped through the water all around him.

The rhythmic thump thump thump of the heavy destroyer's engines reverberated through the water as she slowed and heaved-to. He knew they'd likely stop and search the wreckage and hoped they wouldn't drop hand grenades. He also knew the safest place, for now, was close in alongside the destroyer, so he slipped the air tank harness onto his back, fitted the facemask and cleared the water from it. Diving slightly deeper to over thirty feet, he knew he was entirely invisible. He rolled onto his front and gently kicked towards the engine sound of the approaching destroyer.

Four minutes later, he saw the dark shadow of the 400 plus foot long destroyer as it slowed and finally stopped. He swam to the rear of it before surfacing on its starboard side close to the rudder. Slipping off the regulator to

279

conserve the air he floated close into the hull of the ship. It stayed on station almost a half-hour before he felt the engine note increase. With a panicked kick to get away from the churn and undercurrent pull of the propeller, and after slipping the regulator back in his mouth, he again dove down thirty feet or so to ensure no lookout saw him as the ship moved away.

He stayed at that depth for another ten minutes before slowly rising back to the surface. Slipping off his facemask and regulator to ensure no reflection could give him away, he kept his face as low in the water as possible as he looked around. The wind and swell had increased, but as he bobbed near the crest of a wave, he could see far in the distance the receding shapes of the *Changsha* and the chase launch.

Gently kicking his feet while floating on his back he kept his head above water as he contemplated his current situation. The sea depth was almost 2.5 miles. The nearest land was Surmi Reef where he wasn't welcome, and even that was over twenty miles away. The USS Bradenton would be waiting for him in three hours at the same coordinates as where they'd dropped him, and he had no way to contact them. He was over thirty miles inside Chinese territorial waters, thirty miles plus from the Bradenton, and the prevailing wind and current were pushing him further away. The next nearest islands were also Chinese held and were almost two-hundred miles further. He had no radio, no compass, a near-empty air tank, was only wearing undershorts, had a badly injured hand, and in the chill waters would likely only last seven or eight hours before hypothermia set in.

The human body isn't designed to suffer deep chilling. Our bodies try to maintain a constant temperature. Our skin, fat, muscle and limbs balance the temperature between our hot inner core and the outside world. When you get hot, your body produces sweat to help cool you; when cold, you shiver and your muscles move rapidly to try and produce heat. Usually, irrespective of how hot or cold you feel, your inner core temperature will not vary by more than one to two degrees. Ranges beyond that will rapidly kill you. When your inner core temperature begins to drop, your body reduces blood flow to its extremities drawing heat from your skin and external limbs - fingers and toes are the first to lose sensation. If blood flow drops too much, frostbite and gangrene will set in. If too much blood is removed from feeding your brain, it is deprived of the oxygen and sugar it needs. Gradually you stop shivering and stop worrying. You actually believe you are feeling warm and you drift off into a gradual coma before your body closes down completely and death follows very soon after.

Even trying to be optimistic, Deacon realized the outcome didn't look good.

One of the lessons he'd learned at SEAL training was the ability to conserve energy especially if you didn't have a wetsuit to keep the chill of the water out. Try not to move as every movement uses much-needed energy. In the daytime, the very top few inches of water would be warmed by the sun, so floating close to the surface was best. However, you need to constantly use energy in the form of arms and leg movement to remain horizontal, so floating vertically saved energy.

However, sharks were prevalent in these waters and sharks more often attack humans floating vertically as the vertical shape mimics an injured fish.

Lying on his back, he slipped the air tank from his back to his front. The tank added buoyancy, but he needed the steel to remain underwater. Removing his face mask, he balanced it on his stomach as he unthreaded the straps holding it together and prized out the glass lens.

Gripping a glass lens with his right hand, he manhandled the air tank with his left and started tapping the edge of the lens against the steel. Hard, gentle, gentle, pause, gentle, pause, gentle, hard, long pause. Again and again the same sequence.

The sensitive Chinese underwater listening systems might detect the tapping and might understand, but it was a risk he had to take.

Hour after hour he kept tapping.

When his fingers went numb, he tried swapping hands. The numbness from the cold to his injured hand actually helped, but gradually his tapping got weaker and weaker.

His ears, lips, eyes and nose had all been badly bruised, and bleeding from the beatings and the salt water made the skin swell and crust over.

He tried to keep his head clear of the water, but the wind caused the waves to crest and break over him.

As the day rolled on the chilled waters slowly overtook him, his eyes would close, and his head loll. He'd snort sea water, cough and splutter, and come to for a few more minutes before the pattern repeated itself, while still tapping out his cry for help.

Multiple times his head lolled so much he swallowed seawater, vomiting it back up moments later, the heaving spasms weakening him more and more.

Twice the air tank almost rolled off his chest, but he managed to grab it in time. The third time he was too late, and he didn't even notice it had gone.

The daylight had faded, and the sky had darkened. Low clouds rolled in, but the hope of fresh rainwater never materialized.

With a roaring in his ears, he realized the end must be coming soon. His body was numb from the cold and his eyes so crusted he could hardly see. No one can last forever, he thought, and he'd had some good times. He began to daydream and wondered if his body would be discovered washed up on some sandy beach somewhere. He was actually feeling warm now and thirsty. So very thirsty.

He was trying to fight the temptation to gulp down mouthfuls of clean, fresh water. He knew it was seawater and he shouldn't, but it would relieve the dryness in his throat. He knew he was near the end and was finally feeling relaxed. He wished he'd had a chance to see his parents and sisters again, but they'd understand.

And then just as he was about to dip his head and gulp, something moved across his vision.

Wiping his eyes as best he could with the backs of his hands, he strained to see what it was.

He saw the shape again, and his blood froze in his veins.

SHARK!

Kicking urgently and splashing he spun around as a black fin moved across the surface. Moving away, it began to circle him ten or so feet away. He had nothing to fight it with!

Remembering back to his basic training, he knew any shark would go for an extremity first -- an arm or leg. Anything hanging down or sticking out if the overall shape was too large to get in its mouth in one. He also knew that most shark attacks are attempts by the fish to eat. People swimming often get mistaken by a shark for a seal - the marine mammal variety - and will usually only attack prey smaller than it. They are the perfect killing machine. Its only weakness is its nose or snout, its eye and its gills. If you can inflict enough damage to one or more of these areas, you have a slim chance it may retreat.

Curling his legs and arms in close, terror took over, and he tried to scream at it, although his dry throat only emitted a raspy croak.

Still the shark circled.

Twice it headed further out before turning and aiming straight in, disappearing from view as it dived to investigate or attack. Splashing more water into his eyes to try to clear them, both times it approached Deacon ducked down underwater until he was below its level. Without a facemask, his vision was blurred, but it was easy to make out the gray shape as it approached. It was only just over six-feet-long, but its sharp teeth would still be able to inflict massive trauma. Once bleeding, other sharks would quickly be lured for an easy meal.

On its first pass, it seemed to be sensing what Deacon was. As it became level with him, Deacon kicked out violently, catching it in its gills. Its head snapped around, but it moved further away before heading back towards the surface.

Gasping for air, Deacon filled his lungs as he saw the fin turn and approach again. Knowing almost all his energy was spent he also knew he had to injure it enough to break off its interest in him.

Diving down again and wishing he had anything to fight with, he saw the looming shadow approaching. This time it approached from the other side and Deacon felt the rough skin abrade against his left arm. With his fingers stiffened into a perfect karate blow, he rammed his entire right hand as hard as he could into its left gills, just behind its eye. His hand entered deep into the opening in the shark's skin, and Deacon twisted and clenched his fingers, pulling with all his might the tissue and tendons inside until he felt them snap and give way.

The shark shook violently, accelerated, dragging Deacon along before catching him a glancing blow with its tail and dazing him. Finally, Deacon let go and headed for the surface, gasping.

Urgently looking around he saw the fin heading away, trailing blood. Whether it was gone for good or merely planning a return attack, Deacon couldn't guess. He just hoped he injured it enough to think again.

Taking a deep breath, he dived down again and remained there, just looking. After ninety-seconds, the maximum duration he could hold his breath for, with no sign of the deadly predator, he screamed as loud as he could before surfacing again.

Floating there, within minutes exhaustion overtook him as the adrenaline rapidly wore off.

He floated for as long as possible but the colder his muscles got, the less he could force them to move. His head dipped more and more, and he found it impossible to keep the waves from breaking over his face. Gagging on salt water he had nothing left to vomit up, but his chest dry-heaved, further weakening him.

The energy needed to keep his body floating was just too much, and gradually his legs sank until he was almost upright. With his eyes crusted over again with salt and no reserves left to even raise his hands to clean them, he could see the faces of his mother and father dancing in front of his eyes.

With a bump, something touched his leg!

The shark was back, and maybe it had brought a friend!

Trying to clear his eyes all he could see were more dark shapes closing in on him.

Too far gone to even worry, he sunk below the surface and closed his eyes, just managing to raise a smile at the images of his parent's before him.

50

USS Bradenton

Slowly cruising north-eastwards, the USS Bradenton was on full alert. The waters southwest of Surmi Reef dropped sharply to over a thousand meters deep, but there were shallows around for the unaware. Her speed was hardly faster than a walking pace, and she was at a depth of 400 feet. Still in international waters, and unaware of the problems Deacon was facing, when the time approached she would turn and make the three-mile journey in towards the reef and await the pick-up. Cruising so slowly and at that depth made detection by Chinese forces extremely unlikely.

Captain Betley had just taken the watch over from XO Lieutenant Joanna Gordon. Chief sonar operator Dave 'Wolf' Forrester was working at full stretch. For the last day, they'd been very slowly transiting the area listening and maneuvering away from approaching commercial shipping, fishing boats and the occasional military craft. At their slow speed, they were so silent that fish swimming by made more noise than they did. Like an air-traffic controller keeping track on multiple aircraft at any one time, Ears Forrester's screens showed each and every vessel, its course and speed. It also had a designation as 'container ship' or 'fishing boat', depending on its sonar signature and the complexity of the sonar software monitoring it.

Because of his reliance on sonar, Captain Betley stood in the doorway of the sonar room watching Forrester at work. The XO was standing by the helmsman and relaying speed and direction orders instead of retiring to her bunk.

"OK, Wolf. What have we got?"

"Sir, present course will keep us clear of all commercial shipping. There are two fishing vessels twenty miles northeast of us but they are traversing north, and we should be clear of their stern."

"And their nets?"

"Sir, they're pair trawling and their nets are almost a mile behind them. Unless they change course we will be clear," Forrester said.

"Anything else?"

"Picking up the Chancer in the distance approaching, skipper. She's on course 38 degrees true and has a couple of hound dogs chasing her. Four Chicoms. Computer designates the *Yuncheng*, a type 54 frigate and I think the *Shantou*, a type 53 are both in close to her. I think they are just being awkward and escorting her clear. There are two others, the *Hohhot*, and the *Changsha*, both type 52 destroyers. They are patrolling closer to Surmi Reef."

"What's the Chancer doing?"

"I think she's just doing a FONOP, sir. She's heading back north from Singapore."

Happy that they were now clear of traffic, Betley began to relax slightly.

"Anything else, Wolf?"

"Some other noises I'm just going to run analysis on. Sounded like a couple of faint explosions, but one may have been ashore."

"OK, keep me advised," the Captain said as he moved silently back toward the control room.

Ten minutes later Forrester put a call out to him.

Picking up the intercom he heard Forrester say, "Captain, computer analysis has come back with a number of detonations on Surmi Reef followed a few minutes later with an underground explosion in the same area. Shortly after we could hear high-speed screws. Nothing big - maybe a launch. Followed a few minutes later by more - maybe another launch. Running flat out due north before turning east. I'm monitoring it now. Still seem to be running flat out, sir."

"OK, Wolf. On my way."

"There's more, sir. The additional destroyer, the *Huhhot* has turned and is looking to join her sisters and intercept the Chancer. The other one, the *Changsha*, has continued east chasing the two launches."

As he arrived, comms confirmed a message had just arrived from COMPACFLT - (*Commander, US Pacific Fleet*) stating they were to remain clearly in international waters.

Calling his XO, Lt. Joanna Gordon, back over he said, "X, we've been ordered to stay in international waters. The Chancer is being ushered away by three Chicoms and it's pretty active up there. Plot me a course and distance to get as near to the pick-up zone as we can while staying international."

Lt. Gordon headed off to liaise with the navigation officer while Betley stayed put. Only the Captain and XO knew what Deacon's mission was and they weren't going to leave an American behind if they could possibly help it.

Over the next few minutes, Forrester heard the Chancer, and her escorts turn away slightly and proceed northwest. Twenty minutes later, he reported shells were hitting the sea surface way off the far side of the reef and exploding before a larger explosion occurred and the shelling stopped. There was just faint propeller noise before the *Changsha* left the area almost a half-hour later. She headed north and away. There was also high-speed propeller noise, but only from two outboards, not four, heading back to the reef, so he guessed one launch had been sunk. Then silence.

With the Bradenton still running silently and keeping course as close as possible to where they'd dropped Deacon off the previous day, it was just a case of waiting for him to contact them on the Gertrude.

An hour later, with tensions running high and the meeting time overdue, he turned to Forrester and said, "Update?"

"Strange noise, Captain. Very faint, from approximately where the last explosion happened. Might be wreckage but seems too consistent. Been listening to it almost thirty minutes. I'm running it through the computer now."

"Put it on the speaker."

Clicking a switch over they stood and listened to faint whooshing noises interspaced every minute by a faint, metallic clanging noise.

"Some wreckage banging about from what they were firing at?" the Captain asked.

"Could be, sir, but I don't think so. It's too rhythmic. Listen, it'll happen again," and sure enough, almost a minute later the same repetition of metallic noises was heard.

Pushing his earphones tighter to his head to exclude any other noises and closing his eyes to help him concentrate, 'Wolf' Forrester picked up a pen and started making scribbles on a pad. After fifteen minutes he snatched the 'phones off, turned around and exclaimed excitedly, "Skipper, I think its Morse. It sounds like D E A over and over, just the same three-letter group. Really spaced out, but D E A. Why would somebody be sending out that?"

The captain listened for two more passes of the metallic clangs, instructed Forrester to get an accurate plot location of the source of the tapping, then turned and rushed back to the control room. Moments later Forrester heard the captain dictating a message for immediate secure transmission.

Only the captain saw the reply message, but everyone in the control room sensed his frustration.

"Sir, the noise source is from the other side of the reef, but the land mass is distorting and blocking its exact position. To get a better directional position, I need a second transit. Are we able to head south to clear the reef?" Forrester asked.

For the next five hours, the Bradenton slowly moved south before holding station. An hour previously Forrester's replacement had come on duty to relieve him, but Forrester wouldn't be moved.

"With your permission, sir, I'd like to see this through," he'd asked before being granted permission.

The tapping had slowly become quieter and quieter before almost ceasing entirely and becoming just random, but 'Wolf' had been monitoring it to identify its exact location. Speaking with the navigation officer who showed the tidal drift on a chart, he believed he could place the source of the sound within a two-thousand-yard circle.

Finally, the radio message came through that the Chinese government had reduced their national defense level back to the normal 'Active' status.

Not waiting for any more approvals, the captain's voice came quietly over the Tannoy system.

"This is the Captain. We are currently in international waters, but one of our own is behind enemy lines. We're going to go in and rescue him. You've all done well but the next two hours hold the greatest danger. We'll be on full battle-station alert, but I want the Bradenton quieter than she's ever been before. Forget Ultra-Quiet. If Jonesy in the bow can't hear my heart beating here in the conn, we're making too much noise. Understood?"

There were a few sniggers at his half-joke then everyone became even more businesslike. Those not actively working laid in their bunks. No food or drink was served. Nobody moved about the boat. You could literally hear a pin drop.

With course plotted, the XO steered the boat to within the radius of the circle while maintaining a depth of three hundred feet. Holding station, they gently approached the surface until the periscope was just clear of the water. After raising an ultra-thin ESM mast to guarantee they were alone, Captain Betley then briefly raised the optical periscope to just above wave height and spent twenty seconds looking around before lowering the 'scope again.

"Nothing!" he said. Turning to Forrester, he said, "Could you have been wrong?"

"Possible, sir, bet I'd bet my life I wasn't. That noise source is somewhere very close, sir."

"Keep at it. Anything, anything at all to get a closer pinpoint."

"No sir, nothing."

For the next thirty minutes, the Bradenton was like a tomb. Engines were stopped, and she was drifting with the tide. Not a single person was talking. Only a few of them knew precisely what was going on but they all knew they were deep within Chinese territorial waters and if the Chinese discovered them there, they would be attacked.

"Sir, there's something."

"Put it on the speaker," Captain Betley commanded.

Playing back the recording made just moments ago all most of them could hear were the normal groans and background noises of the sea.

"What have you got? Play it again," the Captain instructed.

"Here sir, listen carefully in about three seconds," Forrester said, pressing 'Play'.

Very, very faintly there was another sound. It lasted less than two seconds.

"I can't make it out. What is it?"

"I've listened to it over and over. The nearest I think, sir, was that someone shouted 'Hooyah' underwater."

"Get me a bearing and distance," Betley demanded, smiling.

It took almost ten minutes to move the Bradenton silently to it.

Holding station at 100 feet, the Captain again ordered the ESM mast up first to establish they were alone. Having confirmed, he raised the periscope until it too was just clearing the waves, making detection by any other craft or fixed-dwelling much more awkward.

Looking around he suddenly saw what he was looking for, ordered the periscope lowered and divers to be launched.

Moments later the secure airlock was vented and the outer door opened in the hull. Four divers exited at a depth of sixty feet and quickly swam towards the surface.

As they approached the lifeless form floating in the water, one of the divers brushed against a dangling leg but received nothing in response.

51

Ningbo, Eastern China

Su Ming had never seen her father so angry. He cursed and shouted, stamping around his office and later, his apartment. He knew the Americans had outwitted him but didn't know how. And he had no proof. He'd received a severe admonishment, almost scolded, by President Xiaodong. Made worse, Zhang suspected, because of the closeness to the danger.

It would take all his courage and nerve, coupled with his deceit and cunning to hold on to his current position. Xiaodong was not a fool, and many had under-estimated him. Few had survived. Zhang knew he'd have to tread extremely carefully.

Su Ming was worried. Worried that the software bug she'd placed on his laptop would be discovered. But she felt she could bluff her way out if challenged. Her father loved her, and it would be impossible for him to consider she'd done anything to harm him.

Impossible that is unless he had heard his father, her grandfather, talk to her on his deathbed. When his father had told her she wasn't of the Zhang family. That Zhang's wife, the woman Su Ming called Mother, had given birth to a healthy son but there had been complications at the birth. Complications that stopped her having a second child. In 1991, Zhang was a mere Lieutenant. One of his missions was to requisition the small island reef known as Surmi from the few local fishermen and their families scratching a living on that barren, desolate reef.

293

There had been three families living there happily in harmony with each other. One of the couples had two teenage sons while the second was older and past child-rearing age, their daughters already sold off into marriages to men across the seas. The last couple's son had left and married but had come back with his new bride over a year before. Eager to carry on the family's fishing tradition, they now had a six-month-old daughter.

None of them wanted to leave. They were all Vietnamese and hated the Chinese. As a group, they refused to move, saying they would call on their government. With his anger boiling over, Lieutenant Zhang grabbed an automatic rifle from one of his sailors and machine-gunned all of them. Apart from the six-month-old girl. Her, he carried back to his wife to raise as their own. They called the baby girl Su Ming.

Su Ming had never hated anyone before. The fact the Chinese and Vietnamese hated each other from past history was not important to her. But that her blood parents had been murdered in cold blood by the man she now knew as 'father' fired up a hatred she couldn't contain. She had been deceived since birth, and there was a price to pay.

She would remain the dutiful, obedient daughter. For now. As she watched and hoped her father's life would crumble. She would do whatever the Americans asked of her. Then she would move to the land of the free, the land of hope. And she would never go back.

52

The Pentagon, Washington

The hot coffee scalded his dried and sunburnt lips as he coughed and spluttered.

"You OK?" Mitch asked.

"Yeah, yeah, just a bit hot, 's'all," Deacon replied.

Sitting in the Admiral's office in the Pentagon Deacon felt relaxed. He'd flown back in a military transport overnight from Yokosuka, Japan, after being rescued by the Bradenton. The divers had grabbed him and pinned his arms as he tried to fight them off in his delirious state. To him, the black faces looked like sharks, and he tried as best he could to fight them off, but four quickly overwhelmed one, and he was soon held firmly with a regulator jammed in his mouth as they submerged him.

To him, he was being dragged down by sharks and whales and the survival instinct cut in, and he fought again, managing to land at least one hard blow, but a swift karate punch to the back of his neck left him semi-conscious as he was finally manhandled below.

He awoke laying on a berth in the sickbay, wrapped in blankets, connected to various pieces of equipment and two intravenous drips rehydrating him, as the Bradenton continued heading towards its base at normal speed.

The following morning the Bradenton liaised with the carrier fleet somewhere off the Philippines and Deacon was airlifted off and taken to the US naval military hospital at Commander Fleet Activities Yokosuka, or CFAY as it's known. By now he was back in the land of the living and had apologized to the divers he'd fought.

After a thorough medical check-up, he caught the evening military flight to Washington.

"You're a brave man to have done that, John," Mitch said.

"Well, after they sank the Argie sub and murdered all those sailors in cold blood ... it just felt good to get our own back."

He stood awkwardly as Admiral Carter walked in.

"Deacon, how are you feeling?"

"Not too bad sir. Aches and pains, but should be fine sir," he said, smiling through chapped lips at the Admiral's insistence of using his family name. The Admiral would only call those he considered equals by their given names - everyone else was family names or rank only.

"You did well. The *Xiangliu* will be out of service for at least eight months, probably longer. Aerials show her lying at an angle, so they've got a fair bit of work do. That'll teach the bastards. How did you do it?"

"Det cord along the aft section of her keel, sir. About thirty feet, with a bit of C4 added. Would have opened her up nicely. The seabed was rock-hard there - all hard coral, so her weight, when she settled, hopefully will have damaged her propeller as well. She might be able to be repaired, but it'll take a bit of effort. She might be a bit radio-active inside as well. I placed the C4 to damage the reactor."

Picking up a folder, Mitch handed over some of the recent satellite aerial photos to Deacon to examine.

"This looks to be water, sir?" he said, pointing to the circular missile silo.

"It does indeed . . . it would seem the coral underneath the silo and building has cracked possibly due to the intense heat of the fire and motors, and the sea has flooded in. Double effect, I'd say. Well done," the Admiral said.

"I s'pose normally the motors wouldn't have fired until the complete mechanism was elevated and the fire doors closed. I know coral is full of air pockets. I guess they expanded and split. Being the entire reef is coral the sea would have just leaked in," Mitch explained. "Either way, it totally wrecked it."

Smiling, the Admiral said, "The President is very pleased. Total deniability, but let them know who's boss. He said he owes you."

"So what's next, sir?"

"We'll increase FONOP's to make it clear to the bastards that those waters are international and 'State is making it clear to Beijing that any interruptions to freedom of passage will be taken very seriously."

"What about Taiwan, sir? What's their current intention to retake Taiwan?"

"Their President Xiaodong dropped their readiness state back to normal after he realized he wasn't being attacked personally. As to the current joint exercise with Taiwan, it's going well and that has put all their immediate plans on hold. The Secretary of Defense has just announced we'll be stepping up further joint exercises with the RoC in the coming months, and the President of the RoC has invited quite a few of our ships for port visits over the next twelve months, so I think that's pissed on their parade," the Admiral said, grinning.

Shuffling the paper and photos back into a folder the Admiral looked at Deacon and said, "So how did you escape and what happened?" and Deacon spent the next twenty minutes explaining in detail the course of events.

"I saw the Chancer being ushered out of the way. After the sled had crapped out and I couldn't get back to the Bradenton, the Chancer was my second option. Once she was gone, and I was in the water I knew I had to do something else. Before I'd been dropped off, I was talking with the Bradenton's XO, a Lieutenant Gordon. She mentioned they'd be on station and listening for the Gertrude from three hours before pick up. I just hoped someone would be listening for anything else and would come to my rescue. It seemed a good idea to just use my first three initials. That way the Chinese wouldn't understand who I was."

"Unfortunately, Captain Betley is likely to face a court-martial. He disobeyed orders to remain in international waters, thereby putting his submarine and crew in harm's way. Had he been detected, I hate to think of the international incident it might have caused," the Admiral said.

"I know, sir. I spoke with him while I was in sickbay. Only he and Lt. Gordon knew my name. Anyone else hearing my tapping would likely have ignored it. He didn't move the Bradenton until after the Chinese had lowered their alert status. He saved my life, sir. He and the other brave men and women on the Bradenton. You said the President said he owes me?"

"I did," the Admiral said smiling, knowing what was coming next.

"Please inform the President that clearing Captain Betley, and his crew of any wrongdoing would totally clear any debt he may feel he owes me."

Finally, Mitch managed to interrupt the conversation and say, "But you were floating alone in the sea, miles from anywhere. Didn't you just feel like giving up? What made you start tapping?"

"I couldn't see anyone but knew some of our guys would be listening. Just hoped someone would understand what I was sending and would come and help.

And as to giving up -- I'm an ex-SEAL. We never give up!"

Epilogue

Ningbo, Eastern China

Admiral Zhang was sitting at his desk in his office ten days after the Surmi Reef incident. Wu Wei had supplied the photo she had taken of the person following Su Ming in Jordan. The Admiral had forwarded it to the Ministry of State Security requesting identification. Their report was on his desk. It showed a grainy picture of an American US Navy SEAL, Lieutenant John Deacon, along with his military service record.

Although these records were classified and kept under strict security, the MSS found it easy to gain access. They paid large sums of money, as well as issuing threats where needed, to many of the employees of Chinese origin working for US companies and for the US Government, especially those with relatives still in China.

Later that afternoon, Zhang's email chimed. The captain of Surmi Reef, Captain Qian Zu, had been relieved of his command and was facing a court-martial. If found guilty, and he would be, the sentence was death by firing squad and his family, both immediate and extended, would be thrown out of their state-supplied housing.

Investigators trying to determine who had set the explosives and destroyed the *Xiangliu* found various fingerprints in the hut where Deacon had been beaten. The result of that investigation had just arrived by email.

For the second time that day, the name of John Patrick Deacon, ex-US Navy SEAL was on the Admiral's lips.

Fact File

- In April, 2014, Boko Haram - the Nigerian terrorist group and keen supporter and follower of al-Qaeda's teachings kidnapped 276 female students and schoolgirls and held them as hostages.

  On February 19th, 2018, Boko Haram kidnapped a further 110 schoolgirls.
  Many of the girls held would be sold as slaves, into marriage or into prostitution, with the monies raised being used to fund terrorist activities.

- On November 15th, 2017, the Argentinian navy received its last update from the submarine ARA San Juan off the coast of Argentina, traveling north of the Falkland Islands. Nothing has been heard from her since. Despite extensive international naval, and air-sea searches, no sighting of the submarine or wreckage has been found at the time of writing this book.

  The previous year, Argentina's coast guard sunk a Chinese ship it claimed was fishing illegally in its territorial waters.

- The Spratly Islands are a disputed group of reefs and islands in the South China Sea lying off the coasts of southern Vietnam, Malaysia, and the Philippines. In 1947 China declared all of the Paracel Islands and Spratly Islands as theirs under their 'Nine-Dash-Line' demarcation. In 1974, Chinese military forces invaded the South-Vietnamese-held Paracel Islands and expelled the South-Vietnamese after a brief, but bloody, war. During 1987, China commenced a slow militarization of the islands, with a rapidly increased build-up and further militarization since 2016.

In April 2018, China deployed radar and communications jamming equipment on two fortified outposts.

About the Author

I am the author of the John Deacon series of action adventure novels. I make my online home at www.mikeboshier.com. You can connect with me on Twitter at Twitter, on Facebook at Facebook and you can send me an email at mike@mikeboshier.com if the mood strikes you.

Currently living in New Zealand, the books I enjoy reading are from great authors such as Andy McNab, David Baldacci, Brad Thor, Vince Flynn, Chris Ryan, etc. to name just a few. I've tried to write my books in a similar style. If you like adventure/thriller novels, and you like the same authors as I do, then I hope you find mine do them justice.

If you liked reading this book, please leave feedback on whatever system you purchased this from.

www.mikeboshier.com

Books & Further Details

The Jaws of Revenge

The fate of America lies in the hands of one team of US SEALs. The US mainland is under threat as never before. Osama bin Laden is dead, and the world can relax. Or can they? Remaining leaders of Al-Qaeda want revenge, and they want it against the USA. When good fortune smiles on them and the opportunity presents itself to use stolen weapons of mass destruction, it's Game On!

Al-Qaeda leaders devise a plan so audacious if it succeeds it will destroy the USA for good. With help from Iran and from a US Navy traitor, it can't fail.

One team of US SEALs stand in their way. One team of US SEALs can save America and the West. However, time is running out. **Will they be too late?**

High Seas Hijack - Short Story

Follow newly promoted US Navy SEAL John Deacon as he leads his team on preventing pirates attacking and seizing ships in and around the Horn of Africa in 2010. When a tanker carrying explosive gases is hijacked even Deacon and his team are pushed to the limit.

Terror of the Innocent

As the Iraqi Forces build up for the liberation of Mosul, ISIS wants revenge.

The UK and USA are in their sights ...

In a daring rescue mission to release aid workers held hostage by ISIS, US Navy SEAL John Deacon stumbles across an ISIS revenge plot using deadly weapons stolen from Saddam's regime.

Masterminded by Deacon's old adversary, Saif the Palestinian, and too late to save the UK, Deacon and the world can only watch in horror as thousands suffer a terrible fate.

Determined to stop the same outcome in the US, it's a race against time.

Using all the resources he can muster including his friends in the Pentagon, Deacon must find and stop Saif before the lives of hundreds of thousands of Americans are ruined forever.

Crossing a Line

Once a respected US Navy SEAL, now shunned by friends and colleagues and wanted by the police, John Deacon has gone rogue ...

Recruited by a fanatical religious cult intent on returning the USA to the ways of God, and headed by a man known as The General, Deacon's weapons skills and combat knowledge are put to treacherous use ...

Deacon has crossed a line ... But has he gone too far? Can he ever cross back?

Check out my web page http://www.mikeboshier.com for details of latest books, offers and free stuff.

VIP Reader's Mailing List

To join our VIP Readers Mailing List and receive updates about new books and freebies, please go to my web page and join my mailing list.

www.mikeboshier.com

I value your trust. Your email address will stay safe and you will never receive spam from me. You can unsubscribe at any time.
Thank you.